MY
MONSTER

MY MONSTER

David Darmstaedter

Ziji

Published by Ziji Publishing
www.zijipublishing.com

Distributed by Turnaround Distribution Services Ltd.
Telephone 020 8829 3000

ISBN: 978-0-9554051-2-9

Printed by CPI Cox & Wyman, Reading RG1 8EX.

I dedicate this book to the spirit of old poppy...
even though he would call me an idiot for writing it.

1

It's six am. And still dark outside. February dark. Winter dark. Cold dark. Depressing dark… or maybe it's me who's depressed. Yeah, that sounds right. I'm lying in bed, staring at the cheap clock radio on the cheap yard-sale dresser, and smoking. I take a drag, blow the smoke out the window then hold the cigarette through a little hole in the screen.

My dog, Shnooky, lies next to me and watches. She is a beautiful mixture of brown, white and gold with Maple eyes and a deep purple tongue. When I found her on the street six years ago she was so filthy and mangy, the vet had to give her three baths to find out what colour she was. Now she is a stunning beauty queen. Shnooky doesn't like the smoke but she puts up with it just to be on the bed, just to be close to me. Dog love, you know how that is.

Anyway, I cut the hole in the screen to get minimum smoke because I share the bedroom with my thirteen-year-old son, Max. He's snoring in the bed on the other side of the mini-dresser. One of the front panels of a dresser drawer is on the floor along with a few pairs of his boxer underwear and socks. I always fucking glue it and it always falls off. I told Max I would buy him a new dresser as soon as we have money. I told him I'd do a lot of things when we have money. He always says, "Sure, Dad, we'll never have money."

"Fuck you! We will too," I always say.

"Dad, do you know you swear like worse than anybody I know?" he says. "Don't you think that's lame for a man of your age?" It is and I am and I know it. We agree on that. But I keep on swearing.

It's 6:04. The alarm goes off. Shnooky wags her tail and jumps off my bed. Breakfast. Walk. She's one second ready like only dogs can be.

"Max, get up," I say as I stub out the cigarette on the window sill.

"Dad, why the hell are you smoking in the room?" he asks, his face still buried in his pillow.

"Just get up," I say. "I was up most of the night trying to find Tony again."

Max turns his apple-cheeked face towards me, opens one of his beautiful, almond-shaped, dark hazel eyes and stares at me with it to give me a reality check.

"Dad, Tony is a loser crack addict."

"Max, he's my friend and my writing partner. As soon as we finish this script…"

Max cuts me off.

8

"Dad, shut up. You'll never finish with him. Just do it yourself."

I can't tell Max I'm scared to write alone, that I don't think I'm capable, so I work with some moron I can berate to feel better about myself. Sick. *I'm fucking sick, Max, can you help me?* is what I want to tell him but Max isn't my mommy, he's my son so I just say, "I can't, we're too far into it."

"Sure, Dad," he says. He knows. He pulls the TV controller out from under the covers (he sleeps with it) and clicks on the TV my brother gave me for Christmas eight years ago. The screen is covered with greasy fingerprints and the box is covered with skateboard stickers. You could say Max has put his mark on it. MTV comes on, some Snoop Dog wit' his posse and ho's video. I start staring at one of the dancers gyrating her ass. I imagine me behind her, naked, gyrating with a huge hard-on as she reaches back and grabs my cock and the other dancer...

I stop my thoughts, hating them, hating myself for having them. I deflect the thoughts by getting angry.

"He wasn't smoking crack when we started," I say. "Okay? I didn't plan it out this way. Just get up and get ready for school... and turn the TV off!"

"Fine," he says. "Grumpy."

He clicks it off and gets out of his bed. He is wearing a pair of GAP plaid boxers. I know because the quality is better than the cheap ones I buy him at the T-shirt outlet. He got the GAP boxers from his school friend, Leo. Max goes to a rich kids' school. Leo is from a rich family, we are a poor family. So what? Why the fuck do I have to think of all this so early in the morning?

Max's hair is long. His bangs are down to his chin. He's getting tall. Tall and thin, like me. That's the only resemblance we have, though. Face to face, you couldn't tell we were related. He reaches up and stretches. He's got a few wisps of hair under his arms. Shit, it must be hard for him to share the same room with me, I think. I was jerking off all the time at his age. What a drag he doesn't have his own room.

"The drawer is broken again," he says.

"I know," I say. He looks at me, disgusted.

"Dad, why do you still smoke?"

"Just get ready."

As he walks to the bathroom he says, "Dad, when you get cancer, I'm not visiting you in the hospital."

"I've been up all night trying to track Tony down in every crack hotel in Hollywood," I say. "So don't give me any shit."

"Okay, Dad," he says, already in the bathroom which is just outside the bedroom door. We're talking small, one-bedroom apartment.

"Okay," he says. "Just get me my own room so you can do whatever you want in yours."

He closes the bathroom door hard. He doesn't slam it. I'm the door slammer. I've slammed it so many times that the wood is splintered on the bottom. I hear the shower go as I get out of bed, drop to my knees, pray to God to help me be happy and have a good day... I feel nothing, no change at all but I know it's saving my life anyway.

I stand up and iron out the wrinkles on my grey, long-sleeved sweatshirt and sweatpants with my hands. I think of changing and say, "Fuck it, for who? I'm driving him to car pool and coming back." I throw on my black wool cap because I'm going bald and can't deal with trying to fix what hair I have left and think of all the jobs I wish I was going to; movie sets, production offices, early writers' meetings.

I make my bed, half-assed. I hear Max yelling, "Dad, this shower sucks, there's like no pressure again." I'm too caught up in my list of things that I don't have to even answer him. I pull his comforter up, slap his pillows a couple of times. Two half-assed made beds now. I look at the framed picture of his mom that is on his side of the dresser, facing his bed. His mom, Keri, who died when he was five. She fell asleep at the wheel while driving through the Wyoming desert on a warm August night. I was here in Los Angeles. Max was in the back seat of her car, sleeping as she passed out, veered off the endless, narrow, dark road and flipped over an embankment. No seat belts. Damnit, Keri! Why? Were you drinking? Maybe. Max said you had wine at dinner. God, I think of this every time I look at you...

As the car rolled over in the air, both were hurled out of the windows. Max scraped and bounced down the pavement, lacerating skin and breaking bones as the car landed on Keri, killing her instantly. He was lying there in the road, five years old, with his mom, mangled to death, less than twenty yards away from him...

Here in the picture she's dressed in a gold cashmere sweater and black flannel skirt, with her almond eyes and apple cheeks all rosy and her skin bronzed from the sun. Her long, straight, raven-black hair falls behind her head that is thrown back in a "devil may care" attitude. Keri laughed a lot. Keri was laughing out loud when the picture was taken. Not a care in the world.

"I love you, Dave. You're doing a great job with Max," I hear her say.

"Easy for you to say," I answer to the picture. "You're dead."

"Oh, brother," I hear her say. "Like I can do something about that now? Stop being such a broken record." I want to keep arguing about the seatbelts, the drinking, but I tell myself to shut up. Keri is free now and watching over us in all her magnificence from the heavens.

Shnooky wriggles around me impatiently, nibbling at my sweatpants. "Okay, okay," I tell her as she follows me through our living room, which is our only other room, cluttered with four decent, but worn, pine wood and leather chairs of Keri's, seated around a varnished, custom-made, plywood and pine table of hers; stacked with bills, papers, magazines and movie scripts. Then there's our two old computers side by side on a little garage sale office desk rammed up next to it, a splintered, garage sale, wood dining/coffee table that we sanded to make look like an antique; that's what I say anyway, it's an antique. Then front of it, our worn out three-piece couch that needs reupholstering (also of his mom's and it was decent once), our one good TV, Sony, not bad but five years old, my overflowing dilapidated bookshelf, numerous skateboards, basketballs, surfboards... just a whole bunch of shit that I stare at and can't figure out how to organize. I have an urge to throw it all out. Everything. Just get rid of everything. Like I own so much stuff, right? Except Keri's, it's all crap. I own a bunch of crap. And I feel like crap and I am crap. I am.

I tell myself to shut up over and over again, like a mantra, as I go into the kitchen. Shnooky rubs against me as I get her bag of dog food and pour some into her bowl. She wants me to be happy. I'm not happy and wish I could remember when I was. There were days, sure, but I can't remember them because today sucks. *One Day At A Time...* okay, fine, today sucks. The sink is full of dishes.

"Damnit!" I say as I stare at them, thinking I just washed all the dishes yesterday. Every day. Every fucking day, for years, I wash dishes.

I look out the window over the sink. The moon is still out. It's that time, seconds before dawn when it's still dark but you can see things better than the dead of night. I get a view even if it is over the top of the building at the back of ours, through black telephone cable wires and satellite dishes. I can see the tops of the palm trees that line Beechwood Street. The long hanging palms look black. Better than the sick green look they have in the light of day. I've been to Hawaii. I've seen healthy palm trees with rich green palms hanging. I think about how I used to go to Hawaii from New York and kick heroin on my way to Japan to clean up for those forty-thousand-dollar-a-month modelling contracts in the eighties. Four rough days curled up in a Waikiki hotel, then gradually making my way back into the sun; going to beaches all over the Island; swimming, snorkelling, surfing, getting all tan and healthy.

Let's not forget drinking and fucking. Drinking didn't count back then, drinking was normal. And fucking a different sun-kissed girl every night… I still beat off thinking about those days. That's when I remember being happy, travelling all over the world, making money. Then I blew it. God damnit… in the past. Takes up a lot of time. Too much. The sun's already set there, buddy. Wake up; it's rising in the present now, before your very eyes. Stay in the present, do the fucking dishes, make Max some oatmeal, walk Shnooky and take Max to car pool. Do it! Get out of your goddamn head!

I wash the dishes and watch the black sky turn orange and blue in the sunrise. I feel a soothing warmth come over my body as I give myself to the sky. I'm in it. In the sky. In the world. In the universe.

14

Melting. Magic. Power. God. The dishes done with a smile. Easy. Sweet. Brief reprieves that keep my monster in my mind at bay.

I make the oatmeal, good Irish oatmeal with spring water. I stir it with a wooden spoon, cut in organic bananas then pour in soya milk and maple syrup. We eat good, no artificial shit, and no short-cut meals. I feel strong in the kitchen because I know what I'm doing. The oatmeal is done. I make a big bowl for Max and let Shnooky lick the rest off the wooden spoon. She loves it so much. This makes me smile because I love her so much. I look at the wall clock. It's already 6:20. Shit.

"Max!" I yell. "Get the oatmeal before it turns cold. I'm walking the dog."

2

I have an old car, a '72 Scamp. The Scamp is almost identical to the Dodge Dart but it was made by Plymouth. Back in the seventies it was not a cool car, not even close. I mean just listen to the name: Scamp. I had a nerdy, ninth grade algebra teacher in high school, Mr. Dietz, he drove one. Somehow we thought that was hilarious, me and my cool little tribe of lower companion friends. We would all sit in the back of algebra class, usually high on weed, hashish, mescaline or acid.

One of us would say, "Scamp" in a stoned, crazy voice then each of us would try to outdo that "Scamp" with another one even crazier. This is how we would get through the class, saying, "Scamp" and laughing hysterically, closed-mouthed through our noses so as not to disrupt the rest of the learned students. Mr. Dietz just let us. He let us and he failed us. I don't remember doing any homework or passing any tests in high school unless I cheated. It was all one big, stoned joke. Now I drive a Scamp. Ha, ha, ha.

I should just be grateful I have a car, right? I got it from a friend for five hundred bucks, so whatever. Most of the time I think practising gratitude keeps you stuck in the same miserable rut but I hear different from so many people that I practise it anyway, hoping one day I really will feel grateful.

The car is parked right outside the building. A rarity. Most days I drive up and down, block after block, looking for a space. Not fun. I used to screech around corners hating the whole fucking world because I lived in a shitty apartment with no parking. I took it very seriously, very personally, just another part of the universal curse against me. Another piece of evidence as to why my life was fucked. No parking. Very big deal when you're in that place in your mind. Bad place.

When Max was younger, he'd fall asleep on the way home, deep sleep like only little kids can do. A few screeches around the corners wouldn't even jar him awake. Then I'd start screaming out the window, "I'm just not one of the lucky ones, am I? Why am I so fucking cursed!" Max would wake up confused and frightened.

"Daddy, where are we? Who are you yelling at?"

Shit, that lady on the corner, is she watching me? Watching me with my son, driving like a lunatic and screaming...

What? Did she just call the police on her cell phone?

I'd cover myself and yell out, "I'm just having a bad day, okay? I love my life and I love my son!" Bad day. Can't find parking. Can't do anything...

You can't do anything right, David. What is wrong with you? You are nothing but a little zero. You will never amount to anything…

Thanks, Dad, for instilling those words in me at such a wee age that I still freak out over daily difficulties. Love you, Dad, forgive you, try not to think of the curse you put on me…

Then I'd drive at a slow pace for about half a block before gunning the engine again. I'd find a place about half a mile away, carry Max out of the car, put him over my shoulder, pick up his school back pack, bags of groceries and shout into the air as I struggled down the block, dropping books, papers and groceries. "Why am I so cursed! Why am I so cursed!"

"What curse, Daddy? You're scaring me!" Max would say.

"My fucking father cursed me!" I'd say.

Then Max grew and watched and learned, and it got to the point when I started screeching around the corner, screaming, he would scream back in a mocking voice, "My name is Dave and when I can't find parking, I act like a big baby and try to blame it on some stupid curse from my Dad."

So I don't do it now… when Max is in the car. When I'm alone I still find the time once in a while.

So I start up the old Scamp to warm the engine for a few minutes. If I don't, it continually stalls when I put it into gear. I just got a new starter so it does start. That was a bitch with the old one, getting under the car, tapping it with a hammer so the starter would work until I could afford a new one. The whole car is a bitch, an old broken down greedy bitch that I dump every dime into just to keep the fucker running.

I'm grateful, though. I leave the car running and walk up the block with Shnooky. No leash, she doesn't need one. Walks right with me, a bit ahead or a bit behind but always stays close. Never bothers anyone. Lots of friends. Maybe the occasional, stuck-up, tightass, dog-hating enemy from up the block. Oh, here comes one…

"Could you put your dog on a leash, please?"

"Could you shut the fuck up, please?"

Give me a reason, right? Couldn't just leave me alone with the dog. Had to say something…

I know if I was going on vacation, I'd be all excited but I'm not. I might as well say if I had no fucking responsibilities and was on a permanent paid vacation, I'd be happy to face the day. But I'm not. I'm walking the dog, taking my son to car pool, waiting to see if my crack addict writing partner shows up and waiting for some lame commercial audition.

I make a meagre living, acting in commercials to, "support the writing." That's what I tell people. I'm supporting the writing, which in harsh terms means I'm not being supported by the writing. I've been close with some things but close don't pay the bills. Ya can't tell the landlord, "Hey, ICM has me as a pocket client and if this script I wrote goes…" Pay the rent, buddy. So, I'm not making a living writing. I'm a struggling writer and a two-bit actor… no, a one-bit actor. Well, I've made twenty-five thousand a year, sometimes more, doing commercials, okay, and sometimes less, so at least I'm not a no-bit actor but come on, I'm just gettin' by.

I don't want to but I look up at the 'Hollywood' sign. I can see it from the street. The towering white looming letters standing so majestic and powerful on the enchanted magical hills, beckoning one and all to come and taste the glory of fame, to bask in eternal sunshine and riches. Every goddamn day I can see that monstrous sign from the street, reminding me where I am… and where I'm not.

"Can you tell me how to get to the Hollywood sign?"

Vacationing citizens from all over the country and all over the world have asked me that. Some days I give perfect directions: "Sure, you go up Beechwood, left on Ledgewood, it's a stop sign, you can't miss it. Then you go right on Rowena and it winds up and around to the top of the hill so you can see the sign really good, get a nice picture. Just keep going where it says, 'No through street'. If you want I'll write down the directions for you."

Some days I just say, "Who gives a fuck about that sign? Why do you care about seeing the Hollywood sign? Did you know up close it's rotten, filthy dirty and pissed on with broken, cheap liquor bottles, used crack vials and rubbers all over the place?"

I look away from the sign. Shnooky has just finished taking a shit. I search my sweatpants pockets for a little plastic shit bag or doggy-poop bag, if you like. It's not a bone or a treat, why can't it just be called shit bag? Anyway, I don't have one. I never do. But I act very upset that I can't find it. Where is it? I had it when I left the house. I blow out a breath of distressed air and say, "Shnooky," in a severe tone, like she should have reminded me to bring one. Her fault, right? Then I walk away telling myself I'm going to come right back and clean it up.

I do this whether or not anyone is watching. I know it's getting to the point where I'm going to have to bring the bags and I don't know why I find that so painful. Change. Changing is so painful. Believe me I've done a lot of it. I'd rather take a nap. Take a nap, wake up and everything is taken care of. Did I just say, "I want my Mommy?" My mom died of lymphoma twelve years ago. I was sharing her morphine, fixing her shot, doing my own in the bathroom, shuffling back into the bedroom, holding her hand as she withered away. One of the last things she told me was that if I weren't so pathetic I'd be a joke. I sobered up after she died, made my amends to her on a beautiful beach as the sun went down.

My mom loved the beach and she loved the ocean. I changed colours like the sunset when I did it. Laughed, trembled, cried. I felt her spirit hold me and kiss me. She loves me now, and she's proud of me even though I'm still a little on the negative side of life's see-saw. A little heavy.

I round the corner and see someone in the Scamp, slumped over the wheel.

"Hey!" I yell out as I run up and yank the door open to see it is Tony, fishing through the ashtray for a cigarette.

"Is that you yellin' so early in the morning?" he says without looking up. Shnooky barks a happy bark, jumps up and puts her paws on his lap. She likes Tony. "Hey, Shnooky," he says, patting her. "Going for a walk with your crazy dad?"

I lean against the car.

"What the fuck, Tony!"

"Take it easy", he says, "I just need a cigarette. What do ya think; I'm tryin' to steal your piece of shit car?" He laughs a low, sick laugh. "Sounds pretty good, though. Someone could steal it, easy, the way you leave it out here runnin'."

He comes up with a good-sized bent cigarette butt. I'm trying to quit so I snub 'em out early. Reality is I smoke twice as many.

"Nice one," he says as he straightens it out and lights it. Unshaven with a filthy, unruly mop of curly brown hair, he looks like a ravaged, beaten, burnt-out version of Harpo Marx with no fun left in his eyes. Just fear. He can't even look at me directly as they shift around, squinting in the daylight. He tries to make it business as usual. "You take Max to school yet? You ready to work?"

"I've been looking for you all night, Tony…"

"So what? I'm here now," he says. "Don't give me a hard time. You wanna work or not?"

"You think you can work?" I say.

"Buy me a pack of cigarettes, I'll work."

"You have any crack left?"

"No."

"You sure? I don't want that shit in my house."

"Yes, I'm sure." I hate asking these questions. I used to be like Tony. Worse, much worse. But I have to because I'm the straight guy now. I'm the responsible, law-abiding one. I've become everything I used to make fun of.

"How the hell did you get here, Tony?" I say.

"Someone dropped me off, okay. Listen, do you wanna work or not? I haven't slept for three days…"

"That's my fault?" I say. "I tried to find you. You were so fucked up you didn't even know what hotel you were in when you called me!"

"I can't work with you if you're going to be angry," he says. I do get angry when we work because most of the time I don't know what I'm doing and he knows less. Very frustrating, but today he's just using it as a loophole.

"Are you fucking kidding me?" I say.

"Dad…" I look around; Max is standing right behind me.

He's got an old army jacket over his vintage, western-wear shirt (actually it's his friend Simon's shirt, fucking thing costs fifty bucks), some old Levis and black, high-top Converse sneakers.

"Max, how long have you been listening…?"

"Dad, like I don't know everything already," he says. "Let's go, we're gonna be late."

"Hey, Maxy," Tony says as he gets out of the car in his oversized crusty grey winter coat, covered with cigarette burns. "Cool sweatshirt. Are those new skate shoes? How's school goin'?" He's feigning cheerful the best he can.

Max mocks him by feigning cheerful back. "Good, how's the crack life goin'?"

Tony's got no punch left in him. Maybe if Max asked him that a few hours before when he was hitting the pipe hard, Tony would have snapped back with a crack-induced witticism, but he's spent. He can only tell the harsh truth of caution.

"Not so good. I wouldn't recommend it, Max," he says.

"Then why don't you just stop?" Max asks, adding in a fierce low voice, "Loser."

"All right, Max," I say. "Enough, get in the car. Shnooky, in!" She jumps in. Max tosses his backpack in after almost hitting her.

"Watch the dog!" I say. Max jumps in, wraps his arm around her and pulls her face into his.

"Dad loves you more than me. Doesn't he? Doesn't he?" She

24

thumps her tail against the seat and licks his face.

"Shut up," I say. As I get in, Shnooky leans into me and licks my face. *Daddy, Daddy, Daddy. I love Daddy more.*

"No, me," Max says. As he pulls her towards him for more kisses, her legs kick out against me.

"Stop it, I need to drive," I say. Our crazy little family all scrunched up in the front seat. I have told people the spirit of Max's mom came back in Shnooky's body.

"Have fun in school," Tony says, trying to join in. Max ignores him. Tony drops his eyes, feeling shattered and left out because he knows he's like family too... when he's not high. Max loves Tony... when he's not high. Tony has given Max Christmas and birthday presents, they've played catch, video games, watched wrestling and MTV together. He's like a generous, fun-loving uncle... when he's not high. He's a lot more fun than me a lot of the time... when he's not high. It's a sad, sad situation. We should all just hug each other and cry.

"I'll wait outside until you come back, Dave," Tony says, his head hanging low.

"Come on, stop with this bullshit!" I yell. "Go in the fucking apartment!" Like getting mad is gonna make him feel better, like getting mad is gonna straighten him out, like getting mad is gonna fix the whole miserable situation. I put the car into gear; grateful it's not stalling. That I'm grateful about.

Grateful, huh? How long is that gonna last? A minute?

Shut up!

"There are cigarettes on the table," I say.

"Okay, thanks," I hear Tony say, sounding a little more hopeful.

"I'll be thinking about the next scene we're writing."

"Sure, okay," I say, not half as hopeful, as I drive off.

3

We take Vine all the way down past Melrose where it turns into Rossmore Street. South of Beverly Boulevard, Rossmore becomes real, old-fashioned class, not Beverly Hills gaudy class. It's lined with huge old maple trees, not a palm on the street. It doesn't even look like California. As we pass Third Street I gaze out at the huge two- and three-storey houses. They remind me of east coast houses.

I focus on a red-brick one with green ivy growing up the sides to the pointed, pale grey slate roof. I get all dreamy and nostalgic thinking of Tammy Pallaro's house on the Westchester Country Club grounds in Rye, New York in the summer of 1975. Her family was so rich and their house was so big and beautiful and she was so beautiful, and I always wanted to fuck her but I didn't really know her. My friend Victor knew her because he lived on the grounds… spoiled, rich cocksucker. And he introduced me to Tammy at a party but she just said, "Hi," and that was it.

But I was obsessed by her smooth olive skin and big eyelashes and big brown eyes and big seventeen-year-old tits, so I drove up there and drove by her huge, red-brick house with that thick, green ivy growing up the sides, in my old 1966 beat up blue VW day after day, always thinking I was just going to Victor's but I drove past Tammy's over and over, and one day I saw her, I saw beautiful Tammy Pallaro as she was getting into her shiny little white Mercedes sports coupé that Daddy bought her, dressed in her tight little white tennis outfit and I wanted to drive in and tear that white skirt off, drop to my knees, rip through her undies with my teeth and eat her sweet little pussy until she begged me to bend her over the hood of her little car and just fuck her and fuck her and wave to her Daddy as he looked out the window…

"Dad, why did you just miss the turn?" Max says.

Holy shit, was I gone! I don't have a quick answer so I just say, "I was thinking." I pull over, back up and go down Fourth Street.

"About what, Dad?"

"About stuff I need to do, okay?" I say as we pull up to the Greenberg's house. Joel Greenburg is in eleventh grade, and is authorized by the school to drive other kids. Max and I wait in the Scamp. Max doesn't like to go inside and wait because he says Joel is a geek and the less time he spends with him the better. So we stare out the window as Shnooky sits in the back seat, watching squirrels, fantasizing she can run as fast and climb trees too. "Max, what are you thinking about?" I ask.

"Nothing," he says.

"Do you think about messing around with girls?" I say.

"Dad, shut up, you're so stupid and sick."

Joel's father is a heart surgeon. He comes out of the house in his sweats for his morning jog before work. They are grey to match his short-cropped grey hair and beard, although I'm sure he didn't plan it that way. He is very tall, very skinny and wears glasses.

He's gonna jog with his glasses on? Nerd, I think, as I give him a stiff, forced smile. He gives a perfunctory smile back, half a wave and starts jogging up the block taking quick, short steps with his long legs, kind of scurrying like some two-legged crab. I laugh to myself a little bit because I've been running for twenty-five years and I know this guy isn't a serious runner. Serious surgeon, okay, but not serious runner.

What a lame ego boost but I don't feel that it's lame. I feel a little superior to the old surgeon, laughing my little superior laugh. Shnooky wags her tail and looks over at me. She likes it when I laugh. She is so innocent; she doesn't know how sick Daddy is. Doctor Greenburg's a nice guy though, I think. He lets Max ride in car pool without charging us for gas money because he knows our financial situation. He's not thrilled about it but he does it anyway. Maybe he's not that nice, he's just charitable. He's one of those guys that would have let me cheat off his exam paper in high school... reluctantly, but he would have let me.

"Thanks for helping me pass high school," I say as he disappears around the corner. Max looks at me and says, "What the hell, Dad, who are you talking to?"

"Nobody... shut up," I say, as Mrs Birnbaum pulls up in her Mercedes wagon to drop off her son, Jonathan, and their neighbour, Zack, for car pool. She is a severely coiffed, stuck-up rich bitch and does not talk to me, just gives a vapid wave. She hated that Jonathan had to ride in the Scamp last year when I alternated car pool with her. I told her I was getting a new car but never did. Couldn't afford one. This year she picks him up from school, won't even let him ride in my car. I wave back and stare her down.

"Don't scare Mrs. Birnbaum, Dad."

"I'm not."

"Dad, you stare her down like a murderer."

"Sorry."

"Yeah, sure."

Jonathan and Zack get out. Both are in Max's class. Jonathan is a fat kid who wants to be a jock and Zack is wack. That's what Max says. Zack has multi-coloured hair and purple pants with a paisley shirt and a zebra-striped jacket and his mom is some die-hard, middle-aged hippie who dresses him and pushes him to be unique, but Max sees through it all and just calls him wack.

"Zack the wack," I say.

"Dad, only I can say that, okay?"

Joel comes out of the house. His hair is neat, combed to the side. He's dressed in a blue turtleneck shirt, tucked in to a pair of khakis. He's carrying a backpack full of books that looks more like a small suitcase. He does look like a geek, a smart geek that will probably grow up to be a surgeon like his dad. I get scared thinking about what Max is going to grow up to be. I feel like I have to give him some imminent warning.

"You know, I wish I hung out with more geeks in high school…" I say, but it sounds so ridiculous even to me, I stop.

"Sure, Dad, right," Max says. "Don't worry, I'm not gonna fuck up like you did. I don't even like cigarettes, okay?" Then little mister sensible adds, "If Tony robbed our house it's all your fault."

"Get out," I say. He gets out of the car. He looks hurt. Maybe I said that a little too nasty.

"Bye… I love you," I say.

"Bye, Dad, love you too… just kidding."

He turns and walks, knowing this hurts me worse. Then he looks back around after a few steps and says, "No, I do, I do, Dad… really. Bye." And he blows me a kiss.

Little bastard - holds my heart in his hand.

4

I get home. Tony is passed out on the couch, crumpled cigarette package resting on his chest. The ashtray that was probably resting there too is now on the floor, tipped over, butts everywhere. Of course I pick up the mess.

"What are you doing?" he asks, his eyes still closed.

"Cleaning up the ashtray you spilled," I say.

"I didn't spill it, it just fell, I guess."

"It just fell?" I say.

"Yeah, I guess."

"Why didn't you clean it up?" I ask.

"I was busy."

"Busy?" I say.

"Yeah," he says. "I was busy thinking…"

"Thinking? About what, Tony?"

"About, ya know, the next scene we're gonna write," he says.

I can't take the bullshit anymore. I explode.

"What about your fucking life, Tony? I mean, Jesus fucking Christ!"

"I'd prefer if you didn't use the Lord's name in vain," he says. Tony is a Christian. He fucks crack whores in bushes off Sunset Boulevard but he's a Christian.

"Which is worse, Tony?" I say. "Fucking a crack whore in the bushes or saying Jesus Fucking Christ?"

"Please," he says. "Don't talk like that. You think I wanna do that stuff? I'm sick. Just don't talk about the Lord that way, okay?" I let it pass; it's just too scary a subject for me. What else can I get pissed at?

"And you smoked all my cigarettes," I say. I count the butts. "Eleven in less than half an hour."

"You're trying to quit anyway," he says. "How about some of that oatmeal you make with all that natural shit in it? That will help get me goin'. I wanna get healthy again. I'm done... no more smokin' rock... really."

I've heard it all before but I'm always compelled to ask. "Why is this the last time, Tony?"

"You don't understand," he says. Then his face starts getting all twisted and emotional, and he starts to moan like some sick, dying beast. Then the tears come. Jesus, his eyes well up with tears.

"Fuck!" he screams out. "The way Max looked at me, he was so disgusted with me... I can't... I can't take it... anymore... I'm done, I'm just really done this time..."

He hyperventilates for a few seconds then breaks down sobbing.

It's a class act. Every time, it looks so convincing because he believes it. I hope he's done too… so we can get this fucking job finished and I don't have to deal with his insanity any more.

But for now, it's a job he can't get fired from because we are writing a movie based on his father's life and his father is paying us. We already wrote a novel about it. Four hundred and fifty-four long, tedious pages, some of which weren't bad, some of which were unreadable because we just did a half-assed job, plain and simple. The incentive wasn't really there for me. His dad paid me two thousand bucks and it took six months to write, with three-day or week-long breaks for Tony's crack runs. I'm afraid to do the math but we're talkin' not even close to minimum wage. We're talkin' masochistic.

Be grateful, you got paid to write.

Fine, fine, I'm grateful. So what?

Anyway, one of his father's big producer friends read the novel as a favour. He said there were, "Interesting parts" and, "It could make a good screenplay." Option money? No. Development money? No, but if they read it and like it, we're talkin' seventy-five thousand, maybe more… so his dad paid us another two grand to write it in high hopes.

I think it's just an excuse to keep his son busy, to try and keep him off crack, and feel like he's actually doing something constructive. But I'm in because I need money to feed my kid and if we do sell it,

Max and I can get a bigger place... so I'm stuck with a little hope, a lot of desperation... and Tony. I'm watching him sob with his head in his hands, rocking back and forth like he's doing some new form of vibrating stomach crunches, snivelling and convulsing on my old, stained, soaked couch, in my messy little apartment at 7:15 in the morning. Here we are, two scared, desperate wannabes taking a stab at success. We are starting our workday.

"You want some fucking oatmeal, I'll make you some fuckin' oatmeal!" I yell. "Then we work."

"Don't start yelling," he says. "I can't take the yelling."

"What can you take except a hit off the fucking pipe?"

Shnooky comes over and gets between us like some peace ambassador, wagging her tail, panting, looking from me to Tony and back.

Stop boys, please.

I know that's what she is saying because we communicate, my Shnooky and me. Crazy? Maybe. So what? I started talking to my dog, Pokey, when I was five years old. I used to crawl under the kitchen table where his bed was, curl up next to him and tell him how my father used to tease me and be mean to me and how nobody in my family understood. *"You're the only one who understands, Pokey,"* I used to say. *"You're the only one..."*

Tony sticks out his snot and tear covered hand. Shnooky licks it.

"Don't use my dog as a fucking tissue!" I say.

"I was just trying to pat her," he says, wiping his hands on his shirt then his nose with his shirt. "Take it easy."

I wanna smash something. Stop what I'm feeling.

Drowning, drowning, drowning.

I stare out the window. It's a beautiful, crisp winter day and I hate my life. I hate what I've made of it and I know there is no one to blame but me. I march into the bathroom, grab some tissues, march back out and toss them at Tony.

"I'm going for a run," I say.

"It does relax you," Tony says. He blows his nose.

"I don't know if I should run up Bronson canyon or the streets," I say, more to myself than him but he chimes in right away.

"Run Bronson," he says. "You love that run. I wish I had your strength, runnin' up that steep hill at your age, you're fit like a fuckin' teenager."

Tony is jerkin' me off. He knows it and I know it. He just can't help himself. He is a con man to the core. I look at him getting more relaxed on the couch, knowing that if I run the streets, I'm back in forty minutes and if I run Bronson, I won't be back for almost two hours. Basically getting me to write the book and the movie with him sharing equal writing credit is a total con but I signed up for it and above all, embarrassingly enough, I need him to boost my fragile ego. I need it so bad.

"All right," I say, and I am feeling that boost...

The ego is so strange.

"I'll make you some oatmeal, you eat, you rest, I come back from my run, we work… okay?"

"You got it, big guy," he says. "And don't forget to pick up some smokes on the way back."

5

So I'm at the light at Franklin Boulevard and Bronson, rush-hour traffic, backed up. You know the story. The light is green but you can't make the left turn because everyone is in a hurry. Even though they're going one mile an hour, they have to block up that fucking intersection so you can't turn. Selfish bastards. I watch them with my hand stuck out the window, pleading.

"Come on! Let me in!"

All these people going to work every day, stuck in traffic, going to work. Real jobs.

So what's your real job, Dave? Do you have a real job? You wanna be a writer but do you have a real job? You need a real job because you won't make it as a writer. But if I worked as a writer it would be a real job. But not for you, you need a real job doing something else. That's what you need. That's what you've always needed. Don't even think the word artist because you're not. You need a real job. A real job.

Realjobrealjobrealjobrealjobrealjobrealjobrealjob realjob…

Shut up! Shut up! Shut up!

Some young guy in a silver BMW stops and motions me to turn. He must have been watching my self-torturous episode and felt pity on me. No, wait, he's smiling, no he's laughing. He's probably some hotshot TV sitcom writer who just discovered a new character to put in his show. As I make the left, I yell out at him, "I don't feel that fuckin' funny!" But I'm grateful he let me turn.

Bronson gets quiet seconds after I pass the Mayfair market. Such a pleasant little neighbourhood. Nice little houses, with nice little groomed lawns, even a few with those sweet little picket fences. Wish I owned one. Fuck. The street swings around. I go past Foothill drive, past a house that a guy used to rent, a guy I put in one of my plays, a guy that won a dramalogue award and LA weekly award for his performance in my play, a guy that's a famous actor now who owns a huge house somewhere that I don't know because I never hear from him, a guy that I shot up with heroin when he wanted to try it to, "really get into the part."

He puked for hours. Puked and whined. Pussy, couldn't handle it. But he could act the part. I gave that little fuck everything I had, poured my soul on the page. He only acted it. I had to live through it for years! They thought he was so deep, so brilliant. Phony fucking actor. He'd be nothing without me!

I should go to the National Enquirer and sell that story, yeah, tell 'em everything, get a nice big fat fucking cheque...

I play that little scene out until I get to the stop sign at Canyon Street. Jesus, I almost ran through the stop sign, I was so blind with vengeful resentment, wasn't I?

Calm down, you're going for a run.

Okay...

I drive up Canyon. More nice houses. It seems like everybody owns houses. What did they all do? I want to go house to house and ask every owner what they did to get to where they are.

Shit. I went over a speed bump too fast and scraped the exhaust pipe.

"Fuckin' speed bump!" I yell.

The speed bump apologizes to me and flattens itself into the road. "Everybody Down!" it cries out to the other speed bumps, "Dave is coming! Dave is coming! Dave is coming!"

I drive past the stone pillars into Bronson Park. Finally, no more houses to look at. Just nature. Shnooky feels the call.

She starts barking, jumping back and forth from the front seat to the back seat. *"Oh, I'm all excited, I'm going for a run with my Daddy!"* I say to her in a high-pitched voice, like I'm translating her barks into English. Every dog owner has their own special voices of translation with their own dog, right? And every one is convinced they know exactly what their dog's barks mean, word for word. You do the dog's voice, you do your voice. You control the whole conversation but it's such a fun and silly little world of love. She barks again and again and again.

Rejoice, rejoice, it's happy times!

We're goin' up Bronson

Goin' up Bronson

Daddy and me are goin' up Bronson!

I pull into the parking lot. As soon as I open the door, Shnooky leaps over my lap and out. I see shattered glass shards on the ground. "Look out for the glass, Shnooky!" Vandals break into the cars all the time. Stereos, cell phones, wallets... stolen in seconds. Fucking bastards.

I have rocks that I run with. They're like weights that fit in the palms of my hands, smooth-rounded by nature, five or so pounds each. Got them off the Bronson trail eight years ago. I never really weighed them. I keep them on the back seat floor, wrapped in a t-shirt so they don't roll around. As I take them out of the t-shirt, I imagine catching a vandal in the act and bashing his head in. It's an extremely violent and gory couple of seconds. Break into my car, will ya! Huh!

Relax; they never broke into the Scamp. Who would? Will you just go for your run and take it easy? Please.

Shnooky is already out of sight. But she knows the trail. I'm not worried. I stretch a little and start my run, nice and easy, looking at the trees, the sky. Oh, there is a brook too, that runs alongside the beginning of the trail, or maybe it's a stream? Water runs through it most of the winter season. I just look at it and listen to the sound of the water running as I'm running. I love that sound.

Okay, I'm starting to cough and hack and spit. This usually happens the first mile or so. I cough so hard that tears come out of my eyes. I'm cleansing my lungs from the smoking. This enables me to smoke with less guilt. I don't just sit around and smoke. I eat well, I run... I'm a healthy smoker. I used to be a healthy heroin addict. I actually wore a little button pin that said, 'Heroin and Health Food'. No candy bars for this junky. Give me an organic carrot and parsley juice with my shot of dope.

6

After I pass over a little stone bridge that the stream runs under, I catch up to Shnooky who is sniffing around in the bushes. She falls in line with me naturally and as we head up, I see a woman I know coming down the trail. I don't really know her but I see her all the time when I go to Bronson. She is usually walking down as I'm running up. She is tall and lanky, kinda has that "Tall drink of water" thing going on like some 1940's movie starlet. She wears one of those leather hats with the floppy brim, a vintage leather jacket over a work shirt and tight khaki pants with hiking boots. She isn't beautiful, she is more like handsome, a handsome woman. Her name is Mary. Mary is close to fifty years old but still very sexy.

"Hi, Mary," I say.

"Well, it's Two Stone and Purple Tongue," she says in her cool, deep voice.

She calls me 'Two Stone' because of the rocks I run with and Shnooky, 'Purple Tongue' because she has one, and the way Mary says it, it sounds like me and Shnooky are some type of cult heroes.

Mary was actually in some late seventies cult movie, where she played a dominatrix nurse. She was very nasty, evil and naughty, not in a pornographic way but in a way that was enticing to the mind. Okay, the sick mind. Okay, my sick mind. Anyway, I jerked off to that movie when I was in my early twenties and I always want to tell Mary I saw her in that movie and jerked off to it but I never do, I just smile at her like I'm about to then keep going.

"Bye, Mary."

"See ya next time, Two Stone."

And so it goes...

Two Stone and Purple Tongue head up the hill on their way to another wild, death defyin' excitin' adventure.

But before it starts...

Two Stone's mind sets in on him. He's headin' up the hill all right but now he's strugglin' because his mind...

What are you gonna do when you get back home and what if Tony did rob you, what if he's high again in your apartment...

And the trail is gettin' harder and steeper by the second...

Because his mind...

If you were working with someone who could write, someone with experience, you could have been so much further along but you're not, you're working with a crack addict illiterate, but what makes you better? Did you go to college, did you really learn how to write...

Because his mind…

And it seems goddamn near impossible to bear, just like his life is goddamn near impossible to bear.

I mean, who the hell are you kidding? You've been at this for a few years now, wrote a few plays, so what? Got a little LA weekly award nomination just a nomination you didn't win but you'd like to think you won you even tell people you won you liar and no agent took you on sure they were interested sure everybody was but your fucking attitude and your lack of experience made you blow it because they wanted you to write a movie and you told them fuck you because you were scared and you hid it because the reality is you can't write a movie oh, you've tried but you can't not a good one a shit one yes anybody can write shit but a good one you can't…

Because his mind because his mind because his mind…

Because you can't because you can't because you can't…

I throw my head back and scream into the sky.

"God help me!"

And I see a red-tailed Hawk, gliding on a wind stream, its wings spread wide. I focus on the Hawk, feel its energy, and drink it up with my eyes. The Hawk lets out a cry as it soars upward, disappearing into the deep blue. In an instant the freight train of fear my thoughts ride on is gone. I run with ease. Almost like magic, I'm at the top. I spread my arms like wings, the rocks feeling weightless and I let out my own Hawk cry in thanks. And Shnooky is there, glowing golden in the sun, vibrating with life, waiting for me.

Do you think you're a Hawk now, Daddy? That's okay, I don't think you're crazy. I love you. You know what else I love? Nice fresh horse shit.

She gobbles down a couple of mouthfuls before I can stop her. I say, "Drop it!" but just for the sake of saying it. I know it won't work. She gives me a guilty look just to make me feel better but she'll do it again. We both know it.

The trail flattens out and winds around for a couple of miles. I'm right there, in the moment, on the trail, running with Shnooky. We are in perfect rhythm with each other and with nature. Swift. Solid. Strong. Yes, we are Two Stone and Purple Tongue. Oh, there's the Hollywood sign in the near distance. We see it from a side angle up here on the mountain and it doesn't even bother me. It's just a sign now. A bunch of big letters that is meaningless. And there is the pointy radio tower with all the satellite dishes on it, the one I thought was being used by aliens to extract information from my brain after I was abducted out of my bedroom one night.

I used to run up Bronson and try to figure out what information they were extracting but at the same time know that it was beyond me, that I was just a chosen messenger. God that was silly, wasn't it? Those runs up the mountain were scary and painful…

I communicate all this telepathically to Shnooky, then say out loud, "Weren't they, Shnooky? But there is no pain right now in this moment, is there? We are free. Happy, joyous and free!"

Why can't you be like this forever, Daddy?

I want to, I want to, I want to, Shnooky but now we're running towards this perfect-looking superior attitude, Ivy League type with a perfect buff body, in the perfect running gear, who is running three times as fast as me, and I wave to him and say, "Hi" as he whizzes past, and see, he didn't say "Hi" back.

Cocksucker. That makes me hate the world again.

But not nature, not nature, Daddy. Let's get back there, come on.

Okay, back into nature. Look at the beauty. Look at the beauty. Good. Run and look. Run and look.

See, Daddy, now we're on our way back down.

And we are. And we're movin' with long fast strides.

Now I see Andy walking up the hill with his scruffy little mutt dog, Augie. Andy is a successful TV writer. Bad sitcoms that make me wanna kick my foot through the TV. But guess what? Andy owns a house on Canyon Drive. He's a fuckin' putz. He knows I don't like him but it gives him pleasure to know he is succeeding in a writing career and I'm not. He likes to see me frustrated. We met at Bronson, had brief talks here and there, got to know things we didn't like about each other. Now there is nothing more to say than, "Hey."

"Hey, Andy."

"Hey, Dave."

Andy is short and fat with long black hair. Augie is short and fat with long black hair. Andy shuffles up the hill. Augie scurries up the hill. Augie is already yapping. Augie always yaps at Shnooky because he always wants to sniff her ass and she never lets him. Shnooky is not interested in Augie so he barks insults at her.

"Hey! Shnooky! Fuckin' bitch! Fuckin' stuck-up bitch! You think your shit doesn't stink? Well it does stink! Bitch!"

Shnooky doesn't even bark back. She just ignores him and trots past. Poor Augie is sexually frustrated. If he was a man he'd be a sexually frustrated little man who would have to resort to hookers to get laid like Andy does.

Andy fucks hookers because he has money to do it. That's what drove him to become a successful writer. So he could pay for hookers and feel like a real Hollywood player and write stupid fucking sitcoms for major networks that make major money because they have major appeal to major America. And Andy is paying hookers to dress up like girl scouts and ass-fucking them and living out all his sick, twisted fantasies.

But he can write a good commercial story. How many Andy's are in this town? Guys that cater to Americans' g-rated needs while spending their earnings in a full blown xxx-rated way. How many? I mean, what the fuck. How many disgusting midget dick bastards – and they run the town – they decide. How the fuck can they decide…?

Oh, man, this shit goes on in my mind almost every time I pass Andy. Just keep running. Forgive Andy for who he is. Be grateful. God Bless Andy. Be happy for Andy's success.

No! Fuck Andy!

You're jealous, you're jealous, you're jealous.

Just run, just run, just run.

Andy's a success, you're a failure, Andy's a success, you're a failure…

Look at the trees, look at the trees. Nature. Nature. Nature.

Failure. Failure. Failure.

PLEASE, NO!

I tear down to the bottom of the hill at full speed, break into a fast walk after I cross the stone bridge then fall to my knees.

God help me.

I do thirty fast push-ups (no, not military style, just the best I can), get back on my knees, close my eyes and take a deep heaving breath in…

Breathe in God.

Then I open my mouth wide and exhale, feeling black clouds of terror leaving my body.

Breathe out fear.

I do this over and over, cleansing my sickened spirit and mind.

Breathe in God. Breathe out fear. Breathe in God. Breathe out fear. Breathe in God. Breathe out fear…

I hear birds chirping - so beautiful. So sweet. I feel the sun. So warm, so soothing and a smile just forms on my face as I open my eyes to behold the beauty of all the earthly delights around me. I am one again with the loving force of the universe.

Shnooky is there, content, lying next to me, maple eyes smiling, purple tongue panting.

You know this is the best place to be, Daddy. Please try not to go away from it so much.

Okay, Shnooky, okay.

7

I walk into my apartment. Tony is still prone on the couch, eyes shut. "Fuckin' Tony," I say. Shnooky looks up at me disappointed.

We just went for a nice run and now Daddy is already pissed off again.

I toss the pack of smokes at Tony. American Spirits. Natural cigarettes. Pure tobacco. No chemicals. What a fuckin' racket, huh? We're all gonna get pure cancer.

Tony doesn't move a muscle or bat an eyelash as the smokes bounce off his head and land on the floor. He had a nice cry, a nice warm bowl of oatmeal, he's out for few hours, minimum. I remember back how I used to sleep for twenty hours or more after a good, three-day run. I have compassion for Tony. Poor guy. But that only lasts a couple of seconds. I don't feel like choking him to death and throwing him out the window because I just came back from my spiritual run but the thought does pass through my mind. Just passes through. I acknowledge it and let it pass, spiritual master that I am. So I call him a "Fuckin' piece of shit" in a soft loving tone and go take a shower.

Hot water cascading down upon my head, my shoulders, the small of my back. The heat, the heat, the heat…

I'm in Phuket, Thailand, 1983, with my girlfriend, Sadie, a burnout model like myself. The air is hot, the sun is hot, we've got pure Thai white heroin coursing through our veins. We are on the beach, getting matching tattoos of Niji birds on our asses. Sadie looked it up when we were in Japan. Some rainbow-coloured bird. She traced it out of some book and brought the drawing to Thailand. It represents a lot to her, this Niji bird. She told me what it meant but I forgot or didn't listen. Something special, though. She says the tattoos will keep us flying together forever. I'm not really into it but I do it anyway. The heroin definitely helps sway me. I'm so stoned, you could brand me with a molten hot cattle-iron, I wouldn't fucking care. We're lying on our stomachs side by side on wooden benches under a huge, palm-thatched umbrella as a little, wrinkled old Thai man copies her drawing onto our ass cheeks with a crude hand needle and some homemade dye. Our voices are so constricted from the one gram a day heroin habit we've acquired, we can barely whine out, "I love you," to each other. But we do, in unison.

Two stoned birds flying straight for the sun. Eventually we burned, we burned bad. Burned each other, burned ourselves. Terrible heart-wrenching breakup. Sizzled and fizzled out.

Now in the shower, I clasp my right ass cheek and look down

at the tattoo. Just a bare trace of the blue outline of the Niji bird left. All the rainbow colours have long ago faded. I tried to locate Sadie a few years ago to make amends for all the shit I caused. Closest I got was a mutual friend that told me she is an ageing, junkie dominatrix somewhere in Florida.

The hot water has run out in the shower.

I'm making myself some oatmeal when the phone rings. As I run into the living room to grab it, I look over at Tony. Fuckin' loser, down for the count... I mean, God bless you man, I love you.

I grab the phone, say an exasperated, "Hello," and race back into the kitchen to finish fixing the oatmeal.

"Hello, Sunshine!" I hear on the phone. It's my commercial agent, Kim, being cute with me. It upsets me a little that I have such an unhappy phone voice but not enough to change it.

"Hey, Kim," I say, not even trying to be more cheerful as I start thinking why she's calling me.

How many fucking times do you have to think things? That is your number one problem, son.

Yeah, yeah, yeah... Anyway, so I'm thinkin' maybe I got some big job out of the blue because some director really wants me in it, or some commercial I did a few years ago is going to be run on TV again because it was so cool, or Kim is going to tell me the agency has to let me go because I'm not working enough and I have a bad attitude. Which is true, by the way.

I never just breathe and wait to hear what she's going to tell me. So she tells me I have a two pm audition for some new TV dinner product. Hungry Man or Healthy Choice or some shit. I'm barely listening now because I think I'm not right for the job. I hate TV dinners. I think they suck. I'd never eat one. Then she says they're looking for a Sam Shepard type. It's always a "type" they're looking for. Some famous TV or movie actor. They think the "type" will remind the public of the famous actor they saw in some movie or TV show and help sell their shitty product.

So I am a Sam Shepard type. Tall, lean, rugged. I do happen to look a bit like Sam Shepard, more like a skinnier, crazier version but at certain angles I do look like him and I get sucked in when Kim tells me I'm right for the job. "Just put on a plaid shirt and be nice," she says, adding, "they requested you." Ego takes over. *They requested me. Maybe I'll get this.*

I start figuring out the money I'm going to make as she tells me the address of the audition. How much money for the day, how much money in residuals if it plays on national TV.

How much money. How much money. How much money.

Say it again and again and again.

I figure each time it plays on national TV I get a ninety dollar residual, so if it plays five times a day for two months, that's well over twenty grand, not even including cable, which equals a new apartment for me and Max. I hang up the phone with Kim. I grab my old dusty copy of Sam Shepard plays, 'Fool For Love and Other Plays' off the shelf of my five-dollar garage sale bookcase.

I look at the picture of him in his plaid shirt on the cover. Handsome, rugged, intelligent, confident. I throw on my own plaid shirt, go to the bathroom mirror. I'm looking at myself from different angles to see which one makes me look more like Sam Shepard. I compare myself with his picture. I don't look like him or feel like him. At all. Fuck. And it's for a stupid fucking commercial for some crap-ass TV dinner that Sam Shepard would probably piss on instead of eat. But he can afford to piss on TV dinners because he's rich and famous and I can't because I'm a poor, third-rate look-alike that can barely pay rent, barely take care of his kid. And I've written fucking plays, good plays, but I didn't get famous like him. Not even close. Why?

"Why?" I say. "Why the fuck... why the fuck didn't I get famous like Sam Shepard?"

I stare into my own eyes waiting for the answer like it's just gonna come out. Because... because... because...

Didn't. Couldn't. Loser. Failure.

"Fuck you!" I scream. Then I walk out of the bathroom. Shnooky is lying on the floor, panting and trembling with fearful concern. Tony is up, off the couch, tearing a cigarette out of the new pack.

"What's goin' on, big guy?" he says. He pops a smoke in his mouth, lights it.

"Nothin'," I say. "Give me one of those." Shnooky comes over and nuzzles up against my leg.

Daddy, please…

"Okay, okay," I say to her. "Take it easy." Like she's the one that needs to calm down, right? Tony sees the book of plays in my hand as he gives me the smoke.

"Another Sam Shepard-type audition?" he says as he lights my cigarette. I take a deep drag, suck the smoke into my lungs. It feels so warm, comforting and soothing, why does it have to kill you? I blow the smoke out, hard.

"Yeah," I say.

"When's the last time you booked one of those?" he says.

I take another big drag off my cigarette. "Long time ago," I say.

"That's because you're goin' bald," he says. "Sam Shepard ain't goin' bald. He's still got a lot of hair. You're more like a Billy Bob Thorton type now. He's skinny and balding like you."

"I don't look like him either," I say. "And stop saying I'm bald. I don't wanna be any type anyway."

"Your good-lookin' days are over," he says. "You're a character type now. You and me both, we're character types."

"You and me both?" I say. "Is that what you think, Tony? You and me both? And when is the last fuckin' audition you went on? For anything?"

I face off with him, stare right into his sunken little pale blue, bloodshot eyes with sheer hatred because I hate it when he compares himself to me because it makes me feel like I'm just where he is, which is nowhere. Tony shrugs and looks down at the floor, taking drags off his cigarette.

"You're just not good lookin' like you used to be," he says. "Why is it such a big deal to you? Character types are much cooler to play, anyway."

"What are you talking about?" I say. "You don't even have a fucking agent, Tony."

"I haven't really tried..."

"Oh, stop with the crap. Are we gonna work or what?" It's just too pathetic a conversation to keep up. And now I've hurt his fucking feelings like I always do.

"I should just go and come back after I'm clean for a few days," he says. "I can't think, I haven't taken my meds for three days..."

"And why do you go off your meds that are supposed to help keep you clean, then get high and then go back on the fucking meds? Why don't you just stay on the meds and not GET high? What the fuck are these meds doing for you anyway? You're on a different med or different dosage every month! For what?"

"I can't take the yelling, I told you," he says. "I got enough voices screamin' at me in my own head."

"Fine, just go, whatever," I say.

"You should try some meds for your anger," he says.

"I don't need any meds!" I yell. "I pray every day for my anger to go away and one day it will! Anyway that shit is too hard on my liver."

I come out of another blackout in a room at the Chelsea Hotel, summer of 1981 in NYC, shooting speedballs with a few strangers. The needle on my syringe is almost bent into a U shape, I've used it so many times. Won't work anymore. I'm sitting across from a guy who is just finishing his shot. He groans and shakes as the heroin and cocaine combination hit him. This guy does not look well. His whole body has a ghastly, yellow glow to it. I ask if I can use his syringe after he is done. He tells me he is really sick with a bad form of hepatitis. I tell him I've had hep before, not to worry about it. He tells me again he is really sick. He is warning me. I tell him to give me the fucking syringe. Three weeks later I'm back in the hospital with chronic, persistant hepatitis, today known as hepatitis C. I live with it, it ain't killin' me but I did some irreversible damage and I regret that day in the Chelsea every day of my life.

"And I can't go on interferon," I say, "because the side effects are severe depression leading into homicidal and suicidal tendencies."

"You already got those," he says. He's joking, doing his best to lighten things up, but I'm on the path towards his throat and can't get off.

"Yeah," I say. "I do, Tony, so the best thing is for me to take care of my health and stay calm."

"When are you ever calm?" he says.

I'm so perversely thrilled he asked me that question so I can unload the answer that takes any responsibility away from myself.

"When I don't have to deal with you! Okay!" I say. Tony starts to walk. "Wait!" I say. I march into the bedroom, yank open the dresser drawer, grab a twenty dollar bill from my big stack of three twenty dollar bills like I'm some bigshot, march back to Tony, shove it into his hand. "Call a fuckin' cab."

"I'll just walk down to Hollywood Boulevard and get one there," he says.

"Get what? A cab or some crack?"

"I'm gonna get a cheap burrito down there, okay? Then take a cab to Patti's and clean out."

"If you get high, it's over!" I say, thinking in the back of my head, this dialogue is amazing, why can't we write like this? The movie would have been done already.

"Why would I get high?" he says, like it's the most absurd question he's ever heard. "I told ya, I'm done. I wanna finish this as much as you do. I wanna get paid too. Ya know, if it wasn't for me and my pop, you wouldn't be getting anything."

"And if it wasn't for me, nothing would get written."

"I come up with most of the ideas, buddy."

"Bullshit, Tony," I say.

"You're bullshit, Dave. You were a bullshit writer without me. Until you met me you never made any money writing. How much money did your little fuckin' plays make?"

"At least I can write," I say. "You're fuckin' lost without me."

"You don't think other writers would be interested in this?" he says. "With all the money it could make? I just tell my pop what an asshole you're bein' and you're out; two phone calls, we find another writer."

"Fuck you then! Get another writer!" I say as I snatch the twenty back out of his hand.

Tony walks. I stop him. "Wait a second, damnit!" I say. "Listen, Tony..." and my eyes start to tear up. I tell him I'm sorry for all the hurtful things I said because I'm on a spiritual path and have to make direct amends whenever possible. I want to tell him maybe it is better for him to find another writer. My heart tells me I'd be much better off without Tony and his dad but my head, my head tells me I can't make it without them. My sick, sick head tells me I'll be fucked out of all that money, all that money I could make. The key word here is, could. The big fucking dangling carrot, could. This could. That could. Right now the money doesn't even exist but I get sucked into the could.

So, as I'm thinking one more time, What the fuck am I doing with this guy? I give him back the twenty, the rest of the cigarettes and a warm, apologetic hug.

"Just get better, okay?" I say. We walk outside to my little patio. My crusty little patio that needs a paint job because the asbestos is showing through the floor. How many times have I asked them to paint it? Fucking apartment owners suck, don't they? I mean, most of them don't care about their tenants, do they? Right? Pay the rent, fuck you on the rest, right? Anyway…

"I'll try and work on the script and we'll go over it when you're rested up," I say.

He smiles with relief, pats me on the back, bends down, gives Shnooky a pat on the head. That's as close as he can get to apologizing to me. He's not really conscious of his part in things yet, not as spiritually evolved as me, the master.

"Okay, big guy," he says, as he pockets the twenty. "We gotta make some more scenes with Mac. I'll be thinking about it, too."

"Great, okay," I say. "I'll work on it here, you think about it over at Patti's and I'll call you or you call me or whatever."

"You got it," he says as he skips down the stairs onto the street. He turns around and waves. "Bye, Shnooky! Take care of your dad!"

What did he do? Came over, ate, slept, got cigarettes, money, left me to do the work and made me feel better about myself. What a great partner I have.

8

So Mac is Tony's dad's best friend in the book we wrote. They pal around in the fifties in Hollywood, do a lot of fun shit then Tony's dad goes to Vegas after Mac dies. Mac is a real charming, fun loving, good-hearted but heavily flawed and tragic character. The producer friend of Tony's dad loves this guy Mac. Mac is his favourite character in the whole story. They love the wild stuff Mac and Tony's dad get into.

They also find it utterly heartbreaking when Mac gets brutally murdered. They want to know more about Mac. Tony's dad told them he gave us all the information he could remember about old Mac and it's just too damn painful to think about anymore. The truth is Mac never existed. The truth is we conveniently made Mac an orphan so no one could check on him and we had him murdered because we didn't know what the fuck to do with him anymore and were half way through the book and not even to Vegas yet. The truth is, the story of Tony's dad is boring except for the few events the story centres around, so me and Tony made up a whole bunch of people and a whole bunch of bullshit to make an exciting lead into those events.

We had his father fucking his aunt and his mother killing his father and her sister then killing herself, with him living above a burlesque house at sixteen with a stripper; all kinds of wild shit. This is before he even gets to Los Angeles and meets Mac. And Tony's dad told his producer friend it was all, "Pretty much the truth." Based on a true story. So we have to come up with some more, "True Story" stuff on Mac.

Me, the true writer, the creative force, is now free from the distractions of my idiot, illiterate, crack addict partner so I can get to some serious work, some mature, professional work. I start to think about Mac. Mac is a loyal friend with a heart of gold but basically a total bullshit con artist. His motto to Tony's dad in the story is actually, "Connections, lies and bullshit, that's what gets you ahead in this town." Tony came up with that line.

Tony is much closer to the character of Mac than I am. Mac is the functioning conman that Tony would like to be. That's why it's so easy for him to come up with ideas for Mac even though his ideas are half-assed; he does come up with them. I come up with the other half of the ass. I flesh it out, make it a whole ass. So as I start to think about new ideas for Mac, I also think, what the fuck am I doing trying to think about Mac when Tony should be thinking about Mac? He knows Mac better than me.

He always starts it off. That's why I'm always stuck when Tony goes on crack runs. Stuck waiting for his beginning ideas. Mainly because it is his dad's story and Tony knows his dad better than me. I mean, he should know his own father's fucking life, right? Even if most of it is a lie, he should know it better than me, right? If Tony's brain wasn't so fried from crack, he could figure it out on his own. If he knew how to actually write, they wouldn't need me anyway. They're just using me for pennies, right? I mean, fuck, I should be thinking about writing my own stuff.

So I start thinking... What? What should I write? About the drugs, the modelling, the porn, the rehabs? The porn. That's always a good one. How I got into porn. Actually they all kind of string together. I was dealing drugs in New York nightclubs when I got asked to be a model, then when I got fired for the last time from the last modelling agency, I got into porn plus I was still into drugs.

I even got fired off the set of a porn movie because I was too high to get a hard-on and that eventually got me into a rehab. Where, by the way, they were still sending me porn movie scripts for when I got out. An attached note from a porn director read: "Lookin' forward to your return, kid. You're a good actor and a real comer."

Anyway, it's 1986. I'm not shooting dope at the moment, just snorting it and snorting a little cocaine and drinking and taking Percodan and Quaaludes. So I'm good. As long as I'm not sticking a needle in my vein, I'm not officially getting high. So I just snort two bags of dope and one of cocaine to get enough confidence to walk into the agency I'm with, which is Elite Modelling Agency.

I've burned through all the other New York agencies; Ford, Wilhelmina, Zoli and most of the agencies in other countries also; France, Italy, Germany, Japan, Australia. Elite is my last chance in New York but it's not working out so well. The healthy, All-American jock models are in. Junkie models aren't even close to fashionable yet. And I'm not about to clean up and go to the gym for some, weight lifting in the mirrors, with those ass-wipe pin-heads. "Check out my pecs, Jeff. Could ya spot me on the bench for a few sets? Loved your GQ cover..."

No, not gonna happen. So I need to get to another country. A new country that doesn't know anything about me. Someone told me that Singapore was taking American models on monthly contracts so I'm thinking in my deluded state of mind, maybe I can get there somehow.

My agent at Elite is Jonathan. He is overweight with thick, wavy shoulder-length hair and wears Indian style clothes. Not Cowboy and Indian which would be funny, but like India, Indian; long linen shirts over loose fitting bright coloured, drawstring pants, sandals, that kind of shit. He could easily pass for some half-way attractive fat girl you might pick up in a bar when you were hammered. Then when he gets you home... surprise! Anyway, he told me he wouldn't work with me if I got high and I told him I wouldn't get high. And in my mind I'm not. That's how high I am.

I walk into his office. Pictures of top male models are on the walls. My picture is not on the wall. I walk up to his desk with all intentions of conducting business but instead I give a meek wave and light the cigarette that is dangling from my mouth.

Jonathan, who is on a business call talking up some other model who is a "Total Hunk", waves me off with a dismissive flick of his wrist, jangling with Indian silver bracelets. But I stand my ground and take manly drags of my cigarette as I struggle not to nod off on my feet. Just as he gets off the phone, I say, "Hey, Jonathan..."

He yells, "Stop!"

He stands up, puts his chubby index finger to his mouth and taps it against his over-glossed, cocksucking lips as he looks me up and down like I'm some piece of choice meat that went bad. He is discouraged and disgusted.

"You look like shit. You're high," he says.

"No, I'm not," I say. "I wanna talk about somethin'. Can you just listen to me?" He waves his index finger back and forth with all the dramatic feminine intensity he can muster up.

"No, no, no," he says. "You listen to me, you little waste case."

"Look!" I say, as I roll up my sleeves and show him my arms free of track marks. "See! They're clean. I've only been snorting it... a little... okay? It's no big deal."

Then he juts the same fat little fucking index finger out and points to his office door. "Get out of this Agency and don't you ever, and I mean ever, come back."

The icy cold fear rips through whatever confidence the drugs gave me and I panic.

"What the fuck am I supposed to do?!" I scream.

"Try getting a real job, honey," he says, all smug and relaxed now that he's seen me unravel. So I come up with the most mature response I can which is, "Fuck you! You fat cunt!" I grab my modelling book off the shelf (where it's been for months) and march out of the agency.

So I'm on the corner of Lexington and 53rd, flipping out in my mind and ready to bring it into some physical action like jumping in front of a fast-moving taxi. I'm fucking lost. It's that "real job" thing. I'm pacing back and forth on the sidewalk saying, "What the fuck am I gonna do? What the fuck am I gonna do? What the fuck am I gonna do?" And the New Yorkers just pass me by. Another crazed man on the street. See it everyday.

Something impels me to grab a copy of the weekly Village Voice free newspaper. Free helps. Anyway, I start flipping through the 'want ads'. Nothing. Nothing. Nothing. I have no experience in any of these things. I'm fucked. Then I see it. Male nude models wanted. 500 dollars. Cash. No questions asked.

And presto... I'm sitting across from Bill, a pasty-faced, mild-mannered scumbag in a cheap business suit, in his one-room office on the second floor of a walk-up apartment building on 19th Street and 3rd Avenue. It's no Elite Models Agency by any stretch of the imagination but there are pictures of models on Bill's walls too.

All nude guys with hard-ons doing tacky, sleazy poses. Bill flips through my book, filled with magazine tear sheets from all over the world, intermittently looking up at me, studying me, wondering.

"What do ya wanna do this for, kid?" he asks.

"Because I need the fucking money," I say.

"Okay," he says. "Let me see your cock."

"What?"

"It's just business," he says. "I gotta see it. Okay?"

"Yeah, okay," I say, as I think, Jesus, *what the fuck am I into now? How did this happen? What am I doing? What the hell am I doing here?*

I shut down the panic, swallow the lump in my throat, stand up and just drop my fucking drawers like a pro and pull on my cock a couple of times to loosen it up. I know I have a good-sized cock so I'm actually feeling okay about that but I never had to show it as a deal breaker. Bill studies it with no emotion whatsoever. Just business, right?

"Nice girth," he says. "How big hard?"

"I don't know... about nine inches," I say because I have measured once before... okay, more than once. Bill doesn't skip a beat.

"I can set you up with a photographer today," he says.

"Can I get paid today?" I ask as I pull up my pants, feeling relieved that I passed the cock measurement test.

"Five hundred cash, after you're done."

Bill makes a phone call and talks to some guy named Giuseppe about taking shots of me as I think… this is actually easier than any modelling audition I've ever been on. Straightforward. Direct. And I'll always have the big cock. Let those top models work out and get their fucking muscles. I have the muscle where it counts now. Fucking midget dicks.

God help me, right? The only thing I got goin' on is cock validation. It's heartbreaking but I don't have a clue.

So the next thing I know I'm downtown on the lower eastside with Giuseppe, this crazed Italian photographer. I'm standing naked in his tiny loft with Playboy and Penthouse magazines spread out on the floor in front of me, trying to get an erection. I'm sucking down Heinekens and snorting the half-gram of beat cocaine he gave me for inspiration and trying to get a hard-on as Giuseppe yells in his heavy Italian accent, "Come on, boy, get de monster up! Get de monster up!"

So I drink and I snort and I concentrate on the tits and ass and pussy in the magazines, and I do it. I get 'de monster' up with a bunch of, *Hey motherfucker, look at this boner!* poses. I mean angry. Angry with a big fucking hard-on. Giuseppe just shuts his mouth and takes pictures. Six rolls of film later, we're done.

I go back to Bill's, he pays me cash. I sign some papers that basically say he can put as many of my pictures anywhere he wants for as long as he wants. And I do it again. Five more times over the next two weeks. And the week after that, Bill calls me into his office and shows me the latest copy of the leading gay magazine called Blue Boy. I'm on the cover with one of my 'Fuck You' looks, naked in a bow-tie.

"Everybody loves ya, kid," he says. "You're gonna be on the cover of Honcho magazine next month and Stallion the month after that!"

"Who's everybody?" I say. I mean I'm just trying to make some get-high money here. I could give a shit about who thinks what. Then Bill tells me guys wanna pay money to have sex with me. I say, "No, I don't do that kind of shit."

"How about hardcore porn?" he says.

"No," I say.

"Pays a lot more," he says.

"I'm not into that kind of stuff," I say. "I'm not gay, okay?"

"It's just a job," he says.

Then he pulls a magazine out of his desk drawer and points to the cover.

"Look at this," he says.

I look. I see the cover shot. It's of a guy with a cock in his mouth and a cock in each hand. Lovin' it.

"See this guy," he says. "He works for me. He's not gay either."

I look again at the ecstatic expression of the cock swallower/ handler cover boy.

"He's not?" I say.

"No, he's not," Bill says, matter-of-factly. Then he holds it right up to my face and says, "He's a family man…"

The sales pitch is so beyond insane that I find myself studying the cover again to see if I can tell if the guy is really gay or not. I try to imagine this guy with his wife and kids.

"He's a family man?" I say.

"That's right," Bill says. "He's just doin' his job and you can do the same thing. Understand? You don't have to be gay."

What a fucking angle this Bill has, I think. I almost went for the bait myself. Unbelievable. Then I tell him flat out.

"I don't do it. No."

Right away he says, "How about straight porn? I got people askin', movie people. They like the size of your cock and they like the way you look."

Now I'm biting. I see myself getting high and fucking women and getting paid for it.

"Yeah?" I say.

"Can you act?" he says.

"Fuck, yeah, I can do it."

Next day I'm on the set of the T&A team, a porn spoof of the TV show, 'The A Team'. I'm dressed in a night watchman's uniform. I'm on duty, patrolling some top security building. Then I hear strange noises coming from the bathroom. I walk in and say, "Is anybody in here?" That's my big line. Then I look over and see one of the T&A team girls standing spread-legged on the bathroom sink with her mini-skirt hiked up over her ass.

"Hey, watchman, come over here and eat my hot, juicy pussy," she says.

I give one of those, "Oh, boy, this is my day!" looks and go over to her and start eating her pussy. Then two other T&A team chicks come out of the stalls. Girl One unbuckles my belt, pulls my pants down and says, "Hey, watchman, wanna fuck me?" Girl Two grabs my cock and says, "I wanna suck his big, fat cock first."

So I eat pussy while I get blown then they all pull me down on the bathroom floor, tie me up and gag me. One fucks me. I come. Two fucks me. I cum again. Then they walk out of the bathroom to infiltrate the security building, leaving me fucked out and helpless. End Scene.

I'm a natural. The porn girls think I'm cute. They love my cock. The director loves me. Same one that called me a real cumer. They pay me six hundred for the day plus four hundred for the extra cum shot.

And so it goes. That's how I got into porn. Only did it for a year or so, did maybe twelve movies. It got a little crazy, a little out of control. In reality it was disgusting. Much more fun to watch than actually do. I started to hate it. I felt like a cheap piece of shit. And my conscience weighed heavy on me.

My mom found out and said she would disown me if I did another one. Then I got fired off the set for being too high on cocaine. No heroin, just cocaine, but I was so high, my cock just wouldn't respond, even when this actress put ice cubes in her mouth and… oh, my cock just shrivelled up inside me as I frothed from the mouth and stuttered, "I ca… ca… can't do it."

"Get outta here kid, go home."

That was really humiliating, getting fired from a porn movie. That's when I stopped doin' them and went to rehab. Was that a sign to get me out of porn? I felt in my soul that it was… but did I follow that sign? No, I read those scripts they sent me and I did a couple more after that. Sober.

That was freaky, saying the Serenity Prayer before a fuck scene. Then I quit. Oh yeah, and one more in California, the first year I moved out from New York. Not sober. I was up for five days on crystal meth driving everyone on the set crazy, ya know talking, talking, talking. I should have been fired but unlike cocaine, crystal gave me an eternal, raging hard-on so I was told to keep my dick hard and my mouth shut.

That was early '85. All the actors had to get an AIDS test before we started. I knew some of the girls were hookin' on the side. Who knows who everyone is fucking off the set? Half the male porno actors fuck guys too. Just business, ya know. And I fucked a couple of girls I picked up in bars during those five blind days. No protection, no questions. *Not good, not good, not good. Scary, scary, scary.*

Something sank in. That was my last one. Then I got my first commercial agent. Got lucky right off the bat. Funny, I had a commercial running on national TV and a porn movie running at the Pussycat cinema at the same time. But I did stop the porn... all right, enough of that.

*

I'm back in Hollywood in my crappy little apartment... yeah, I'm back in Hollywood at the apartment. I'm getting nowhere with this Mac character. Caught in the past again. My wretched porn life I regret so much... so much that I'm actually on an internet porn site myself looking at how hot the porn chicks are now compared to the ones I fucked in the eighties. I'm playing with my cock and wanting to get back into porn so I can fuck these hot new porn stars and hating myself for thinking that. I go from site to site, staring at tits and pussy and fucking and sucking... and hating myself and looking and hating and looking...

Oh, God, I gotta stop, please…

Shnooky lies on the floor pretending to ignore me. She knows. But it's hard for her because she loves me so unconditionally. I feel what I think she is thinking and I tell her, "Shut up, just shut up, Shnooky!" Of course she wags her tail and beams at me.

I love you, Daddy, I don't care what you do… maybe you care what you do but I don't. My little furry gift from God. My little messenger of love. Okay, what's the message?

Get off the porn site, you'll feel better.

"Okay," I say. I click off the porn site, relieved. I feel better, better than if I jerked off in a napkin over some porn star sucking cock. Maybe if I had the porn chick under my table and she was sucking my cock as I was writing… I close my eyes, think about that for a few seconds, get the visual… and feel like jerking off again.

No!

So I get back to writing but it takes about half an hour to get the porn visuals out of my head. Then I stare at the page where I think I'm going to start re-working the Mac character. That takes another hour. Just as I get a glimmer of where to go, I realize it's already time to get to this commercial audition.

I think I better call Patti to see if Tony got there so I can go over my ideas. Plus I gotta check up on him, right? Make sure he got home okay.

Just let it go. You can't control what Tony does.

Sure, I listen to that voice for a second then make the call.

"What? I thought he was at your house," Patti says. "He told me he was going to be there all day working."

"Fuck," I say. "He was too burnt out so I told him to take a cab to your house. I only gave him twenty bucks."

"Well, that's enough to get him started again. Who knows what he does after that?"

She knows. I know. Tony will do whatever it takes. Patti laughs. She has known Tony for twenty years. Seen him through all his struggles. She just loves him pretty much for who he is and lets him stay with her whether he's high or not.

I don't know how and I don't know why. He'd be dead on the street if it wasn't for her. Maybe he'll die on the street anyway. Every time he goes on a crack run, I never think he'll make it back. I always think the worst. I get off the phone, my mind races with panic. No Tony, no script. No script, no money. No money, no nothing for me and Max. I wanna kill Tony. I hope he just dies and gets it over with.

So I wash the dirty oatmeal dishes with vigorous anger and hatred because I can control my goddamn dishes. Then I put on a pair of Levi's to complete my Sam Shepard wardrobe, fuck with my hair a little, placing the long hair over the balding spots with careful attention...

"Oh goddamnit! Forget it!" I say. "Come on, Shnooky!"

And me and the dog are out the door.

It's turned into a lovely day. The sun is up high in the sky, puffs of clouds passing by. The winter air is fresh and clean. The palm trees sway in the breeze. Oh, look! A Hummingbird hovers over the crimson sage bush, sucking nectar out of the deep red flowers, right outside your building. Look at its bright green little belly. Oh, my God! Look how fast it flies. Whoosh... there it goes. Life is so wondrous, so beautiful. Did you notice that, Dave?

9

I'm in the commercial casting office on Ivar Street in Hollywood with all these Sam Shepard lookalikes. Some don't look anything remotely like him and some are pretty damn close. This one guy who is a better looking version, more like a fashion model version - taller, bigger muscles, perfect hair - is strutting around, staring down the other inferior versions like, "Dude, you don't have a chance against me."

I fucking hate this guy. I kill him in my mind many different ways. Smug cocksucker. He's not a widowed dad trying to bring up a kid on his own. He doesn't need this job like I do. And he'll probably get it too. Fucking prick. I got more Sam Shepard in me than he'll ever have. But he has the look, the commercial look. When he stares me down, I stare right back. He winces. I actually unnerve him a little bit or maybe he just winces like, "Dude, you look fucking crazy."

That's right! I'm crazy!

They call me in for my audition. The usual drill is that a casting agent assistant directs you through the audition while he puts you on video tape. Sometimes they have you do an improvisational bit, like for this crappy product; pretending to eat a satisfying TV dinner or telling your wife how it tastes like home cooking, some bullshit, or sometimes you read a few lines of ridiculous, unrealistic dialogue.

I've seen this assistant before, kind of a quirky guy, stocky, built like a pitbull but still nerdy. He's auditioned me before and knows I'm a little edgy. He always acts kind of nervous around me even though if he wanted, he could beat the shit out of me, easy. I ask him what the deal is and he tells me, "Just gonna ask you a few questions, Dave." Great, my favourite type of audition. A personality test.

Some of the commercial directors want to get the feel of the, "real you" so they have the casting agents ask all these personal questions to decide whether or not you're good material for the callback audition. So I stand in front of the camera.

"Hey, what's your name?" the assistant says in a cheerful tone.

"Hey, Dave," I say back, trying to muster up my own cheerful response but it comes off more like, "Hey, I'm fuckin' crazy and I hate this shit."

This sucks, this sucks, this sucks, oh God, this sucks so much. Be nice, be normal, relax, relax, take it easy...

"So, Dave, what are some of your favourite things to do?"

I imagine fuckin' pretty boy Sam Shepard lookalike saying, "I like to work out, hike mountains and eat healthy," as he flashes a perfect smile, and I know I can't compete with that so I just say what's in my head.

"When I'm not eatin' Healthy Choice?" I say, staring right into the camera. "Shoot speedballs and fuck pussy." The assistant bursts out laughing.

"Dude, you want me to keep that on tape?" he says.

"Yeah, why not," I say. "Does this director have a sense of humour?"

"Dude, not that kind. I mean, I think it's funny but we're talkin' TV dinners here. Ya know, you're like a regular American guy."

"Any of these fucking people ever read a Sam Shepard play?"

"Dude, I don't care. I'll keep it if you want it..."

I think, fuck the director and the TV dinner people but I need a job, bad. So bad. All I'm getting is a few trickling residuals from the last commercial I did over a year ago.

"No, forget it," I say. "Let's try it again. I'll be nice."

So I do it again as nice and normal as I can. I say I love to run up hills with my dog and go to the beach with my son but I come off all pensive and melancholy so I get one more try to be all-American and positive (because that's how we are all supposed to be, right?) and I come off all uncomfortable and unnatural and it sucks and I leave.

It's not that I don't wanna act happy, I just don't have it in me. Not that kind of happy. I mean, if I could say, "Eating TV dinners sucks but if ya have to eat one, at least make it Healthy Choice," then maybe I could pull it off. As I pass smirking, perfect Sam Shepard smug-ass on the way out, I feel like such a failure that I can't even fake being happy. I get that scared... *what am I doing with my life?...* feeling but I push that down as quick as it comes up.

"Fuck these stupid commercial auditions," I say to Shnooky, who rides shotgun, as I drive down Vine Street trying to keep my eyes off all the gutter life that still seems to fascinate me. She smiles, thumps her tail on the seat, gives me a love wink with her eyes and beams at me. *It's okay, Daddy.*

"No, that audition sucked, Shnooky. I sucked."

Don't worry, Daddy, I love you, you're my favourite.

Not enough right now, I need more. My ego is starving. I need something. I need to look better, younger, right now. I keep checking myself out in the rearview, I mean like every few seconds thinking maybe on the next look I'll be younger, more handsome, more hair... I mean, how many times can I look in the rearview mirror and expect an instantaneous change?

There, I just did it again! You look the same, okay, the same as you did three seconds ago. Moron! Try doing something constructive.

I take a right onto Santa Monica Boulevard. Fine, I'll go get dinner at the Whole Foods on Fairfax for Max and myself before

I go back home and stare at the computer some more. I make a lot of vegetable and Tofu dishes, pastas with fresh ingredients, homemade sauce and once in a while get a good piece of fish so I'm thinking maybe some Albacore tuna or halibut if it's on sale, and get an avocado, some toasted seaweed, make some rice and we'll have our own Japanese-style fish wraps.

I can't afford it but I rationalize because we don't eat out or go to fast food crap-ass joints; Taco Bell, Pizza Hut and worst of all, McDonald's. Those cocksuckers, forcing their bullshit worldwide commercials and suck-ass food, all over the world, taking over the planet and wasting it away with their tons and tons of sick, chemical-injected cows, chomping, chomping, chomping the rainforests into extinction just to get slaughtered and made into garbage burgers with barf-tasting special sauce. Billions and billions sold. Billions and billions made. How corrupt. How disgusting. How utterly despicable. I HATE MCDONALD'S! Just my opinion.

Anyway, I love cooking good meals for us at home. I feed my son well. Get it? I put good, healthy food in his growing body. And just as I'm thinking how much I love my son, I get a call from his school, from the Principal's office. What's this? Max fell asleep in math class and when asked why he was so tired, he told his teacher he was up late worrying about his dad who was looking for his friend Tony in Hollywood crack houses.

"So is this true?" the assistant principal asks me.

Her voice is even tempered and concerned so I try to stay even tempered and concerned.

"Well, it's partially true," I say. "I was trying to find a friend who is sick, who is addicted to crack."

"Excuse me," she says, "but did you leave your son at home alone to go to a crack house? Because that is what he said."

I get a little defensive.

"I don't think that is any of your business," I say.

"Excuse me, but it is our business," she says. "We have concerns for all of our students' well-being here and this is definitely a concern. Could you please explain what happened last night?"

Now it sounds like she's got a snotty, private school, superior attitude and that she is accusing me of being a dead-beat, drug addict dad. That's what I hear and I answer accordingly in the best way I know how.

"Excuse fucking me!" I say. "Number one, I don't take drugs, any drugs. I happen to have a partner who is on them who I am trying to help, okay? I'm trying to save his life! And my wife, as you are aware of, is fucking dead! So I didn't have anybody to stay with Max when I left at two in the fucking morning AND I'M A GOOD FATHER, OKAY! AND I LOVE MY SON AND I WOULDN'T FUCKING EVER PUT HIM IN ANY DANGER, UNDERSTAND?!!!"

I wait for a response but she's already hung up on me.

"You fucking bitch!" I say, feeling the rage that starts throbbing through me. Shnooky jumps in the back seat and starts shaking.

"Not you, stupid!" I say. "I'm mad at Max's assistant principal, okay!"

She thumps her tail against the seat, fast and scared.

Take it easy, Daddy, take it easy…

"No I won't!" I mean, I'm saying this right to my dog.

"I'm gonna drive down there right now and talk to that woman! I'm gonna give her a big fuckin' heads up!"

I speed through traffic with fierce determination. Someone honks their horn at me.

"Fuck you! Let me pass, damnit!"

I mean, I'm in a hurry now, I have more important issues at hand than anybody else on the road, know what I mean? I'm on a righteous mission. I'm gonna take care of things, set everybody straight.

They have no idea what I go through down at that snot-ass rich kids' school! Who the fuck do they think they are to talk to me like that? They don't have to bring up a kid alone with no fucking money. They don't know how hard it is for me just to get through the day. They don't have the fucked-up past I have. They wanna know what's going on in my life, I'll tell 'em everything! I'll tell 'em it's a miracle that I am even alive! Shock the shit out of those sheltered motherfuckers! I'll walk in there proud, tall and justified and I'll pull my kid right out of that place. Phony-ass Cocksuckers!

Suddenly, I hear Keri's voice. Kind. Soothing.

"Dave, he needs to stay in that school. I think what you should do is go and apologize."

I hear it but I don't pay attention. Her voice in my mind. So what? I even say, "Fuck off," under my breath.

Then I hear her voice and it's loud.

"Dave, you're an idiot! Go apologize now!"

I'm stunned. I'm floored. I glance over at Shnooky.

Sorry, Daddy, you're wrong.

Did she hear it too? Or is Shnooky really Keri?

"Are you Keri, damnit?" I say to her. "Go ahead! Say it if you are! Say it!"

Shnooky hops in the front seat and licks my face. Just laps away on my cheek.

It doesn't matter, it doesn't matter, it doesn't matter, Daddy.

Love, love, love, love, love…

I don't want to accept it but it's too strong. Maybe Keri's spirit is in her. I don't know and it doesn't matter how. It just is. My rage is broken by her love.

"Okay, okay…" I say as I crash down from my fury, realizing, realizing, realizing…

Now I have tears in my eyes. I remember when Keri came to me in a dream and said, *"Please, Dave, try to get him in a good school if you can."* He was in fifth grade then, going to a shitty little public school on Beechwood, getting C's and D's, just kind of scraping by with no interest and no one there was showing much interest or giving him any direction, either.

He said he learned more watching Discovery channel than at school. He spent more time drawing and painting than he did on homework. I just told him he had to go but I wasn't exactly the best role model (I was skipping school and smoking weed at eleven). Every day he said he hated the school, hated his teachers. I went to meet with his teachers and I hated them too. His academic future was grim. I knew it and Keri knew it too... knew it from beyond... *please get him into a good school.* How?

Then I got an unexpected call from an old friend of hers, Barbara, who along with all of Keri's friends was crushed when she died. They all loved her so much. I can't honestly say they had the same feelings for me. Barbara cornered me once and said she just couldn't understand why Keri was ever with me. My self-defeating, drug-induced, slurred reply was that maybe I was just a good fuck and a good time.

"How about a good fuck and a bad time, Dave?" she said. And every time Keri threw me out of the house, Barbara was relieved. She wanted to call child services and tell them I was nodding out on heroin while changing my son's diapers (which I was) but she didn't for Keri's sake.

Even after I sobered up, she didn't trust me. Even though I was showing up for Max and becoming an honest, trustworthy, loving dad. Barbara was waiting for me to fuck up, waiting for me to fail, waiting to prove to Keri that I was a loser piece of shit. But I kept showing up. I was becoming a good dad, a toe-the-line, teetotalling, stand-up guy, telling Keri not to drink around her son, or as she would say, "a tea-pot calling the kettle black." And Keri and I lived together off and on up until the day she died, fighting, separating, getting back together, right up until the night the phone call came… shit… the phone call… telling me that Keri was dead… and Max was in intensive care…

After the accident none of them could imagine me being able to take care of Max on my own and neither could I. I could barely take care of myself. I carried him around in his body cast for three months, held him over the toilet so he could pee and poo, scratched him where it itched with a coat hanger, brought him to physical therapy, put him in a new school, made him breakfast, lunch, dinner, cried with him about his mom, worked two to three menial fucking minimum wage jobs… and stayed off the drugs and the booze although some nights I wanted to just end it all, end the pain and the fear and the desperation of being a broken single dad, day by day by day…

And the years went by and Keri's friends waited and waited and waited as I changed and changed and changed and rose and rose and rose to every occasion, not very gracefully but I rose to become a sober, responsible dad and mom... Fucking hard job, let me tell ya, especially when all bets are against you. Barbara used to call a couple of times a year just to check up on how we were doing... just in case. Cordial but not friendly. Sense of duty to Keri. I knew she probably wished it was me instead of Keri that died but I'd be cool, tell her things were okay with us, a little rough but okay.

Anyway, I hadn't heard from her in about a year when I got the call. "Dave," she said. "I'm only calling because Keri came to me in a dream and asked how Max was doing in school. It was so clear and she seemed really concerned."

I just flat out told her about my dream. I also told her how Max was doing in school. Barbara gave me the number of a tutor she knew and told me not to worry about the money. Then she hung up. I reluctantly called, Max reluctantly went. Her name was Sarah. Very wealthy, married to a successful TV writer/producer, Lawrence, very smart nice guy playing the game right in the business and reaping the benefits which I hated right off the bat.

Oh, he must be a phoney sell-out. *Why, Dave? Because you couldn't do it? Anyone who is successful is a sell-out, right? Okay, enough, go on...* but what about that time he said he had a days' work for you on his ridiculously silly sitcom and you showed up and it was only an extra job and you had to wait six hours before your big part which was serving the star of the show a Burrito from a Burrito truck and they shot your scene, showing you from the elbow down, serving the Burrito as the star carried on with some piss-ass unfunny dialogue with his co-star while Lawrence and the director and creator and the other fucking idiots running the network boat of stinking shit, laughed, "Ha, ha, ha, ha, ha," over and over, take after take after take. Five fucking ha's every time. No more, no less. Empty flat laughter. I mean what the fuck... live canned laughter on the set before they cut in the recorded canned laughter. Fucking twilight zone! Just horrifying... and they're all getting rich while you're a charity case for his wife.

But Sarah was special. She was genuine. She was kind, loving, patient and tolerant of both Max and me, of our personalities and our attitudes. Let's just say she was a fucking Saint. After a few sessions she told me Max was one of the brightest kids she had ever worked with and a true Artist and that she was going to look into a private school that suited him.

"I couldn't even pay you for tutoring, how do ya think I could pay for fucking private school?" I asked.

Sarah laughed. She thought it was funny that I swore all the time. Made me wanna swear less but I still swore. She told me although the school she had in mind was one of the best in Los Angeles and very hard to get into, they made a point of seeking out diversity in their student body and gave financial aid in certain special cases. She was sure that Max would be one of those cases.

She told me to just go forward with applying, not to worry about money. "It will work out," she said and it did. I remember before the interview I heard Keri's voice say to me, *"Play the violin, Dave, milk it for all it's worth."*

So I told them the story of how she died and how Max and I struggled without her and I cried and cried and they cried and told me Max was a wonderful kid and for me not to worry and they accepted Max in the school on a ninety percent scholarship.

Yes, it is a gift that he is in that school and maybe Keri's spirit did pull some strings from beyond and I want to yank them all down because I don't like the way the assistant principal talked to me.

I replay my pleasant little phone conversation over in my mind, and over and over and over. Regretting, regretting, regretting. Why couldn't I have just stayed even and explained what happened like a normal, responsible parent?

Because you're not! You're a fuck-up! You'll show them, right? Fucking moron. Idiot!

No! Please!

I get another call on the cell. Oh, no, it's gonna be them. Max is expelled. Oh shit… Maybe I should answer first.

"Hello…" I say, ready to get reamed by the Principal.

"Yeah, mothafucka, this is Tony's secretary," I hear on the other end. Okay, he's high, he's with a street hooker and she's calling me… but I'm still baffled.

"What?" I say.

"I work for Tony now an' he ain't goin' over to your sorry ass crib no mo'. He's sick a your shit-ass attitude. You come to his office from now on, mothafucka! Tony is the mothafuckin' boss now!"

"What office?" I say.

"Tony got an office now…"

Then I hear Tony in the background, his voice all nasty and weasely, like it gets when he smokes crack.

"Shut up, you stupid ho' bitch, get off the phone…"

"Hey, don't you call me no stupid ho' bitch, Tony," she says. "How many times you sucked dick for some rock? And you told me to call the mothafucka, you told me to give the mothafucka the heads up!.." Then the line goes dead.

Jesus! This is all I need! I mean, this is my life… my life sucks so bad! Oh, God, I gotta calm down, I gotta calm down.

I grab a cigarette butt out of the ashtray, shove it in my mouth and push in the three-decade-old cigarette lighter.

"Come on, come on, come on!" I say, waiting for the lighter to pop out. I see my gnarled-up old, angry, leathery face with the crumpled butt sticking out between my lips in the rearview. *Look at you, suckin' on that dirty old butt. Disgusting. Smoke the feelings away, you desperate bastard. Better hurry up!*

I wish I didn't know exactly why I smoke. I sure didn't when I started at ten years old. Smokin' was cool. I couldn't wait. Didn't know shit. Now I know so much information, not only the physical but the why, the why I smoke. *Hiding, hiding, hiding.* I have so much self-knowledge that I fucking hate myself every time I light up. So I toss the butt back in the ashtray.

Wimp. Loser. Can't even smoke.

Okay! Stop it! Stop it! Stop it!

I pull over to the side of the road, a block past La Brea, jump out of the car and race around to the passenger side like I just discovered a flat tyre. But I don't have a flat, I need an excuse to drop to my knees and pray myself back to some sort of sanity.

So I pretend to check out the tyre in case people are watching. Like anybody cares, right?

"Look at that man! He doesn't have a flat tyre, he's praying!"

I notice a couple of skinny teenage gay hustlers on the corner of La Brea, looking my way. Shirts open, jeans pulled down low. I know they're tweakin' on speed because they're so flighty and animated with each other.

In a flash I think of Max. I mean, shit, he's just a few years younger than them and look what could have happened if I didn't take care of him and love him and get him in a good school? Just as I get a shot of gratitude, one of the teeny-bop hustlers grabs the other one's hand and starts hurrying over. What the fuck? Do I look like an old cruisin' fag now? Is that what they think? I just wanna pray. So I stay there on my knees with my eyes closed, hoping they'll just pass me by. Then I hear one of them right behind me say,

"So… what are you doing here, mister?"

"Doesn't look like a flat to me," the other one says.

"Really? Maybe he just wants us to get in the car. Is that the game, honey? What do ya think?"

I feel like I'm gonna lose it, go crazy, crazy, crazy, tell 'em what I been through, tell 'em how utterly fucked their lives are gonna be if they don't… but somehow I just say, "Please, just no, please…"

"Well, call us when you get the nerve," I hear, and I feel them huff away, justified in their own little pathetic delusions.

And I pray… God help, please help me, please help me, please help me, faster and faster until it sounds like, pselpmeselpmeselpme…

Breathe in God. Breathe out fear. Breathe in God. Breathe out fear. I can't believe just breathing helps so much. I always forget but it always works when I do it. I stand up.

Okay, okay, it's all gonna be okay. "I'm going down to the school and apologize, now," I say. I just say it into the air, like Keri is listening or God is listening. Somehow it makes me feel better. I see the blue sky again, feel the silver winter sun on my face. I get back in the car. Shnooky wags her tail.

Okay, Daddy?

"Yeah, okay, okay, I'm sorry I got so upset. I love you."

She beams at me. *Say it again.*

"Okay, okay, I love you, I love you a hundred million times."

10

I park the car and tell Shnooky to be a good girl and wait.

Okay, Daddy, you be good too.

I look up and down 21st street at the school campus. Bunch of fucking brick buildings wedged up next to some industrial site by the freeway. Where do all the millions go? All the huge tuitions and donations… for what? It's not like some sprawling campus where you can see where the money went.

There are even other businesses on the same block; some sheet metal shop and some air industrial offices. They turned an alley in the back into a lunch hangout for the students and put in a couple more buildings; a little theatre, an arts centre, a library built by some famous architect… but I'm thinking still not millions. Somebody's makin' out somewhere, gettin' richer and richer.

Hey! Why are you concerned where all the money goes, you're on financial aid!

I go into the middle school office ready to make my amends. I'm calm, and relaxed… okay, somewhat calm and relaxed. I mean, I'm progressing on my spiritual path, I'm no saint, right? I still have

94

voices in my head telling me to pound my fists on the table and say, "I wanna talk to the fucking principal! Now!"... but they're little voices, little chattering demons, so I ignore them and tell the plump little olive-skinned secretary with a thick black mane of hair, my name, my son's name and grade and ask if I can please talk to Principal Morganson.

Pretty good, huh? Please. That's the humility right there or maybe that's just how everybody is supposed to do it. Must be, Dave, because the secretary doesn't say, "You are such a fine man for saying please." She just asks me what it pertains to. *You wanna know what it pertains to, huh? Fuck!* Stop. Don't tell her.

"It's a personal matter," I say, surprised myself at how I'm responding. "It's important that I speak to him."

She looks at me for a couple of seconds like maybe she failed to recognize my importance, like maybe I'm some rich and famous parent.

And then... I feel like I am that rich and famous parent. I don't know who, I just have that, I'm rich and famous feeling and it feels good. I say, "You're Greek, aren't you? Ya know, I went all over Greece in the eighties; Athens, Rhodes, Mykonos, all the islands." I don't tell her I went there from Thailand with Sadie to kick our bad heroin habits and we ended up whoring ourselves around the islands after we ran out of money, but the memory does take some air out of my egotistical rich and famous feeling.

"I'm half Greek," she says, somewhat impressed. "My father is from Spain."

As she picks up the phone and calls the Principal, I wanna tell her I've been to Madrid too, but my mind flashes back to a visual of me fucking this wild, insane Spanish model, Carina, on a liquid morphine/ecstasy combination as this decrepit, prehistoric, 'Count Pepe' from some obscure province, watches and peels off mucho pesos.

The secretary says, "Principal Morgan will see you in his office now."

"Huh? Okay," I say, as I realize he must have given her the heads-up on my nobody status when I was off in another sordid fuck story from the past, because she gives me a condescending smirk then points to the open door about ten feet behind her desk.

Rich and famous feeling flattened, the little chattering demons growing and guffawing in my head, telling me to yell out, "Hey! Want me to dick-slap that smirk off your fat little greasy face?" I give the secretary a meek, forced "Thank you," and walk back to the Principal's office.

Go with God, Dave. Bring God in the room with you.

Okay, okay, okay, fine, fine, fine.

Principal Morganson stands up from behind his desk. He is a tall, severe-looking man with close-cropped hair, donning gold wire-rimmed glasses, wearing Ralph Lauren khakis, crisp white button-down shirt and tie. He is the middle school principal at an exclusive private school and playing the part well. He is not happy to see me. He gives a superior and irritated, "Hello," and tells me to, "Sit down."

Back in the Principal's office again, Dave? Jesus! Didn't you have enough of this when you were in high school?

"I, ah… I just came to apologize for…"

Morganson cuts me off, saying, "I would like Alice to be present for this, she will be here momentarily."

He takes another phone call, obviously showing me how insignificant I am and how I've interrupted his busy day… anyway that's how I see it as I sit down in one of the chairs across from his desk, feeling my pulse throbbing through every vein in my body.

How long can I sit here like this? I can't stand it!

Yes you can. Stay humble. Relax

No! I can't, I wanna jump up and scream out, "You cocksucker!"

Wait, wait, okay, okay… okay.

Alice, the assistant principal, walks in. She's got short, prematurely grey hair, bookworm glasses, no make-up over her ruddy complexion and she's wearing a conservative, navy blue pants suit. *Librarian lesbian type, hates me, hates me.* She skirts around me avoiding eye contact and sits in the chair next to Morganson's desk.

She looks at him, tense. He gives her a reassuring look back. Then she stares down at the floor like the violated victim that can't face her filthy rapist while Morganson reams me out for verbally terrorizing her.

I stay humble, apologize to her for my inappropriate behaviour. I tell her I'm sorry if I hurt her feelings in any way, making sure I don't tell her if she wasn't such an accusing fucking bitch none of this would have happened. I hear Keri in my head say, *"Good choice not to say that, Dave."*

Alice accepts my apology and tells me she was only concerned for Max. She says the math teacher came to her, concerned, then she called me, concerned. Morganson adds, "We were all concerned because we care about our students' welfare here. Would you rather we weren't concerned?"

Now is the time, Dave. Stand up, grab your cock and balls and say, "Concern this, you fucking stuck-up moron! I know what the fuck I'm doing with my kid!" Just a little voice, just a little voice, just a little voice…

I tell him I'm very grateful that they were concerned and stress that I appreciate all they have done for Max. I do a little violin playing, adding I never had the chance for an education like he's getting. I remind him about my past with drugs and that I was trying to help a friend who is taking them.

Morganson cuts me off again saying he knows my past enough

to understand our situation but basically tells me it's no excuse to behave the way I did. He suggests if I have to leave Max alone, to notify a relative or neighbour. I agree with him as I think, *Notify? What are you, a fucking cop? Yes, I'll notify a neighbour. Why don't you just say, call a neighbour? Notify. Do you say vehicle instead of car like cops do, too? I should fucking ask you that, huh? Do you?!...*

Anyway, I tell him it won't happen again. I say all I want is for Max to stay in school and that I will do anything they want to keep him there. Morganson tells me they have no problems with Max. He is a good kid, a bright student, a very talented artist and they love having him there. He says, "If we ever find it necessary to suspend or expel Max from this school, you will most probably be the reason why."

Alice likes this. She loves this. If she had any guts she would burst out laughing but she remains composed just widening her eyes enough to give her glee away as she nods her head in agreement with Morganson.

I say, "I understand," holding back a, *So what... it's all my fucking fault! Fine! You two pieces of snot-filled shit!*

Morganson tells me Max will be out of class in a couple of minutes and I might as well take him home early so he can rest up for tomorrow. As a concerned parent I ask, "You think he should miss class?"

Alice tells me, "It's okay, his last class today is gym."

She's reassuring me. No, she's making fun of me because I don't know his schedule. Patronizing me? Is that what she's doing? Before I can figure it out, Morganson dismisses me like he would an eighth grade student after a scolding, and I take it because I have to. Right, Keri, right?

"Oh, shut up, Dave, you big baby."

11

So we're driving home. I ask Max, "Why didn't you tell me you were so worried that you couldn't sleep?"

"Because I wasn't."

"What? Then why…"

"Take it easy, Dad."

"You take it easy. What happened?"

"I just didn't wanna take the math quiz."

"So you… Why didn't you just take the fucking quiz? Then none of this would have happened! I screamed at Alice, swore at her, everything."

"Good move, Dad. If you just acted like a normal parent none of this would have happened. You make such a big deal out of everything."

"When they think I'm going to crack houses, it is a big deal."

"No, you made it into a big deal."

"Fine, I apologized okay, it's over. I kissed Alice and Morganson's asses."

"Morganson is a big dickhead anyway and Alice is a big mean

Lesbo. All the kids hate them."

"Why?" I ask, glad that I didn't know this information before or I would have really blown it in the office.

"Because they treat us like fifth graders. I can't wait until I'm in ninth grade."

"Well, just behave so you make it into ninth grade," I say, like I'm the mature parent closing the issue.

"How about you behave... Dad," he says back like he's correcting me on who the mature one is in the family.

Now that pisses me off but I let it go. No, I wanna let it go but I can't so I just stop talking, let it simmer as the traffic builds. Olympic Boulevard is already jammed and believe me I've tried every other way home; Pico Boulevard, across Sepulveda up to Wilshire over to Santa Monica or straight up to Sunset, which works until you get into Beverly fucking Hills.

And forget about the 10 freeway, it's like a parking lot after two pm. You just can't avoid it. Rush hour has started and it's not even three o'clock because there really is no rush hour, is there? That is such bullshit. One little hour from five to six? I mean, come on; it's from five to six fucking hours long, right? And I never get used to it. Especially when I'm simmering over what Max just said to me or how I'm gonna get work, money, pay the bills, deal with Tony and on and on....

"Look at this fucking traffic! I can't believe this fucking traffic!"

Listen up, cars: Dave's coming down the road! Everybody out of the way! And the cars part to the side as I pass, muttering in unison, "Oh, sorry, sorry... sorry, Dave."

Max ignores me. He turns on the radio and changes stations trying to find a song he likes. Station to station to station, it's the same when he watches TV, switching from channel to channel to channel.

Wasn't like that when I was a kid, we had to get up and change the damn channel... and we used to watch the whole damn show, like it or not... and a hot dog used to cost a goddamn quarter...

He's actually pretty savvy in his choices. He doesn't like the new bands very much, hates commercial bands, thinks most hip-hop is funny (thank God he doesn't take it seriously). He likes the old stuff, though, from the sixties and seventies. All the bands and all the songs that I used to listen to at his age, stoned to the gills, I might add.

He leaves it on a classic rock station. Led Zeppelin's 'Babe, I'm gonna leave ya' from their first album is playing. He likes the song for the song. He likes Robert Plant's voice, Jimmy Page's guitar, he drums along with John Bonham on the dashboard while, for me, I mean shit... I drift back to a 1971 summer memory where I'm sucking Arrid extra-dry deodorant through a towel for the free-on while peaking on purple micro-dot acid, in my friend Pete Bono's black-lit, psychedelic painted basement, all to blot out my broken little fourteen-year-old heart over Becky Newirth who moved away to Boston. And the song is blasting and I'm peaking into oblivion and crying and singing, "Babe, I'm gonna leave ya'... leave ya when the summer..."

And somehow I just wanna go back there to that time and change it all around so I wasn't such a lost, fucked up, drugged out little kid but I can't and I miss it all at the same time because it was so fun and crazy and I had no responsibilities or pressures. But I was wasted and I wasted it and I wasted so much...

"Max, change the station," I say.

"What for?"

"I just don't wanna listen to that song, okay!"

"Dad, it's just a song. Why do you always have to make it into something?"

"It's not just a song for me, it brings back stuff. You don't understand."

"Sure, Dad, I don't understand. I don't understand why you're such a big sensitive baby."

"I don't wanna be like that, I just am like that, okay!"

I hate that I'm so sensitive. I hate it more than he does. I remember when I was in sixth grade, kids used to make fun of me all the time. I'd get so upset. Then I asked this kid, Pete Byrnes, why they all made fun of me so much and Pete said, "Because it's so easy."

And it was easy until the drugs took over, covered up all that sensitive shit. I turned into a cool, dark little Demon. No one could touch me. But those days are long gone and I live with my super sensitivity again… and I know that… and yes, I pray just for it to go away. But it's still there every fuckin' day and I still hate it.

Just get a pack of smokes. Push it down, push it down. No, no, no! Wait a second, you're simmered to boiling… think about it, think about it. Breathe. Let it go. No? Okay. Boil, baby…

"And don't do that again! Don't make up excuses why you can't take a test!"

"Quiz, Dad."

"I don't care! And don't ever tell the teachers anything about drugs! They could think all kinds of shit… This fucking traffic! I hate it! Fuck!… You know how hard it is for me to keep everything going for us? Huh? What if they cut off our financial aid, huh? Then you'd be in some shithole fucking public school in Hollywood! And your life would be fucked! God damnit! My life is hard enough as it is… now Tony's on crack again… I don't know what the hell I'm gonna do about work. Damnit, I hate this traffic! Change the station!"

"Fine, Dad. Blame your life on me."

"It's not my life, it's your life!"

I'm just plain blackout screamin'. I don't even know what I'm saying anymore. Idiot. I don't know that yet but I will. Soon.

Max turns off the radio, leans back in the seat and stares out the window. Straight out and far away. I hear Shnooky panting and thumping her tail in the back seat. I clench the wheel and fume and drive and... yup, here it comes... I feel like a remorseful piece of shit.

"Okay, okay, I'm sorry, I'm sorry I got mad at you, okay? It's my fault, okay? I know it... I'm sorry."

Max shakes his head, keeping his gaze out the window. "Sometimes when you yell," he says, "it makes me not wanna be here. It makes me not wanna be in my skin."

I know what he's talking about. He is so right I can't even think to deny it. My desperate, end of the world, fuck everything yell. Horrible. I glance over at his sweet, young face. It looks worn and sad and pained. I love him so much, so deep. No mom. Crazed me as a dad. I feel the tears forming in my eyes. I blink hard a couple of times to stop them. I wanna say I'll never yell again but I probably will. I know it. He knows it.

"At least I apologize sooner than I used to," I say.

"So what, Dad? You still suck."

"You know I love you."

"Sure, Dad."

"I'm getting better. I'm trying."

"You can do better, Dad."

"Okay. And you can do a little better helping me."

"Fine, what's for dinner?"

"Do you love me?"

"Yeah, yeah, yeah, sure… What's for dinner?"

So we work things out the way we do, like we always do. I glance back at Shnooky.

Oh, you boys…

The traffic is better now. It's still jammed but the traffic is better.

We stop at the Whole Foods Store. As far as grocery stores go it's the best for fresh organic fruits and vegetables and it's got great meat and seafood selections. And a very good bakery.

We hit Trader Joe's for packaged goods, which are way cheaper. Fuck Ralphs and Vons with all their fucking artificial this and partially hydrogenated that. They're not that much cheaper and they suck. And their fresh produce? Tasteless vegetables and fruits, flabby, fat-filled, steroid-injected meat, hormone up the ass chicken… Just my opinion again. Eat what ya want.

Anyway, I grab a few Mejool dates (yeah, organic ones) and a handful of roasted cashews (no salt, goes better with the dates) on my way over to the fish counter.

Max says, "Dad, you're such a thief." Then he grabs some of the cashews out of my hand. Just petty stuff. Better than at the Mayfair Market (the most expensive of all) a few years back when I used to put four or five steaks on the rack underneath the shopping cart then throw a fifty pound bag of dog food on top to hide 'em from the counter clerk.

Ah... hum... excuse me, Miss Clerky there, don't forget to charge me for the dog food under the cart, please... or I'd put a wedge of imported Parmesan cheese in my pocket just because it was eighteen dollars a pound.

How dare you taunt me? How dare you insult me with those prices? So what if I'm broke? So what if I'm on a Kraft budget? Kraft sucks. Kraft makes fucking Velveeta for God's sake! I need cheese for our pasta and I need the good kind. There, I'm justified so I'm taking it. *How do you justify that, Dave?*

Shut up! I'm not even paying attention to you. I mean, which voice are you anyway? Keri would have told me to take it...

I am the voice of God within you...

Please, not now, I need the cheese.

When I lived in Tokyo I used to, on occasion, shove a piece of Ahi tuna (sealed in plastic wrapping, okay) in my underpants while shopping at the market, if I saw it was overpriced. I would confess at the checkout counter... in English. "Listen, I just wanna say that I have a big piece of tuna in my pants. I stole it and I'm sorry. If you want me to return it..." The Japanese clerks would just smile and nod their heads. I'd pay for the rest of my groceries and walk out. It was hilarious back then. Kinda feeling shitty about it now. If I ever get back there I owe a financial amends.

Anyway it's not like that anymore. A few dates, a few cashews, maybe grab an oatmeal cookie from the bakery counter. Shop a little. Eat a little. No big deal.

Albacore tuna is on sale. Nine ninety-nine a pound. Good. As we pick out a nice piece and wait for the counter guy to weigh and package it, Max observes me with disdain as I crane my neck for every attractive woman shopper that passes by, then he gets fed up at the vegetable section when he sees me staring at some stripper-type chick's insane tit job while I'm feeling for ripe avocados and calls me a "Disgusting pervert."

What's happening is that she is in the fruit section feeling melons and her tits are right up against them and I can't stop staring because it all seems so bizarre. Only to me, though. She isn't staring at me over at the vegetable section. She isn't like, "Oh, my, look at you, you handsome dashing man over at the avocados and hot little me here at the melons with my own big melons and both of us just squeezing and staring and squeezing and, oh, isn't it bizarre and freaky and like so hot and I just want you to come over here and...."

She could give a shit. And my son thinks I'm an old pervert. So he caught me. What can I say? "Okay, I'm disgusting. Fine. We need water." So we get one of those big bulky 2.5 gallon plastic containers of Arrowhead spring water with the little handle on top and argue over who's gonna carry it.

"Max, just do it."

"Dad, it's too heavy. You do it. Pervert."

He has to add that like I have to carry it as punishment for being caught by the pervert patrol. So I end up carrying the water and we get outta there.

12

"This place is a fuckin' mess."

I think I say that every time I walk in our apartment door.

"We better clean it up," I say to Max, who dramatically struggles carrying the container of spring water with both hands.

"I carried the water in okay, Dad? You clean it up," he says as he goes into the kitchen with Shnooky following. I put down the grocery bag and his back pack which I'm carrying, look over a handful of junk mail dreading another bill tucked in between…

Wait. What's this envelope from my commercial agency? Looks like a residual cheque peeking through the little cellophane window. I feel an immediate rush of excitement. How much ya think? It's for five-hundred thousand dollars! Oh, please… shut up, ya big fuckin' fantasizer. Wouldn't it be great, though? Think of you and Max in a new two-bedroom apartment, no a house, a house with a living room and a dining room and big bedrooms for both of you with separate bathrooms and a front yard with a luscious green lawn for Shnooky to hang out on, eat bones, roll around, bask in the sun… You deserve it. I mean, why not? People are making millions in this town. Assholes. Hacks. Lames. Cocksuckers. Okay, okay, some are hard-working and talented but I'm not thinking about them, I'm thinking about the phonies, the sellouts, the cocksuckers, all making money. Why them? Why them? Please. Stop it. Don't get into that. Open the envelope, maybe the cheque is for a couple of thousand; maybe they upgraded the commercial from cable to national TV. That's it. Okay, a couple of grand. Haven't seen it, though, on cable or national. Shit. It's probably for nothing. Probably not a cheque at all. Asshole. What were you thinking?

I open the envelope: it is a cheque, it's a holding fee for three hundred and eighty three bucks. They're not playin' it but they're holdin' it in case they wanna play it. Ahhh… I was expecting more. Wait. I just thought it was for nothing. Jesus, I'm so crazy, always expecting more, always expecting less, never just what it is. Kinda like my life. Fuck, I gotta stop that. Just feel grateful that I got a cheque at all. Okay. Grateful, grateful, grateful, grateful, grateful. *Still want more though… don't you… don't you!* Okay, okay calm down, what's next? Gotta clean this place up. No, I should get back to work.

"Dad, help me marinate the tuna," Max shouts from the kitchen.

"I gotta get back to work here," I say.

What am I gonna write, though? Just thinking about it floods me with anxiety. I mean, I know I'm stuck. Haven't heard from Tony in hours. He could be dead... fine, I don't care. Fucking idiot. Oh, man, I gotta pray for him... God bless Tony, blah, blah, blah... but what about me? What am I gonna write? I sit down in front of the computer with my head in my hands, thinking....

What? What? What? What? Nothing. Nothing. Nothing. Nothing!

"Come on, Dad... please."

I jump out of the chair. *I'm free! I'm free!*

"Okay, I'll come help marinate the tuna," I say, like I'm doing him a big favour. Just a few more minutes away from the dread of it all is such a relief. I walk into the kitchen. At least I know what I'm doing in there. I don't just stare at the food like I do at the computer screen, waiting, waiting, waiting for an idea, and manically massaging my temples to keep my veins from popping out of my fucking head.

Max has already lined up the sesame oil, olive oil and soy sauce bottles, peeled a few cloves of garlic, a nice piece of ginger, got the garlic press out and put the tuna steaks into a bowl. I run the tap in the sink. "Wash your hands. Max, did you wash your hands?"

"Yes, Dad... then I stuck 'em in my butt."

"Fine, I don't care," I say as I wash mine. "Shred the fucking garlic and ginger."

"Okay, Dad, mister fuckin' fuck, fuck!"

"Very funny," I say. "Just use two cloves and cut the... cut the ginger in half before you put it in the press."

Shnooky sits between us, tongue out, eyes moving from me to Max to me, waiting for anything to drop. Max cuts the ginger, puts two garlic cloves in the press and flips the extra clove to her. She catches it in her mouth, spits it out on the floor, tries to eat it again, spits it out.

"Why is Shnooky so stupid?"

"She's not fuc... she's not stupid."

"It's hard not to swear isn't it, Dad?"

"Listen, I haven't smoked all day so give me a break."

"Really?" He looks at me, impressed.

"Yes, really," I say, then I remember I had one in the morning with Tony and I remember the ashtray is full of butts and I get an immediate urge to go get one and smoke it and I know I will smoke one, sooner, later, maybe go buy another pack when Max is asleep... I just know I'm not done with smoking.

"Fuck..." I say to myself.

"Dad, did you just swear for no reason?" Max asks as he squeezes the garlic and ginger over the fish.

"No, I mean, yeah... don't worry about it," I say, as I mix up the oils and soy sauce and pour it over.

"You're the one that should worry about it."

"Okay, okay, fine," I say. "Rub the garlic and ginger over both pieces and flip them around a few times. Then squeeze a little orange over the top and put 'em in the fridge. I gotta get back to work."

"Is Tony out smoking crack again?"

I turn and snap at him.

"What are you trying to say? I can't work if Tony is on crack?"

"Dad, I didn't say anything, I just asked you a question."

As he stares at me with a mixture of pity and bewilderment, a flash shoots through my head of me at his age standing in the kitchen, asking my mom what was for dinner.

"If you don't like it, you don't have to eat it!" she snapped back at me.

"Mom, I didn't say anything, I just asked you a question," I said, and I looked at her the same way Max is looking at me now and Max is saying the same thing I said to her. What does it mean? What does it mean? I can't grasp it. It's floating by in my subconscious, knocking, knocking to get into my consciousness so I can get the message, it's some message of mending but I can't seem to get it... these things happen all the time, I know they do but my mind is always moving so fast... slow, slow, slow it down... there, okay, here it is... my mom's spirit is just stopping by...

Hi, Mom... I miss you, too... I know... Okay, I'll just answer the question... I feel a warm kiss pass through me.

"Yes, Max, he's smoking crack again," I say, calm and even. "But I'm going to try and work without him."

Max looks at me, incredulous at my sane, mature answer.

"Are you okay?" he says.

"Yeah… I'm fine. Try to get some homework done."

I walk into the living-room feeling calmed by my little spiritual experience, as if it will help me come up with some brilliant idea, but that experience has come and gone. Mom has rocketed back out into the infinite heavens and I am here, hands on my hips, staring at the computer screen again. I can't even sit in the damn chair… Ah shit, why can't it be easy for me? Why can't I just be a fucking genius? I grab the broom and start sweeping the floor. At least I can clean up some of this mess while my mind is circling around some ideas, which could be better defined as fearful procrastination. Shnooky comes in to watch. Cook, clean, take care of the kid… I'm nothing but a house mom. Who's gonna bring home the bacon, Shnooky, huh? Are you? Why can't you write something? Why can't you get a job?

My job is to love you, Daddy.

Max comes in, turns on the TV, flops down on the couch.

"Come on, Max, please, don't distract me."

"Dad, you're not writing, it's not like you have to think when you clean up."

"But I'm thinking about writing… okay? Go in the other room."

"Dad, when are we gonna move so I can have my own room?"

"I don't know. I told you, I'd put a partition out here and sleep on the couch until…"

"Dad that is so ghetto."

He gets up and walks into our three-foot hallway that leads into the other room, the only other room, our bedroom. I let out a little sigh of exasperation then continue to clean the best I can but it's always half-assed. I just get the obvious dirt out of the way, sweep up the floor… wait, excuse me, hardwood floor. I live with my kid in a little box but at least we have hardwood floors. Do you have hardwood floors? What the fuck is it with hardwood floors? I think they used to be just called floors, like most all floors were all made out of wood, then people started putting carpets over them and now it's like ya struck gold if ya pull up your carpet and find a wood floor underneath. Look! They're Hardwood! I don't know. Anyway, I never really sweep all the way under the table or behind the couch, I kinda re-organise the messy papers on the desk, maybe throw a few in the trash, try to blow the dust off with my mouth until I feel like I'm gonna faint. Wait. Oh, yeah, I find the crusty old fake-feathered duster behind the bookcase and start dusting off my books. Shit. I'm supposed to dust first then sweep up. I'm not gonna sweep again. Oh, man. That's what I mean, half-assed.

I look at the way the books are stacked, some side by side, some on top of each other. They're so unorganized. I used to have them in alphabetical order. When? Liar. How many have I just lost, left behind somewhere, half read? And these ones here, the covers are bent, the pages are frayed. I see my ancient copy of Fantes' 'Ask The Dust' in a plastic zip-lock bag because the pages started falling out. My Raymond Carver hardback copy of 'Where I'm Calling From' has the plastic cover falling off. God, if I could write like him, I think. I look at an old paperback copy of 'Narcissus and Goldman' by Hesse. It was one of my favorite books because I identified so much with... which one was I most like? Narcissus? No, Goldman was the wild one. I can't even remember. Why was it so important when I read it? You fucking idiot, Dave! Boy, that just comes out so easy with me, doesn't it? And these - Hemmingway, Fitzgerald, Steinbeck - all just meant so much to me... at one time. What time? In your youth, stupid, old... Okay, none of that. Oh, look at this, I open my Edgar Allen Poe book, 'Tales of Mystery and...' shit, eighty pages are missing. Here's my copy of 'Last Exit To Brooklyn'. Man, the way Hubert Selby Jr. wove Poe's 'The Raven' into those pages where Georgie is the Queen of all her little drag queen friends, all hyped up on benzedrine, reciting Poe, wanting tough-guy Tony, wanting so desperately just wanting, wanting, wanting to feel love, to be loved, to be the love itself... and Charlie Parker blowin' his sax on the radio through it all. God, that was so twisted, glorious, resplendent and so devastatingly painful. Can't forget that... Fuck. What else? What am I doing anyway? I'm supposed to be cleaning up. I hear a few seconds of some MTV music video through the wall on the bedroom TV then a couple of seconds of Discovery channel, some shit about polar bears or something, then a bit of a Seinfeld re-run... do they show those all fucking day long? Anyway, Max is doing his channel surfing. I tap on the wall with my hand.

"Do your homework!"

"I'll do it later!"

Ah, I know he'll do it, he always does. Such a good kid. I don't remember ever doing homework. I was fucking hell-bent, insane... no discipline, no... that's why I never and now I can't... oh, shit... stop it. I'm getting crazy again looking at these books, thinking about the authors. How did they do it? Why am I so... stop. Again. Stop. Oh, here's my Carl Jung, 'Memories, Reflections Dreams'. Keri gave it to me. I forget every fucking thing I read in that book. I should look at it again. It might help me. Ah, maybe not... I don't know. I thought it helped me before. I even preached Jung, blabbed to everybody, Jung says this, Jung says that. I didn't have a clue. I was all fucked up. He's the one that knew, not me. Just because ya read doesn't mean you're the same as...

Wait, here, 'Ramakrishna and His Disciples'. I used to read this over a lot. Christopher Isherwood, another great writer, wrote it because he was an avid follower of the Vedanta religion which began in India with Ramakrishna, who was an Avatar that lived in the 1800's. I got it when I worked as a gardener, okay part-time gardener, okay pretty much just a weed puller for six bucks an hour at the Vedanta Temple in Hollywood, nestled up above Franklin

Boulevard off of Vine Street. Very unassuming. You'd never see it unless you were seeking it out. Kind of like the religion of Vedanta, which is... can I remember? It's a Hindu philosophy based on the ancient Veda scriptures which accepts all gods and all religions; Krishna, Jesus, Buddha, Mohammed, everybody, something like that. I knew how to explain it better when I worked up there, read more, went to the Temple to meditate. Not really, I just read the pamphlet over and over, which I fucking forget now. And I never really knew how to meditate, I just went when I was freaking out in the garden (I mean I had a reason to, Keri had just died, I was just off dope, didn't know how to take care of Max) and would sit there in the temple with my eyes closed. I guess that's kind of meditating. Sometimes I would think I heard Ramakrishna or one of his disciples, Vivekananda, talking to me in English with heavy Indian accents. *Don't worry, be strong, take care of your son... you will be just fine.* Sometimes I'd laugh, sometimes I'd cry, then I'd go back to pullin' weeds.

God, that garden helped me a lot. Shnooky was a little youngster back then. She used to sit and watch me stabbing and digging into the ground with a hand hoe, tearing out weeds around the Iris beds, the earth absorbing all my black energy. That place saved my life. At one point I thought I was destined to become a monk and I asked one of the Swamis what he thought. He told me in a loving way that he didn't believe it was my path, that I should stay in the world and take care of my son, find another woman. In blunt terms he coulda just said, "Hey, you're not monk material." Then I booked a couple of commercials and I figured... I don't know what I figured... didn't need the six bucks an hour, wasn't gonna be a monk. I stopped reading the literature even though it was a bridge to God for me. I should read some more of this book again. No, I gotta clean up some more.

Why can't I just fucking sit down and write? Oh, I need help. I take the book in my hand. I no sooner glance over at the couch than I'm lying on it. Now I'm too tired to read. As I drop the book on the cluttered coffee table, I remember the metal plaque of Ramakrishna that one of the Swamis gave me is in my wallet. I take it out. It's bent from sitting on it for... it's been a few years. I look at his picture engraved in the front. Man, I mean for this guy, Nirvana was everyday, he went way beyond that into Samadhi, which has been described as super consciousness... a man knows his absolute identity with God... and that's how he looks in the picture.

What is my identity? I just wanted to clean up and now all this is happening. What does anything mean? I turn over the plaque which has a simple quote written on it: *"The breeze of God's grace is always blowing; Set your sails to catch this breeze."* That's what I needed. That's what I needed. I clutch the plaque, put it to my heart. Oh, man, am I crying again? Just relax. Close your eyes. Set

your sails. Catch God's breeze. Set your sails. Catch God's breeze.
Set your sails. Catch God's breeze. I'm sailing away, sailing away,
sailing away.

13

"Dad, wake up. Dinner"

I open my eyes to see Shnooky sitting in front of me, wedged in-between the couch and the coffee table, fixated on two plates (Keri's good china ones) of Albacore tuna, seared to perfection with crescent-shaped slices of rich green avocado on the side. Next to them are two of our cheap plastic bowls we got in Chinatown (for a buck ninety-nine each), full of rice. Max is walking back in from the kitchen carrying two cups of green tea (also nice jade coloured China ones of his mom's) with the package of toasted seaweed clenched in his teeth. I sit up, look out the window; it's already dark. Fucking long nap I took. Max spits the package of seaweed out on the table.

"Hey…" I say.

"Dad, I made the dinner so you be quiet." He puts down the tea, picks up the TV controller.

"Homework?"

"Done."

"Anybody call?"

"No."

"My commercial agent?"

"No, Dad."

I'm gonna ask him what time it is but he clicks on 'The Simpsons' so it must be seven o'clock. He just loves 'The Simpsons', watches the reruns every night he can and the new episodes each Sunday. He's been watching them since he was five years old and it's one of the only shows he watches without changing the channel. It is very funny, silly and also controversial in a cartoon kind of way. Somehow those cartoon humans can get away with so much more than real humans because they're only cartoons, right? Fucking genius. So we eat and watch and laugh together even though we've both seen the episode twice before.

"You made the tuna good tonight," I say.

"Better than you make it, right, Dad? Say it. Say Max is the best."

"Max is the best."

"The best what?"

"The best cook."

"The best everything. Right, Dad? Right?"

Yup, we got our own little show goin' on here, don't we?

We finish eating, let Shnooky lick the bits of tuna left on our plates and gobble up the little rice we purposely leave in our bowls for her. I look over at Max, his eyelids getting heavy as he watches the TV with long, slow blinks. Maybe he was up until late last night worrying about me looking for Tony. He's learned how to be so strong from such a young age that I wonder how many of his fears he hides from me, what kind of lid he keeps on them out of concern for me and my already overburdened life.

"You can tell me if you were really worried about me last night," I say.

"Dad, shut up, 'King of the Hill' is coming on,"(another one of his favourite shows).

He won't tell, the little tough. Maybe it will come out in therapy when he's older. Then I remember we both did go to therapy to process his mom's death and after the fourth or fifth session the therapist said to me, "I believe your son will be fine but you, you need to come back." Of course, I took it personally and told her to go fuck herself. "I'm just as fine as he is, damnit!"

No, I don't think you are.

I nonchalantly look around for the ashtray full of cigarette butts figuring since he is tired, I can get him to bed early, fish a nice long one out and smoke it. I spot the ashtray. It's emptied out. Not a butt in it. Fuck. I can't mention it, though, because I told him... oh, man... my eyes pop wide like a fiend as I take a deep quivering breath in and blow it out hard.

"What's the matter, Dad?"

He knows, right away. Jesus.

"They're in the garbage, go get one if you want."

I actually stand up, nicotine slave that I am. Max keeps his eyes on the TV, his voice even. "I hacked lugies on 'em, though..."

"What the hell, Max!"

"I haven't had a cigarette all day," he says, mocking me.

"You're such a little..."

"Such a little what? A little shit? A little fuck? A little son that cares about his stupid Dad's life?"

"All right, all right..."

"Move over," he says as he curls up on the couch and rests his head on my shoulder. Neither one of us acknowledges it but I feel the sweetness of the moment. I wanna put my arm around him and hug him but I know he would push me away so I just let him rest his head there, feeling the weight get heavier as he starts to fall asleep.

There's a knock on the door. Shnooky barks and races towards it, growling, hair on her back standing straight up in a line from head to tail. Max sits up, winces with his eyes still closed.

"Damnit Shnooky!" he says.

Whenever there is a knock, she goes, kind of like that Pavlov experiment with the drooling which is one of the only things I remember from high school, or did I learn it from a Rolling Stones song? "You make me drool like a Pavlov dog," or salivate I think it was... but the Pavlov dog drooled when it saw the food, then the bell rang, then Pavlov took away the food, rang the bell and the dog still drooled, right? What a Cocksucker, I'd never do that to Shnooky... so I guess it's not like that experiment... okay, someone knocks, my dog barks, like most dogs, right... shoulda just said it's instinct or something. Anyway, she's at the door already wagging her tail so it's someone we know.

"Come in!" I say. The door opens.

"Hola, Shnooky, mi muy muy bonita..." then the Spanish gets so fast, high-pitched and breathy, I can't understand a word Carolina, my Argentinian ex but not really (you know how that is) girlfriend is saying. Shnooky wriggles around her in circles, moving towards the couch, then plops over on her back and spreads her legs out wide like a cheap hussy. I feel the temperature change in my body as I watch Carolina squat down, her fleece-lined Levi's jacket opening to show her sweet, braless breasts push against her tight vintage Santana tank top with her short, suede skirt inching up over her strong, smooth, bronzed thighs, covered with light sun-bleached golden hairs. As she strokes Shnooky's belly, she shakes the long locks of her dirty, blonde mane away from her sultry, rich deep brown eyes, and smiles at me with them as she purses her full, luscious lips and blows me a quick kiss.

Even though I see how devastatingly sexy and voluptuous she is, I also remind myself of who she is, a thirty-two-year-old, unemployed single mom, living in a two-bedroom apartment with her unruly thirteen-year-old daughter, alcoholic mother and forty-year-old, divorced, crack addict brother. Toxic and complicated. Don't get swept away in her beauty, I tell myself, while at the same time I'm hoping we get to fuck later.

"Hi, Max," Carolina says, as if not to bother him.

"Hey..." he says, staring at the TV with hooded eyes.

"How are you?"

"Good."

"How's school?"

"Good."

"Sasha says hi."

Max doesn't answer, just kind of nods his head, his eyes still on the TV. I know what he's thinking, I can almost hear it. *My dad and I were just relaxing, I was falling asleep on his shoulder, he would have carried me into the bedroom, tucked me in, I still like that once in a while to be tucked in... then you come over and ruin it... you never even call, you just come over whenever you feel like it...* And he just stares at the TV and Carolina strokes Shnooky's belly and I get all huffed up like I gotta do something, fix the situation.

"Max, you wanna answer her, please," I say. Carolina reaches out, touches my leg, reassuring me, like it's no big deal. She has known him since he was seven. Her daughter Sasha went to public school down the block with him. That's where we met, actually, in the Principal's office because Max and Sasha were constantly teasing each other in class so she called us in to discuss having a group conference with our kids. We both basically told the Principal we'd work it out without her fucking help and after leaving the office, complimented each other on our mutual immature responses and rebellious attitudes (although we didn't identify them as that). We talked about our woes as single parents and she told me Sasha's father was a junkie that disappeared when she was three and I offered up my junkie past, telling her I stopped heroin just before Keri died and she told me about her mother, her brother and another brother, that had just recently been murdered in Columbia. Some bad drug deal or something. He was tall, lanky, intense, moody... crazy... she said I reminded her of him. She took it as destiny that we met and even though I was trying to move in a different direction away from all that insanity, it wasn't hard to play the part, I mean I had been the part. She even told me if I got strung out again she would take care of me.

I should have run right there but I took it as flattery and we started in a dark, desperate, passionate romance, writing dark, desperate, passionate poems to each other and having dark, desperate, passionate sex whenever and wherever it was possible, which wasn't easy, let me tell ya; Carolina living with her whole family, me with Max in our little one bedroom... the kids still teasing and hating each other whenever we got together and me over at her place trying to convince her mother to stop drinking and her brother to get off drugs and them goofing on me in Spanish and her brother telling me stuff like, "Hey, whito, what makes you better than us?" and, "You look like YOU need a drink, you wound up motherfucker." Sometimes we talked about running away to an island together, living off the land, ya know; fish and fruits and nuts and shit… stuff I did years ago that always turned into a nightmare when the money ran out. Reality is, though, neither one of us could really commit so we've just kinda gone on like this, seeing each other less and less over the years… and Max wishes it was less than that, like never.

"Max… you gonna answer?"

"What, Dad? You want me to say, Oh wow! I'm so excited, tell Sasha I said hi, too! Like she cares. We both hate each other."

"Don't be so fucking rude!"

"Nice, Dad, real nice."

Yeah, I fucked up the situation with my everlasting patience, understanding and tactful finesse. Carolina looks down embarrassed as Max gets up from the couch, shuffles to the hallway, looks over his shoulder at me with a wry, sarcastic smile and says, "Hope you get some writing done… Dad." He closes the hallway door, then the bedroom door, making sure not to slam them because he knows slamming them would be stooping to his Dad's level.

"Sorry," I say to Carolina.

"You want me to go?"

"No… he's just, I don't know… such a little…"

"Sasha's worse. She treats me like shit. When I served her dinner tonight, she told me to get my big ass out of the way, that it was blocking her view of the TV."

Carolina takes a pack of Marlboro reds out of her jacket pocket, puts one in her mouth, offers me one. As I think, I didn't notice her ass was bigger, I have to check that out later, I say, "Go ahead, I'm trying to quit," although I know if she had American Spirits I would have taken one.

"Are you sure?" she says as she lights up, takes a long drag, blows the smoke out of the side of her mouth away from me. As soon as I say, "Don't worry about it," I know I'm gonna smoke, Marlboros or fucking not. The nicotine clock is ticking down. The bedroom TV starts blaring through the wall. I jump up, go over, yank open the hall door, the bedroom door.

"Come on, stop it, Max."

"So, you're smoking again."

"No, mister smoke detector, I'm not. Carolina's smoking."

"You will be." He shuts off the TV and pulls the covers over his head. I'm pegged again, rendered tongue-tied.

"Fine. Good night…" I say. No response. I take a deep breath. What to do? What to do? God help me.

"I love you," I say.

"I hate you," he says.

"I love you," I say.

"Hate."

"Love."

"Hate."

"Love."

"Hate."

"Love."

"Okay, shut up, Dad. I wanna go to sleep." I take that as he loves me, close both doors, come back into the living room. Carolina is already cleaning up the table. "Come on, you don't have to," I say.

She hands me my little Ramakrishna plaque.

"I found this on the couch."

"Thanks."

I kiss Ramakrishna's image, put the plaque back in my wallet. Carolina watches me. Just as I say, "What?" she clasps both hands around the back of my head, pulls me in and drives her lips into mine.

"You're so beautiful sometimes," she says. Then she picks up the plates and bowls and walks into the kitchen. I remember once I was weeding the upper iris garden at the temple on a hot sweltering summer day, dressed in shorts, shirt off, covered in sweat, and Carolina came up, watched me, watched me weed; then she drew me into the shade under the huge avocado tree, un-zipped my shorts, slipped out of her sundress and we kissed and we touched and we fucked a slow, steady, hot, sweaty fuck, both of us on fire inside and out, and at the same time I felt like I was going to hell because we were fucking in the sacred garden of my salvation while the Monks and Swamis did afternoon meditation in the temple, and she kept saying, "This is so beautiful, this is so beautiful…"

So why am I thinking about this? What does it mean? Is there something to figure out here? Is this another thing I feel but I can't put my finger on? I look down at Shnooky. She wags her tail. *Don't worry, Daddy, let's go in the kitchen, see Carolina, maybe get something to eat.* I laugh at her, my own insanity, I don't know what. I even mouth, "Okay" to her, as I pick up the tea-cups and go into the kitchen.

So I'm in the kitchen putting all the stuff Max left out in the cabinets as Carolina sponges down the counter. I take a big chew stick out, give it to Shnooky. *Yeah, Daddy, yeah, yeah, yeah.* She trots into the living room to chew to her heart's delight. I ask Carolina how her brother, Miguel, and her mother, Jacqueline, are. She says, "You know how they are." She lights another cigarette, keeps it in her mouth as she starts washing dishes.

"How's Tony, you still writing with him?"

She leans over the sink and scrubs the plates.

"I'll, I'll tell ya later, first I gotta see something." I step back and look at her ass move under her skirt.

"What are you doing?" she asks. I kneel down behind her.

"I'll watch your ass instead of the TV anytime."

She laughs.

"Keep washing," I say, as I run my hands up her legs, cup them over her warm, smooth, full cheeks, feeling them vibrate as she vigorously washes.

"I need to look at something else here," I say, as I slip one hand under her thong and run my two forefingers over her pussy. It's wet and it's heating up. I bring my fingers back out, lick them and slip them back in, rubbing her pussy, putting the tips of my fingers inside, taking them out, licking them again, tasting her honey-pepper taste, slipping them back in. She reaches down with one hand and digs her nails into the back of my head.

"Get up here and fuck me."

I stand up, legs trembling. As soon as I unbutton my jeans my cock bursts out of them. I lift up her skirt. She stands on her tip-toes, leans over the sink a little more, arching her back… and her pussy just calls my cock inside. She sucks hard on the cigarette, blows out the smoke in a deep, sexy, guttural sigh. I feel like I'm gonna come right there. I take the cigarette out of her mouth, suck it down almost to the filter in one drag, pull the smoke deep into my lungs and blow it out like a demon. It's okay, it's okay, I'm smoking again. I knew it would happen. The nicotine courses through my body. I'm calmer. I can last longer. My favourite thing used to be reciting poetry with a cigarette in my mouth, high on heroin while fucking for hours and hours and hours. I know I could go to hell with this woman, that's why I fight it. That's why. Maybe. Who knows. Shut up. You go to hell by yourself. I drop the cigarette butt in the sink. I feel my cock starting to soften. Don't drift. Don't drift. Carolina doesn't know, she thinks it's so beautiful. She thinks it's so beautiful.

"You okay?"

"Yeah, yeah…"

Get back there. Get back there. Get back there. Okay, my hands are under her skirt on her hips and I'm pulling her into me, thrusting into her, my cock throbbing hard again. Out of breath, both of us.

"You still washing the dishes?"

"Yeah…"

The way she says it, I feel like I'm gonna come again. "Wash the dishes, wash the dishes, wash the dishes, wash the dishes…" I say over and over so I can last, so I can come when she does… and we fuck, faster and faster and harder and faster until she screams out, slaps a plate down in the sink and cracks it in two… and I come so hard I swear her feet lift off the ground.

"Dad!"

"Oh, God, did he hear?"

"I don't know."

I yank up my pants, almost trip over Shnooky who's still devouring her chew stick as I race into the bedroom.

"What happened?"

"Carolina was helping me wash the dishes and she dropped a plate. Go back to sleep."

14

Max is fast asleep again. Everything is cool. Carolina and I giggle. She apologizes about the plate. Keri's plate. Pang of guilt. This some sign? Then Keri's voice. *It's no sign, Dave. She just broke the plate. I wish you fucked me like that.*

Carolina tells me she has to get home before Sasha goes to sleep or she gets screamed at by her mother, well into her second bottle of Chablis. Plus she has to get in the bathroom by nine before Miguel locks himself in with the crack pipe. The usual routine. We laugh about that. I ask her for a cigarette. "You sure?"

"Maybe just leave one on the table in case."

She puts one on the table, sees the residual cheque on top of other bills and strewn about papers.

"Oh, you got a cheque."

"Shitty one."

"Wanna give it to me?"

"I wish. I can't even afford to pay my own bills."

"Tell me about it," she says. "I'm sick of it."

She starts separating my bills from the junk mail from the index cards from the post-it notes.

"Come on, you don't have to do that," I say, wondering why she is doing it. She's kinda hedging about something. Maybe she does need money. I can give her fifty, I guess.

She picks up a City of Los Angeles stamped envelope with a cheque lying on top of it. "You gotta send these or you'll get booted," she says as she puts it in, licks and seals the envelope.

"Fuck, I thought I sent that!"

"You made it out to Parking violation Nazi Cocksuckers?"

"Oh, yeah…" I say. "I was a little angry when I wrote that one."

She laughs but it's not a big ha-ha, I love your crazy ass laugh. Something is just off here. Then she says, "I thought you were trying to be less angry."

"I am… I mean, what are you… why are you asking me this stuff?"

She hugs me. So tight. Too tight. What? I'm breaking her heart. What? She can't live without me. What?

"I just wanna know you're going to be alright," she says. "Because I'm… I'm not going to see you anymore."

My heart sinks but it had to happen but I can't swallow but it's better like this. She's waiting, I can tell. What am I supposed to say? Obviously something, get mad, something, but I don't, I just stand there limp in her arms.

The phone rings.

"I gotta get that."

She pushes herself away from me, puts her hand on the door.

"Bye."

"Wait…" I say as I get the phone. It's Patti, filling me in on the latest about Tony. Carolina stares at me disgusted, lights another cigarette. I mouth to her, "It's about Tony." A hint of compassion on her face. She knows what it's like.

"I don't know… I'll look into it… I'll call you back," I say over the phone then I hang up. "Fucking idiot he is," I say to Carolina.

"What happened?"

"Tony's holed up in a crack house on a conference call with his dad and Patti telling them he's sorry, it's over, he's gonna turn himself in tomorrow, first thing in the morning and he'll go to rehab… but he wants them to find one with a golf course. So she's calling me…" Carolina shakes her head a couple of times, laughs a little bit through her nose but she doesn't laugh out loud and hug me again. She's done with me.

I even say, "It's so crazy, isn't it?" like I wanna draw her in again, make everything the way it was so we can kiss good-bye and I'll see her in a week, couple of weeks.

It's just all messy and awkward.

"Look, neither one of us can ever fuckin' get it together, okay?" she says. "And I met somebody… somebody who's gonna move me and Sasha into his house. I just gotta get away from my mother and messed-up brother… I'm like some low rent fuckin' Cinderella over there… and… and I don't love him but…he's nice and he said I don't have to work... ever... and you would never fight for me anyway would you? Would you!?"

Now there are tears in her eyes and I'm not talkin'. I'm just hearing somewhere... *you gotta let her go, you gotta let her go, you gotta let her go.*

Shnooky, the love ambassador, trots over, gets in-between us, wagging her tail. Carolina bends down, pats her head and kisses her.

"I'll miss you, Shnooky," she says. "Take care of him."

She walks out the door. Maybe that broken plate was a sign. Was it, Keri? I search my mind for a reply. She's not even available for comment this time.

I lay down on the couch, unlit cigarette sticking straight out of my mouth... just sucking on the filter. You could never take care of her even if you wanted to. Could you? Could you? Jesus, I sound like her to myself. It's true, though. I don't have money to move out of here. How can I ever have a decent relationship with anybody? Am I gonna live like this forever, just scraping by with the rent in this craphole until Max goes to college? College? Who the fuck's gonna pay for that? I'll fucking die in this place like Mrs. Churchill downstairs did. She wanted to be an actress, ended up doing movie extra work, lived here forty years. Not so bad, she had a kid, too, that came over and visited once a month, something like that... yeah, I'll end up sittin' around The Gumbo Pot down at the Farmers Market on Fairfax all day in my pyjamas and slippers, with some other old, angry, crotchety Hollywood losers complaining and lying my wrinkly ass off about how I coulda made it and who I used to know and who fucked me over. *Ahhh... that movie sucked anyway... cocksuckers. Yeah, those cocksuckers... they were all cocksuckers...*

Oh, man, what am I gonna do?

The phone rings again. Here's a place to channel all this crap. I grab it and say, "I haven't found a rehab with a fucking golf course yet! Okay!"

"Dave?"

"Yeah... who, who is this?"

"It's your sister. Are you on drugs again?"

"No... shit... I'm sorry, sorry, Margaret... I'm just... I'm fine."

"Well, you don't sound fine. How's Max?"

"He's okay, he's sleeping. What's going on?"

There is a pause then she says, "What's going on is old Poppy is in Intensive Care at the Coronado hospital."

15

I hope he lives. I hope he dies. I hope he lives. I hope he dies. I hope he lives. I hope he dies. I hope he lives. I hope he dies.

So me, Max, Shnooky and a duffle bag are packed in the Scamp and on our way down to Coronado Island which is just south of San Diego. My Dad moved there from New York about a year after my Mom died of cancer. Sold the house and bought a condo on the beach. Funny, when my Mom wanted to move to California, he told her he was too old to move. Bastard. See, my Mom wasn't supposed to die before him because she was gonna leave me the house because I was the artist in the family... Oh, God, how many times did I go over that one? That should have been my house! How could she die before him? Jesus, how could I judge anybody with thoughts like that? But I do. Especially good old Poppy; that's what my sister's kid, who is also named Dave, used to call my Dad when he was little and we all just started calling him Poppy after that. Margaret named her son after me because I was strung out to the hilt when he was born and she was sure I was gonna die from a drug overdose, and wanted to keep the name David alive in the family. Well, I made it through and now there is a Dave and an Uncle Dave still alive, and me and my sister, we're okay with each other now. She still thinks I'm a loser. She still tells me she'd kill herself if she had to live like me but we're okay now. She sends Max very generous Christmas and birthday cheques. Even helps with the school tuition sometimes. Me getting off the drugs helped. A lot. She is proud of me for that and raising Max but like I said, she still thinks I'm a loser.

"It doesn't look good," she said the nurse at the hospital told her. Poppy had some pains in his chest and called his cleaning lady. The cleaning lady called the ambulance then she called Margaret and Margaret called the hospital. That's how it happened. "You should definitely fly out from New York," the nurse told her.

"What about Jessica?" I asked. "Isn't she taking care of him?"

Jessica is his thirty-year-old girlfriend. He pays for her but he calls her his girlfriend. He had a lot of those kind of girlfriends even when he was married to my mom. Poppy is ninety-three years old by the way. Can you say sex addict?

"They had a fight a couple of weeks ago," Margaret said. "And if you called him more often you would know these things. You should call him at least once a week."

"I know, I haven't been." I asked her if she called our brother Paul which is also my father's first name although there was never any Paul Sr. or Paul Jr. goin' on between them. "Did you call

Paul Jr. and tell him about Paul Sr..." ya know what I'm talkin' about. That junior and senior shit is a fuckin' waste of time in my opinion. And some fathers and sons hold on to it like it's of the utmost importance, right? So and so senior and so and so junior and so and so... fuck you. Anyway, Paul did follow in my father's footsteps... *not like you, Dave, you black sheep loser... shut up...* Paul was a straight A student in high school, went to a top college, became an engineer, but he couldn't follow those footsteps when he started cheating on his wife. He had a little more of a conscience, tripped up a little bit, couldn't handle it... so he left her. Poppy thought he was very weak to do that. He didn't approve of what he considered to be weak behaviour.

See, Poppy grew up in Germany, half Catholic/half Jew. He was an accomplished student and linguist with a doctorate degree in engineering. When Hitler took over, he fled to the United States and joined the American army to fight against the Nazis and he saw a lot of horror and tragedy, things that he used to say would "make us shit in our pants..."

"So that makes it okay to cheat on your wife and stay with her?"

"You don't understand, Paul, men have to do things. I stayed married to your mother for forty years."

"Well, I can't do those things, I have to get a divorce."

So they haven't been very close since. But Margaret called him.

He's gonna show up. Not that anybody in my family is that close, especially after my mom... she was such an angel... I loved my mom... more than anyone else... and the way they treated her... oh God, the dyke of memories has opened. Stop the flood. Stop the flood. Stop the flood!

We pull into the Chevron before getting on the freeway so I can fill up the tank and put some oil in the Scamp. Scamp needs oil. Scamp eats up oil fast. I go in and buy a couple of quarts... okay, so I buy some smokes too... just in case, and a pack of peanut M&M's for Max. He likes peanut M&M's. He loves the bright green ones. Yick. They all fuckin' taste the same, why are they different colours? I walk back out to the car, tap on the window. Max rolls it down. Wrapped in a blanket. Wool cap on. Sleepy eyed. Horrible mood.

"What?"

I dangle a pack of M&M's. He grabs it from me, rips it open with his teeth.

"Dad, why do we have to go down there now?"

"Because Auntie Margaret said Poppy might be dead in the morning."

I pop the hood, unscrew the cap of the crankcase and pour the oil in, straight in because I'm too lazy to get the funnel out of the trunk. I think if I tip the quart of oil fast like the pros do, it will go straight into the hole but I'm no pro and oil spills all over the side before I actually get it in.

"Fuck!"

Some guy filling his tank at the next pump tells me to take it easy.

"You take it fucking easy!" I say. "My father is dying!"

I finish pouring in the oil and slam the hood.

"Sorry, dude."

"Yeah, yeah, yeah... me too."

I get back in the car. Max is sitting there chomping on M&M's, judging me.

"I don't wanna hear it."

"Dad, you're so stupid."

"I said, shut up!"

There goes Shnooky's tail in the back seat. *Love, love, love.*

"You shut up, too."

"You don't even care about Poppy," Max says.

"I do care..."

"You said he messed up your whole life."

"It doesn't matter, I still love him." I feel that as my spiritual self, speaking through me and I allow it.

Max has four of the green M&M's he separated from the others left in his hand. He eats them one by one. Then he says, "I don't, I think Poppy sucks. I don't want him to die but I think he sucks."

Max has his own fond memories of Poppy, like the time when

146

he was seven and we went down to go deep sea fishing for a day in San Diego and old Poppy (who, by the way, was fifty when I was born so he was always old) called to make the reservation on the boat and he made it for two and a half people. Max didn't understand and Poppy told him in his superior, demeaning way that Max was too little to be considered a whole person, that he was only half a person… and the time we were playing a fun family game of Monopoly and when Max landed on Park Place after already owning Boardwalk, he screamed with joy because he was gonna own both and buy houses and hotels and maybe win the game, but Poppy didn't want to land on them. See, Poppy had to own Boardwalk and Park Place and laugh at Max when he landed on them. Poppy didn't laugh that game. Poppy called Max a cheater and quit. But I don't believe Max's memories haunt him that much because he's already back asleep as we head down the 101 south.

Whereas me… well, I'm haunted, oh yeah, lifelong, big time but I have my spiritual tools… I breathe in, I breathe out, I ask God for guidance… and at the same time wanna get off the Alvarado Street exit, barrel on down to Sixth and buy a big fucking load of heroin. Fuck. Need. Again. Need. I turn on the radio. 88.1 Jazz. I hear the piano, trumpet, bass and drums introduction to a song… Bop ba - bop ba dap ba da da - Bop ba bop ba dap ba da da… I know it. I know it… and then… and then Dexter Gordon's smooth so smooth Alto Sax playing takes over and I glide right past the Alvarado exit as the song gives me all the relief I'm looking for and takes me just where I need to go right now with the title so fitting… yeah… 'One Flight Up'… One Fight Up… One Flight Up

Bop ba - bop ba dap ba da da…

16

We're passing downtown San Diego on the 5 south, almost to the Coronado Island exit. Max is still asleep with Shnooky snuggled in-between us. I've been lost in music the whole way.

"Ain't no change in the weather ain't no change in me,

Ain't no change in the weather ain't no change in me

I ain't hidin' from nobody,

Ain't nobody hidin' from me for me.

I got that green light baby…"

I'm singing along to an old JJ Cale tape, wanting my life to be just like that. I rest my hand on Shnooky's head and sing to her… *"They call me the Breeze I keep blowin' down the road, they call me the Shnook…"*

"Dad, shut up."

The King has awoken. He turns the volume down. The breeze is gone and I sigh myself back to reality.

"Where are we?"

"Almost to Poppy's. We have to go to the hospital first."

"What if he's dead? I don't wanna see him dead."

I have a vision of my mom in the hospital on her last days when the cancer had gone to her brain and she was telling me there were condors flying around the room. All her body, mind and spirit just ravished. Eaten away. I don't wanna see Poppy dead either. Then I see the dread in Max's face.

"Are you thinking about your mom?"

"No, Dad… okay?"

"Okay," I say.

I'm not gonna push it. Maybe he's not. But how can he not? He lay there scraped and cut from head to toe with his femur bone sticking straight out of his leg and saw his mom dead on the road next to him. When I sat next to his bed in Intensive Care and told him his mom went to heaven, he said that her spirit flew out of her body, came down and kissed him. It has to be true. He is a miracle. So I let it pass if that's what he wants, and get back to talking about old Poppy.

"He's not dead," I say. "He's as strong as a bull. He'll probably go home tomorrow. He's probably gonna live to be a hundred and twenty."

"I'm not gonna let him fuck with my kids," Max says.

"Okay, fine," I say.

"You really think he's gonna live that long?"

And we used to joke about that, me, my brother and sister, that Poppy would be at all our deathbeds because he, my God, he just never seemed to age after seventy-five, like he just stayed there and he was gonna stay there for eternity. He still swam laps, walked on the beach, did push-ups, sit-ups, complained to his girlfriends sixty years younger than him that they were too fat. Maybe it was his refusal to let go of his manhood, his desire to still fuck that kept him so youthful. I laugh to myself, thinking he's probably flirted with every nurse, probably invited one to go to Puerto Nuevo, Mexico and eat lobster with him when he gets out of the hospital. Makes me laugh, makes me sick at the same time.

One of the only times he was proud of me was back in New York when he went to the Pussycat Cinema on 48th and Broadway to catch a little after lunch porn movie and by coincidence saw me in it. "You vere very good in zat party scene vith zose two lovely big-chested young girls."

He still had his German accent after all his years in the U.S. He'd refer to it as an international accent because he was fluent in at least four other languages... but it always sounded pretty fucking German to me.

"Please don't tell Mom."

"Of course not, she vouldn't understand. Perhaps you can bring me to vork vith you one day."

And my mom eventually found out because she got an invite to attend 'Jack and Jill 2' or something, one of the movies I did. I guess I used my parents' address on one of the releases I signed.

Anyway she got it in the mail. I think there was a still picture of me inside the card, doggy stylin' Jill while she gave a blow job to Jack. *Come and see your son!* That's when my mom threatened to disown me. If I did one more porn. Yes, I promised and yes, I did one anyway because like my dad said, she wouldn't understand. Me and him had bonded on that issue. Makes me sad to think it was one of the only times we ever bonded and sadder to think he still asks me, "Have you done any more of those movies?"

So my sadness kind of amps up to anger as we cross over the Coronado Bridge which winds around like a rollercoaster track all lit up, high over the San Diego bay with the downtown skyline shimmering under the fucking moon and the cute little marinas full of yachts and sailboats and the big navy ships in the distance on the other fucking side and yeah, I see the whole view but it doesn't register as some breathtaking magnificence. I mean I'm not sayin', "Isn't this a spectacular view from the bridge, son?" No, we're drivin' over the bridge to see if my Dad, who I don't have fond memories of and don't wanna see, is dead.

No wonder I'm back out of myself again and start thinkin' it reminds me of the 79th causeway in Miami Beach that I used to zoom back and forth over in my 64 corvette convertible to meet my connection on Collins Avenue when I lived there as a twenty-year-old, long-haired, sun-tanned, cocky-cool-carefree, cocaine dealer.

"Escape, escape, escape…" I say to myself in a not so friendly way, "…back into your stupid fucking past."

"Dad… what?"

"Nothin'… Jesus! Why can't I stay in the moment!"

"Maybe because the moment sucks, Dad."

Wow… once again the omniscient one speaks.

"So where are you…" I ask, "…if the moment sucks?"

"I'm like three years old in Pt. Dume where we used to live, naked, spraying the hose all over the lawn."

"You used to run around naked and spray that hose for hours."

"I loved it more than anything."

"I know you did," I say and I picture Keri and me on lawn chairs at the little beach house we rented, watching him.

"Dad?"

"What?"

"Did I really eat my own poop when I was like, two?"

"You took a little dump right on the floor, picked up a piece and ate it."

"I just tasted it and then my mom ran over and slapped it out of my hand and you and her started laughing."

"You ate it all."

"I did not. I just wanted to see what it tasted like."

"I have pictures."

"Shut up, Dad."

So we're back in the moment together, jokin' around, trying to avoid the moments to come. I guess somehow memories of his mom did slip in...

the ones he wanted to...

the good ones...

the funny ones.

17

I'm on my knees again, parked in front of the Coronado Hospital, which is nestled in a quiet neighbourhood off Third Street. It's so small, only like a three story building, so it doesn't need one of those major pain-in-the-ass parking structures where you drive around and around and around looking for a space and use up an hour of the five dollars every twenty minutes fee you have to fuckin' pay. What a relief, easy street parking, and there is a little park right there dotted with a few pine trees and some shrubbery. So Shnooky jumps out to sniff around while I lean into the Scamp and pray under the guise of looking for my wallet I can't find... just in case anyone asks... only I have the wallet in my hand which is lodged under the front seat... just in case I have to say I found it. I'm concerned about what some security guard or cop cruising by might think of me in that position with my thirteen-year-old boy sitting across from me. I know how crazy I look... just not the normal dad type and I don't want to have to explain myself to some authority figure. "I was praying."

"Sure, pal, just get up slowly and put your hands over your

head."

"But that's my son."

"I said hands over the head!"

I remember once I dropped Max off at school, I think he was in the second grade. My car then was a step down from the Scamp; a dingy brown '74 two-door dodge dart with cardboard and tape on the broken back windows, cracked Lynrd Sknyrd and Marshall Tucker band stickers on the bumpers and big tyres on bogus Mag wheels. Hey, it was given to me by a mechanic friend, the only price attached was that I looked like a deranged, desert crystal meth dealer drivin' it. So I was there parked in front of the school, Shnooky sitting in the front seat with me, all cute and young and puppyish, watching Max go in, just adoring him, thinking of what a strong little boy he was. Then as soon as I drove off, this fucking cop pulls up behind me, red and whites flashing. He does the whole license registration thing which is fine by me because it's all good, all legal, all up-to-date. But then I figure out it's just a ploy to see if I have any warrants out for drugs or child molesting or something because he starts interrogating me about what I was doing there in front of the school.

"Excuse me?"

"How do I know you're not out here with your cute little dog trying to lure kids into your car?"

"What the fuck! Are you a fucking moron? I just dropped my

kid off. He goes to fucking school here! Are you fucking kidding me?"

I didn't get arrested but I did get some miscellaneous tickets. So, it's easier just to say I'm looking for my wallet... sir... offi... cer... sir... surly midget dick moron cocksucker... sir.

Max is still wrapped in the blanket, half-asleep, half-ignoring me because he is used to me praying and he knows it helps, even if only a little, he knows it helps. And so I pray, I pray for love to come into my heart for my father.

"Let's pray for Poppy to be all right," I say.

"You do it, Dad."

"God help Poppy be all right."

"But Poppy doesn't believe in God. You told me he said God was for weak people."

And he did over and over and over. Drilled it into my head, growing up. And I wanted to believe, I wanted to believe but I couldn't believe. Weak. Weak. Weak. And now I have my own understanding of God and it's where all my strength comes from.

"Come on," I say. "Let's think good thoughts about him. What did he do that was good?"

Max is silent and nothing is really jumping into my mind right off the bat. I close my eyes and try to remember good things. He was a decent provider. He took us on vacations. Never got me braces or bought me a car like he did for my brother and sister. I hated him for that... Come on, good things, good things, good things. He got me out of jail when I got busted, paid for a lawyer, but then he told my girlfriend I was a hopeless loser and she dumped me. Come on! Come on! Good things. He did the best he could with what he had. That is the spiritual approach I was taught to follow, supposed to wipe the slate clean, make you beam with forgiveness, understanding and love. I'm still waiting for that to work.

"He named Shnooky, Shnooky," Max says.

"That's right!" I say.

When we first got her Max wanted to call her Purple Tongue Golden Wolfie. "Here, Purple Tongue Golden Wolfie!" Can you imagine? Then we shortened it down to Purple Tongue and eventually to just PT. And being who she is, she brought out the love in everybody, even old Poppy because he always had food for her when we came down to visit and always patted her and always let her sit in his place on the couch and then one day when Max and I came back from the beach where Shnooky was banned... natural bird reserve or some shit the Ranger said, I mean she doesn't even chase birds... anyway we walked in the door and Poppy was watching his favourite, 'Married With Children' rerun because he couldn't get enough of that young Christina Applegate's cleavage, with PT (as she was known then) sitting next to him on the couch. He patted her head and said, "This little PT, she's such a good little Shnooky."

"What's a Shnooky?" Max asked.

"It's kind of a German slang word that you say to someone very dear to you," Poppy told him, "someone you love very much."

"I'm gonna call her Shnooky from now on," Max said and the rest is history.

"That was one good thing Poppy did, huh, Dad?"

"Yeah, that was a good thing," I say as she comes trotting back to the car and jumps in. Both of us grab her and kiss her.

Shnooky! Shnooky! Shnooky!

So we go into the main hospital entrance and see a lone, silver-haired lady easily close to eighty, sitting behind a desk in the cute little cosy lobby. Yeah, cute and cosy but I still smell hospital. Sickness. Pain. Death. I feel myself getting weak just bein' in there. She smiles at us. She's happy to see anybody.

"Excuse me, my father was admitted here tonight and… can you tell me where the Intensive Care Unit is?" I say.

"Why of course," she says. "You go down the corridor, take a left then a right. You can't miss it because if you do, you'll already be out the back entrance." She chuckles to herself. And how many times have you said that fucking line, I think. I don't ask. I stay respectful, polite and I say, "Thank you."

Max and I head left down the corridor with the wood support railings all along the sides and take the right to see some gurneys and wheelchairs lined up on the side and I feel my heart pounding.

I feel scared, scared to check on Poppy.

An orderly comes out of a door. "Is that intensive care?" I ask.

"No, sir, that's the emergency room, ICU is the next door down after the waiting room." He grabs a wheelchair and wheels it back into Emergency.

"Dad, see, it says Emergency on this door and Waiting Room on that door, ICU on that door and there's the back entrance that the lady said…"

"Fine, fine… I see it, okay?"

"Okay, Dad, just telling you." He senses how frightened I am so he's not giving me shit.

"I know, I know," I say. "Fuck. I don't feel like going in there."

"Me either."

"Okay, you go in…" I look into the cubbyhole-sized waiting room. "Jesus, it's fucking small in there… Go in there, I'll get you if… I'll get you if I need you… it's probably no big deal… just gonna check on him, okay?"

"Okay, Dad."

He's looking right into my eyes with the concern one can only have for someone they love. He loves me. I see it and I feel it, and I love him.

"I'll be right back, okay?"

I poke my head through the door of the Intensive Care Unit. Why don't I just walk in? It's small so I don't need to, right? That's what I tell myself. I mean, I can see the nurses' station right there in the centre and I can see the rooms spread around it in a semi-circle. Only seven beds with numbers over the doors. 1, 2, 3,5, 6, are all empty. There's a nurse in room 7 fixing some IV drip for an old, old lady wrenched in agony, screaming but no noise is coming out of her mouth. She looks like she's already dead. I'm hoping it's morphine for her sake. Fuck, I could use a little shot of morphine. I'm so nervous here. I look at room 4. I think I see his outline in the bed; yeah, that's my dad. His head is cocked to the side, eyes shut, jaw dropped. He's got that oxygen thing in his nose so he must be okay. He couldn't just be there lying dead. That emergency light or whatever it is over the door number would be flashing if anything was wrong plus the nurse behind the station has that monitor right in front of her. Bleep… bleep… bleep… is that him? If something happened, she'd be in his room in a second. Everything is so close in here. Fuck, he's okay; I don't even need to ask. Oh, she sees me and gets up. She a cute, heavy-set Hispanic woman, maybe thirty, long black ponytail with huge bulging tits strapped down inside her nurses' uniform that I concentrate not to look at even though I do as she comes over. I step in the door. "Hi, sorry, I'm just checking on my dad… that's him in room four…"

She gets his chart and ushers me out into the corridor. She tells me although he's critical that his condition is stable at the moment and he's peacefully sleeping. "Yeah, I saw."

"Would you like to spend some time in the room alone with him?"

"I don't know," comes out of my mouth even though I didn't mean to say it. I was just thinking it. Shit. I feel like a bad son. I just can't handle it right now. Wait, am I saying this or thinking this?

"Excuse me?" she says.

"I... ah, I'm sorry, I'm just really tired... I'll come back when he's awake since he's okay right now, I mean he's gonna live until tomorrow... right? I mean..."

"Presently, the signs are that he will. He is very strong considering his age and the severity of his condition."

She also adds that he is still quite the charming character, that he was quite talkative after they relieved some of his pain.

I'm not gonna say, "So did he flirt with you, tell you you'd look much cuter if you lost some weight?" or, "Ya know, he'd fuck you if he could," because I'm coming from a place of love so I smile and say, "Yeah, my dad sure is some character." We both laugh a little, each I'm sure with our own thoughts about what kind of character he is.

"Which son are you?" she asks. "The one from Hawaii?"

"No, the other one, from LA."

I'm waiting for her to say, "Oh, the ex-drug addict?" but she doesn't. "Oh yes, you come down to visit with your boy..." Then she whispers, "Your father told me about what happened with your

162

wife and son. I'm so sorry. I hope you don't mind."

"No, it's okay." She takes a peek at Max zoning out on the TV in the waiting room.

"Is that him?"

I nod.

"Oh, he's a cutie. He looks like a nice boy, too. You should be proud of yourself."

Did my father say he was proud of me? Huh? Can you tell me fucking that! I scream in my head as I say, "Thank you."

"Well," she says, "I suggest you and your son go get some rest, and come back in the morning."

"We'll be staying at my father's place in the Coronado Cays," I say. "Do you have that number?"

"Yes, we do."

"If there is any emergency, please call me immediately."

Cordial. Nice. Mature. Kind of brief and anti-climactic but so far so good, I think, as Max and I walk out of the hospital. In a way, my prayers about my dad were answered.

18

We ride through the quaint little town of Coronado, most of which is shut down for the night. As we pass the Hotel Del Coronado, which was the location for the famous Marilyn Monroe, 'Some Like it Hot' movie, I remember watching it with my father on TV when I was a little kid and how he laughed and laughed at Tony Curtis and Jack Lemon all dressed up as women, fumbling their way through and how I didn't really understand it but laughed too because he was laughing, because I just wanted to laugh with my dad. I think of how many times I passed by the hotel on the way to his place and never remembered that and I get a strange, empty, sick feeling in my stomach. My father is gonna die.

"Why are we even going to Poppy's?" Max says. "We should just drive back home."

"No, we gotta stay."

"But the nurse told you he was okay."

"We just have to wait and see."

"I'm gonna miss school."

"Big deal. Tomorrow is Friday. One fucking day. Anyway, he's in critical fucking condition. You call that okay?"

"What happened, Dad?"

"What do you mean?"

"You're all, like, mad again."

"I'm not mad… okay? I'm sorry, I'm just thinking."

"You know what I'm thinkin', Dad?"

And I'm waiting for something, I don't know what, something profound, some insight, some realisation.

"I'm thinkin' I gotta take a crap," he says.

I laugh. And it is profound because it gets me off my own crap, so to speak… but I still gotta push a little bit.

"Why didn't you go at the hospital?" I say.

"I didn't have to go at the hospital."

"But you were probably thinking about it because you were reminiscing about taking a shit before we got to the hospital, right?"

"No, Dad, it doesn't work that way with me, I just gotta take one, okay?"

There we are. He's just gotta take one and I'm trying to make something out of it.

"Fine, we'll be there in a minute," I say.

So we drive out of town and take the 75 south over the Silver Strand, which is a long, narrow strip of land (one of knowledge may refer to it as an isthmus) with the San Diego Bay on one side and the Pacific Ocean on the other. It's a popular resort area in the summer for campers, crowded with trailer homes and Winnebagos parked all along the Pacific shore for miles, but in the winter, it's barren and desolate and the Navy Seals who have their national base there do these training exercises on the beach that they have set up like some fucking combat zone with old tanks and burnt out fuselages and trenches and nets and beached P boats or D boats or whatever the fuck they are.

"Look at this stuff," I say. "It gives me this creepy, end-of-the -world feeling, especially at night."

"Dad, see that hollowed out airplane? I wanna take a shit in it."

"Yeah, and they'll come in and shoot your ass off."

"Dad, I'm serious, I gotta shit."

"We're almost there, okay? Just hold on."

Now we're on a mission to get to my dad's before Max shits his pants. The urgency takes precedence over everything else and I'm glad it does. I can control this, I can drive faster, get him to the toilet on time. So I zoom down to the Coronado Cays exit down the ramp, wind around to the Coronado Cays Village which is this whole, marina-style retirement community on the bay, filled with houses and condominiums. I slow down for a second as we pass the little guard house making sure to wave to the retiree, rent-a-cop guard, who hobbles out and waves back (he lets everyone who waves through, anyway). I speed down to the complex where my dad's condo is, and pull up to the call-box at the gate.

"I forget the code."

"Dad, please."

"Remember how we always call Poppy and tell him we forgot the code just to piss him off?"

"I don't care, Dad..."

I do my father's accent.

"You don't remember za code? But I've told you zo many times."

"Dad, I hate you so much right now," Max says.

"Tell me you love me."

"No."

"Tell me. Scream it out or you shit in your pants."

"Okay, I love you! Open it!"

Now I have to deliver. I press 0133. The gate opens. I screech into a parking spot. I jump out of the car. Max jumps out of the car. Shnooky jumps out of the car and we all tear down the path past one old blue shingled condo after another with Shnooky leading the way to Poppy's place. She gets to his building across from the pool, hops three stairs at a time and sits right in front of #43. She doesn't know Max has to take a shit. She's hoping Poppy is going to greet her at the door with a nice treat like he always does. I follow her up with Max right behind me, breathing down my neck.

"Look, Shnooky knows where to go every time."

"Dad, shut up! Open the door."

I know he's at the moment of truth. He's literally hanging on my back. I don't kid around. I shove the key in the lock, twist it, turn the knob… the door swings open as Max pushes past me and flies into the downstairs bathroom like the Flash. I hear a loud, painful, groan of relief then, "Dad, I'm gonna kill you after this!"

"Okay, okay," I say, as I'm grinning and laughing through my nose and feeling one of those silly moments that fill your body with warmth. I turn on the living room light and the immediate sadness of my dad's absence hits me. He may never come back here. I look at the two couches he still has from the house in New York; the blue one with all sunken-in pillows, faded and frayed… I remember jumping up and down on those pillows with my brother when I was about five, bouncing off, banging my head against the radiator and getting two butterfly band-aid stitches. They were almost like real stitches. It was important to say that to other kids… and the pastel red couch he has lined up across from it… my mom replaced the blue one that she said we all ruined as kids with the red one when I was about fourteen, and moved the blue one up to their bedroom. She figured we were all grown up enough not to abuse the new living room couch which had some expensive soft velvet cover and pillows on it. And I didn't jump on those pillows but I came home drunk in the wee hours for years and partied on those pillows and fucked on those pillows and passed out on those pillows and my mom used to find me in the morning, sometimes clothed, sometimes naked with a girl squeezed in next to me or one of us sprawled out on the floor under the antique mahogany table in front of it. My father still has it sitting between the two couches here. My mom used to keep it finely polished and dusted, now it's all dull and dirty and chipped with his ancient little portable TV sitting on it. She would have had a fit… and speaking of fits, I'm getting a gripping nicotine one, of the worst kind. I gotta have one. I feel my pockets. Shit, where are they? In the car. The duffel bag is in the car too. Good.

"Max, I'm goin' to get the duffel bag," I say and I sprint back to the car. My eyes bulge as I see the smokes sitting right on the front seat. I tear the pack open, light one up, keep it in my mouth, and just suck drag after drag as I grab the duffle bag from the back seat, throw it over my shoulder, close the doors, and head back down the path, senses now calmed and cool even though the torture and pain is still behind them like I'm some famous method actor (you pick the name), strolling to some dramatic destiny, cigarette dangling from his lips.

I sit on the stairs of my father's place, reflecting, smoking… in that cool, smoking/reflecting way that once you've quit, you know means absolutely fucking nothing…

"Dad?"

Shit. I blow smoke into my chest, cup the cigarette.

"What?" I look around. Max is poking his head out of a crack in the door.

"Dad, I don't care if you're smoking. I know this is all really hard for you."

"Sure, what do you know?"

"Dad, I mean it."

I ponder that for a moment, pop the cigarette back in my mouth, take a long drag.

"So what are you doing?" I say. "Why don't you come out here?"

I figure we might finally sit down and talk, talk about some heavy stuff; how we really feel and what it really means and how things really are... I kinda know in the back of my mind, I wouldn't even have thoughts like that if I wasn't smoking but...

"Dad, you need to come in here," he says.

"What for? Where's Shnooky? What happened?"

"Nothing, she's in the kitchen licking the floor. Dad, I think I hurt my butt."

"What?"

"It felt like I shitted out wood splinters or something. I need you to look at it."

"Max..."

"Dad, I'm serious, I think it's bleeding."

"What?"

"Dad, it hurts... please... like really bad."

He sticks his hand out to show me a piece of tissue paper, soaked red.

"Jesus, Max!"

I leap up the stairs like a lion, like a lioness, I mean what the fuck, I'm both, right? My hurt little cub! My hurt little cub! Even though I know, I know something is just a little off here... but it's too late. I've pushed the door open and the big, plastic bowl full of water has fallen down and bounced off my head and I'm standing there, drenched, with the cigarette butt in my mouth, the soaked tobacco dribbling down my chin and Max is laughing and laughing and laughing and Shnooky comes trotting out of the kitchen, wiggling and waggling with ketchup all over her snout.

"You little bastard!"

"I told you I'd get you back. Stupid smoker."

19

"Max, I want you to help me clean up in here."

"Sure, Dad, get me a blankey."

He's lying on the red couch, with Shnooky next to him, eating the scrambled eggs with smoked salmon I've made out of Poppy's fridge. Poppy always has smoked salmon. It's his favourite. Margaret sends him ten pounds of it every Christmas so he practically lives off it until March and always offers it to us when we come down. "Zis is a good one, from Nova Scotia, very expensive."

Yeah, so Max is eating and watching TV and wanting me to get him a blanket while I'm wiping the rest of his ketchup tissue mess off the counter and washing the rest of Poppy's dirty dishes, which are so dirty. Even the ones in the dish rack are dirty, even the ones in the cupboards are dirty. I re-wash them every time I come down which Poppy disapproves of. "Zese dishes are perfectly clean," he says. "Wash zem if you vant but zere is nothing wrong wis zem."

"Yeah, Dad, there was nothing wrong with any fucking thing you ever did, right? The dishes are fucking dirty, okay!"

And I used to talk like that and he would call me an idiot, no good, little zero and I'd tell him he ruined my life, storm out and slam the door. Used to. Used to. Used to. But not for years. Now I still wash 'em and he still says the same thing but I pause and I ask for God's help and I say, "I'll just wash them anyway Dad, okay?" and he says, "Okay, if you must, you must," and we go on getting through the day. What a spiritual giant I have become.

"Dad, blankey."

"Get your own blankey, lazy!"

And I actually say that as I'm walking out of the kitchen to go upstairs to get him one. I skirt by the old white Formica-topped kitchen table. It's got some dirty plastic placemats on it... well one lone placemat is out, the others are stacked up for guests. I'll sponge them off for him and he'll say they didn't need it but he'll appreciate it. And the chipped wicker fruit basket only has a couple of brown spotted bananas in it. He usually fills it up for us but he didn't know we were coming down this time. Poor Poppy... I guess I'm missing him. He eats the rotten bananas anyway, he doesn't care. He says food isn't that interesting when you get to be his age, that it has no taste anymore, but when my sister takes us out to the fancy restaurants in San Diego, he loves to order that fresh halibut. Always asks if it's fresh. He's real interested in that. Eats it all. Tasty, right, Dad?

Who knows? What do I know? I should throw the bananas out though, Max won't eat 'em with the spots. Then Poppy will ask what happened, ask us if we ate them. Can't lie about the stupidest things, right? So I'll eat 'em, I'll eat 'em, I'll eat 'em... okay? I grab one, peel it as fast as a tree monkey, and shove it in my mouth as I walk upstairs saying through a mouthful, "Getting the blankey for the little baby." Max ignores me. Damnit.

Can't escape the corniest old modelling picture of me on the wall as soon as I walk into the little guest bedroom. There are some other family photos but I always get stuck on this one. It's from one of the first jobs I did in Paris for this Sears type department store. I sent it home to my mom for I don't know what reason. Oh, yeah they made a subway poster out of it and put it in a bunch of magazines... *doing well in Paris, Ma.*

I'm in a blue and white striped, short sleeve polo shirt and some ugly maroon jeans. I have my arm around this big bucked-toothed stuffed donkey. We both have the same dorky smiles. I remember the only way I could smile was by making fun of the donkey's smile. I was so wasted. Young wasted. Cute wasted. Get away with it all wasted with nice little dabs of cover make-up on my track marks. My mom framed it, she was so happy. She didn't know the cute little story behind that smile. I hate looking at it. I guess I don't smash it to pieces for my mom's sake.

And then there's this painting I did in art class in seventh grade of this kid, Willy Conners. I remember he broke his arm, it was in a cast and he couldn't draw so the art teacher had him pose for the rest of the class all the time. This time she had him kneel down on a table, steadying himself with his good arm and we had to make something out of it. I had him looking for a golf ball on the golf course. I painted the grass, excuse me, rough, he was looking through and the golf ball with the clubs in the golf bag on the side and some little guy in the background, putting on the green. I remember the art teacher was impressed with my idea but I really couldn't paint for shit so she helped me a little and gave me an A. My mom framed that too. She was proud. I didn't tell her the art teacher painted more than half of it. I always wanted to tell her that. Oh, God, get me out of this room. I'm not sleepin' in here, I'll sleep on the other couch next to Max. I grab the blanket off the bed. I'll need one out of Poppy's room, too. Oh, man, I gotta go in his room. Why is this so creepy? I never feel like this when he's here, when I know he's gonna live, right?

I go into his room, grab the blanket off his bed, the old bed my mom used to sleep in with him. It's so sunken in on his side now, almost thirteen years she hasn't been in it. What I used to do in that bed too as a teenager when they went away, like some crazy little Caligula. Did I say I was sorry for that, Mom? I think I did. Well, I'm sorry again.

The light is on by his desk, so is his electric typewriter next to the old portable radio made by the electronics company he used to run in the sixties: high-end stereo equipment; tape decks, speakers, language labs that he sold all over the world.

Then when he retired, he messed up his pension with some crappy lawyer. He had to pay hundreds of thousands in back taxes and went broke. Did I blame him for that? Yes. Had to keep the fuel going in the hate-the-father fire so I could keep destroying myself on his behalf, right? I mean in those days it had to be all his fault, know what I mean? But now, it is just a radio.

When I stop thinking so loud I realize it's still on, very faint, on a nice soothing classical station. It sounds like... Chopin? Could be. Fluttery. Melancholy. I don't know. I don't know classical music. Maybe Mozart I could tell. Ah, bullshit. I listen, I like it, but give me a quiz on classical composers, I'd fail it. Anyway Poppy loved to listen to Chopin so I'm leaning towards that. Now he doesn't really care about music either, just keeps the radio on at low volume, like a quiet little friend in the background. Maybe he was here at his desk when he got those chest pains. What was he writing? He's written a bunch of books. None of them published, all about his world travels and his accomplishments and conquests. He is always the hero, always helping people and never does anything wrong nor thinks about it... and it always gets down to sex with a girl or woman which he describes as lovely and beautiful and they have relations of love and sex and sex and love and sex. One of his books was entitled, 'The Most Important Things In Our Lives.' It was basically about him jaunting around the world on business ventures over the years with his many, "girlfriends" (better known as escorts and even better known as women who travel with you and fuck you for money). He even had xeroxed pictures of about thirty girls that he wrote about. My mom's picture was not in that book. When I asked him why she wasn't one of the most important things in his life he said that was a whole different story.

What's he writing here? What's this title? Bohemians? He told me something once about tracing back Bohemian ancestors on his mother's side. Oh, here I see on one page he writes, "Our family has a great deal of craziness in their genes and my Bohemian grandfather may explain these genes," which would mean along with some other historical points, this is another rationalization for him being a total fuck-hound all his life. I can't bear it. Maybe if I was someone else, I'd be interested, impressed, thrilled but it's just too hard for a son to read. *And you have those genes too, don't you? Yes. Yes. Yes. I know...*

I look at the old framed picture over the right side of his desk. It's him, dressed in his flight jacket, sitting proudly in his single engine reconnaissance plane. He was very valuable to the American Army, he told me, having grown up in Germany, knowing the terrain so well. He was very brave and bold, even got a Purple Heart, was hit by shrapnel from a hand grenade or something, got a metal screw in his shoulder. I study his facial structure, his forehead, cheekbones, chin and nose.

Then there is the one picture he has of my mom on the left side of the desk. A forties modelling picture of her tall, slender, blue-eyed, blonde body, in a low-cut, black evening gown, leaning up against a mahogany piano, her finger on one of the ivory keys, as she gives a sultry look into the camera. She was a big model in the late forties. She modelled with Lauren Bacall and shot with Richard Avedon and was asked to come to Hollywood to be a big star, but turned it down to take care of her two younger alcoholic sisters. Yeah, I've got her blue eyes, maybe her lips, but when ya get right down to it, when I look back at my father's picture, I'm the spittin' image of this man, this man, who I've hated and resented and wanted...

I wanted him, I wanted him to be...

And I remember the story my mom told me of when she was nineteen. Of when she was engaged to the tall, strapping, handsome Sterling Hayden, who she coaxed into modelling before he became a famous actor and how she left him because he drank too much. And I remember as a teenager, seeing him in the movie, 'The Killing' and wanting to look like him and getting mad at my father and screaming...

"I could have been Sterling Hayden's son! Not yours! I could have been Sterling Hayden's son!"

And it's screaming in my head now, as I'm staring at my father's picture. I'm still staring at it. Am I breathing? I almost choke on my swallow. Fuck this. I gotta get back downstairs with the blankeys.

Max and Shnooky are sound asleep. I lay a blanket over Max, kiss him on the cheek, kiss Shnooky on the snout. I drop to my knees again, thinking, how many times in one day do I have to pray? But I do it anyway. I pray just for my mind to be calm, and I remember the monks at Vedanta Temple, who prayed in Hindu before every meal, ending with…

Shanti Shanti Shanti

Peace Peace Peace

Please, God, that's all I want.

20

"Dad, why are we here so early?"

"Because Auntie Margaret wants to meet us here."

"Fine, wake me up when she comes."

"She's supposed to be here at eight o'clock, Max, it's like five to eight."

"Fine, wake me up in five minutes."

"Fine."

So we sit in the car, back in front of the little Coronado hospital waiting for my sister to arrive. Max closes his eyes and I watch Shnooky sniffing around on the lawn, hoping that she takes a discreet shit somewhere in the bushes. My cell phone rings.

"That's her," I say but Max is already sleepy, slack-jawed with his head lolling into his chest, slumping over on the seat... amazing how kids can do that.

"Margaret?" I say.

"Who the fuck is Margaret?" I hear on the other end.

"Tony?"

"What's up, big guy?"

"Are you in rehab already?"

"Almost, buddy, almost."

"Almost? What does that mean? You're still high, aren't you? Why didn't you go to rehab?"

I'm so worked up I'm not even aware that I've gotten out of the car and lit a cigarette... but I have, I'm just not recognizing it yet.

"Take it easy," he says. "I got good news for us. We're getting seventy-five grand to finish the script but here's the catch. I have to do the three months or six months or whatever it is first, my dad says... and listen, we can work on it over the phone because this is a top-of-the-line rehab in Arizona. A lot of celebrities go there. I don't even wanna get into all the big names I heard went there at this moment. And get this, I got a private room so I'm just gonna tell 'em I have to work on my screenplay..."

"What the fuck are you saying!" I scream into the phone as I watch Shnooky chasing a little brown squirrel across the lush green lawn, glistening with silver dew drops under the rising morning sun. I see the whole beautiful moment so clearly but I don't feel a part of any of it.

"Hey, I'm giving you a chance to work with me here," Tony says. "I got other writers..."

"Good! Bullshit them, okay! I don't wanna ever work with you again until you're off crack for five fucking years... at least!" I turn off the phone and take big, livid drags off the cigarette.

A horn honks behind me.

"What!" I say as I swing around, ready to kill.

And... it's Margaret, sitting behind the wheel of a brand new white Mustang convertible rent-a-car, waving to me.

"Hi, Dave..."

"Oh, shit... sorry... did you hear that?"

"I heard some of it."

"I just, my writing partner... is just so messed up, he just blew a seventy-five thousand dollar deal." And I say it so unconvincingly, catching myself trying to impress her with a line of bullshit as I'm saying it.

"Okay, whatever..." she says. She's never really interested in what I'm doing anyway. Maybe if I showed her an actual cheque for seventy-five grand it might be different.

"I can't believe you're still smoking," she adds.

I drop the cigarette and step on it like it wasn't even there.

"I'm not really... just one here and there."

"It's your life," she says.

Oh Christ, I hate it when she says things like that along with some of her other favourites; "You made your bed, you lie in it," or "You've got no one to blame but yourself," or "You should have thought of that a long time ago."

Maybe you should just have a fucking cue card that says, DAVE YOU LOSER, in capital letters, you can hold up whenever appropriate,

I think as I nod my head and say, "I know, I know."

"Where's Max?" she says as she gets out of her car.

She looks so much like my mom now. She's lost weight; fixed her nose, cut her long, mousy brown hair. She bleached it blonde and put turquoise blue contacts over her dark, hazel eyes. She used to be so jealous of my mom's beauty and she turned that jealousy into hatred. It made my mom so sad because she knew the truth. She knew where the hatred came from. Still, Margaret treated her like shit.

Margaret had my father's intellect so she would torture my mom mentally. "You're so stupid you can't even balance a cheque book," she'd say and maybe my mom couldn't. So what? She was kind, sensitive and loving, qualities Margaret didn't give a shit about, qualities she considered flaws.

Then my mom died and it seemed like that was what Margaret was waiting for so she could finally inhabit the look she always wanted... along with my father's brainpower plus the ample sized breast implants, she landed herself Doctor Steven Sudlow, a very prominent and wealthy orthopaedic surgeon, a few years back... took him right away from his wife, actually his second wife. Look out, Margaret!

Anyway, now she is smart, beautiful and rich, so she's also decked out in a Prada or Versace or Donna Karan... some fucking designer navy wool pants suit, and has about a quarter million of jewellery hanging off her. Every time I see the eight-carat marquise diamond ring on her hand I just stare at it and think, *this is enough to fix my whole life* and to tell ya the truth I get the urge to just chop off her finger and take it.

And I hate myself for it because she does show her love through generosity now, which is the best she can do. I look at her again. She appears sweeter. Maybe Mom snuck some love inside her too, that was part of the deal Margaret didn't know about. And I feel my mom's spirit giggle and say, Shhh... Dave... like it's our little secret.

"Max," I say as I open the car door. "Wake up, Auntie Margaret is here."

"Hi, Maxy!" she says. "Wanna go out to a nice big breakfast after we see old Poppy?"

He rises up off the seat like a dreamy teen, Jack In The Box, hair sticking in every direction, blinking his eyes open, cracking a sleepy grin.

"Sure," he says. He loves his Auntie Margaret.

I blow a short whistle to Shnooky who trots up, hops in the car.

"She is such a good dog," Margaret says. "Aren't you, Shnooky?" Shnooky looks at her like, *That's no news to me.*

So we go into the hospital. I tell Margaret what the nurse told me about Poppy being stable and ask her if she thinks he might recover. "Dave, I talked to the nurses extensively over the phone and he's going to die for sure. He has acute bronchitis accompanied with an aortic aneurysm dissection that is inoperable. The only hope is that it stabilises and at his age the chances of that are slim to none."

Margaret used to be a registered nurse and worked in the cardiovascular department at Doctor's Hospital in NYC so she knows what she's talking about. We shared an apartment back then, 1978 I think it was. She just worked and drank and worked and drank to ease her mind from all those people, sick and dying day after day and I was out in all the clubs and all the after hours clubs, every night pushing my career and coke and Quaaludes. We'd meet at dawn when I was coming in and she was going out and I'd be fucking some girl when she was making breakfast, or she'd be fucking some guy when I was making dinner. One time I partied in the clubs with my friend Robbie Huntz from high school and he needed a place to stay. We got home at four in the morning and as I was passing out, he stumbled into Margaret's room and I heard her scream, but Robbie was a real good lookin' guy so by the time I pulled myself up and careened across the floor to her rescue, I heard them goin' at it like wild animals behind her bedroom door...

And I wanna say, "Remember Robbie Huntz?" just to joke around, ease the blow of her words but I don't because Margaret has shut the door on her past and is now a serious, sophisticated spouse of a conservative surgeon... yes, shut the door on her first marriage to an LSD dealer when she was eighteen and her weekend dabbles in prostitution in Manhattan and her second marriage to a sheep herder in the south of France and her third marriage to a jungle dancer at Club Med in Bora Bora… unmentionable, all in the past.

"So how long does Dad have?" I ask.

"I'm surprised he's still alive," she says.

21

There is blood trickling out of my father's mouth. I'm not as shocked as when I first saw my mother up close in her hospital bed, emaciated, eaten from the inside out by the cancer, but I hold back a gasp and it shoots up to my eyes and tears come out. I feel Max grabbing my arm. He's scared seeing old Poppy lying there, helpless, tubes connected everywhere and the blood... oh, it's hard to take.

"Just say hi to him," I tell Max.

"Hi, Poppy."

"Who? Who is zat?" my dad says as he strains to look at us, his weak, aged eyes glazed over and fluttering. Margaret comes over from the nurses' station.

"He doesn't know who we are," I say.

"He's disorientated from the aneurysm, Dave, and he's on morphine because he's in a lot of pain. Just act normal, okay?"

She goes up to his bedside, takes a Kleenex out of her purse and wipes his mouth.

"Hi, Dad!" she says with professional forced cheerfulness. "It's your daughter, Margaret, and David."

"Your little David?"

"No, your little David."

"Who?"

"Your son, David, and his son, Max."

"Oh, vhere is your son David?" he says.

"He's in college in Ohio," Margaret says. "He sends all his love."

"And Steven, how is he?"

"Steven had an early surgery today in New York but he should be here early this afternoon."

"Oh, he doesn't have to come to see me, he has too busy of a schedule."

"He wants to see you, Dad."

"Such a fine man, your husband."

I feel myself getting angry and wanting to walk out. Can't even fucking acknowledge me and Max. God help me take the opposite action. I step closer and lean into him.

"Hi, Dad."

He looks at me for, I don't know, maybe ten seconds. Then he puts a trembling hand with tape and IV needles stuck in it on my cheek.

"You're my son, David, aren't you?" he says. Then he focuses and looks at me very seriously. I anticipate something important will come from his lips next, something monumental.

"Did you eat za salmon?" he says.

I can't help but laugh at the absurdity of my own expectation, and I'm grateful I can laugh because that expectation ten years ago would have sent me into a rage, screaming, "Is that all you can say? How about saying you're sorry for how you treated me my whole life. I'm glad you're dying. I fucking hate you!" And I would have stormed out of the hospital in search of an overdose. Maybe that voice is still screaming but it's a little scream only I can hear. So I answer with a warm, loving smile.

"Yeah, Dad. Me and Max ate some salmon."

I feel Max stiffen as I pull him next to me. "Remember Max?"

"Of course I remember Max. Don't be an idiot. Zese drugs they put in me makes everything so fuzzy I can't see anything clearly. Where is za doctor? I want to see za doctor."

He called me an idiot. This is gonna get bad. Time to take a break.

"I'll find him," I say, then I put my finger on my chest, point to the door and mouth to Margaret, "I want to go."

"Relax, Dave," she says.

"I want to leave too," Max says.

"Shhh…" I say.

"I vant to leave too," Poppy says. "You think I vant to stay here? Zese nincompoops have stolen my car keys. Zey are trying to keep me here against my will making me all fuzzy with zese drugs."

"Dad, you are in critical condition," Margaret says.

"Nonsense," he says as he struggles to sit up.

My mom once said, "When your father dies he's going to die like a soldier with his boots on."

He clutches on to Max's arm to steady himself.

"Poppy! What are you doing?" Max says.

"What does it look like I'm doing? What is za matter with you people?" Then he breaks into a coughing fit. It's bad with hacks and gurgles.

"Get the pan, Max," Margaret says. "You're closest to him. Get the pan."

As Max grabs the little kidney shaped pan from the bed table, Poppy leans over and spits in it. "I have to save zat for za doctor to look at."

"Ahhh!" Max says when he sees the huge yellowish-green and red mass of death floating in the pan. It's not pretty. I wouldn't wanna eat it on the half-shell, if ya know what I mean.

"Don't be such a little baby," my dad says.

"I'm not a baby," Max says.

I take the pan from Max and feel like cracking Poppy over the head with it but I put it down on the table as he slumps back in the bed, exhausted. "Please, I want za doctor," he says. God he is so, so weak… and such a pain in the ass, too.

I notice my brother coming into the ICU, looking worried and annoyed at the same time as he goes up to the nurse's station. He sees us in the room. I give him a half wave and a grim smile as he walks in. He's dressed in a grey suit that matches his grey hair, his full head of hair. *Why the fuck did I have to be the one to go bald? I'm not grey, though, and he's fatter… oh, shut up!*

"Hi, Paul," Margaret says. "When did you get in?"

"I got into San Francisco at five am to pick up the kids and then the flight was delayed… and I'm supposed to be in China on Monday morning… and Katy is going to show up any minute so I have to deal with that…"

"Sorry I asked," she says.

Yeah, sorry Dad had to be dying on your busy schedule, I think, but I just stand there. Don't wanna add to the family tension that is beginning to rise.

"How is he?" Paul asks.

"See for yourself," Margaret says.

"Hey, Max," Paul says. "Michael and Jeffrey are out in the waiting room if you wanna see them…" Max's eyes light up with relief. He's definitely not thinking, *no, I want to stay with my favourite Granddaddy…*

"Bye, Dad," he says and he bolts. As Paul moves closer to our father, he pats me on my shoulder and solemnly says, "Hey Dave," not the usual, "Hey, Daaaave!" with a punch to the arm. He's feeling down, this is hard for him.

"Is zat za doctor?"

"No, that's Paul, Dad," Margaret says.

"All za way from Hawaii? What is he doing here? What are you doing here, Paul?"

"I came..." and he starts getting choked up... "I just came to see how you were doing." Then he almost pukes when he sees the specimen my dad left in the pan.

"I don't know what all zis fuss is about. Did zey tell you I was dying?"

"Dad, you had an aneurysm in your aorta," Margaret says. "The wall around your heart has been torn."

She says it detached and matter-of-factly but it sounds so poetic and I wish if only he would have said something like that to me... *My son, the wall around my heart has been torn, the wall that kept you out for so many years, and now in my dying days, my love, my strong love I have always had for you, is seeping through...*

And as I work on that poem in my mind my father says, "I don't vant to talk to you Margaret, you are not the doctor."

"I've had it," she says. "I'll go find the damn doctor." And she walks out.

"Oh, such a difficult girl," he says to Paul. "And how is your Katy? She is so lovely."

"She's coming any minute."

"Zo you are back together?"

"No, Dad…"

"Oh, no, you must stay together. I always stayed with your mother."

"Dad, we already went through this…"

"We went through nothing…"

"Dad, Katy and I are already divorced. Okay!"

And then Katy walks in, drained and stoney-faced, hair pulled back tight, dressed in a serious pinstriped business suit of her own. She's some CEO of something or other in San Francisco now. "Oh, Jesus!" Paul says. "Sorry, Katy."

"What for? We are divorced," she says as she shoots scornful eyes and skirts by him to the other side of the bed.

"Hi, Katy," I say. She cracks a forced smile. She never really liked me, just kind of tolerated me as the crazy younger brother, which I was. I think I still owe her an amends for giving Paul a quarter-ounce of cocaine for his thirtieth birthday. Fucked him up for a month, almost lost his job, cheated on her three times, I think.

Anyway, I am sorry and I have changed. Kind of bitchy to still look at me that way, though, maybe I won't make amends. Who cares? She's only here to see my dad. She was always very fond of him since she and Paul began dating as freshmen at Colombia and I think my father actually convinced him she was the one he should marry. She did tolerate his cheating which is right in line with what my mom did. Paul was the one that wanted the divorce. Katy places the palm of her hand on my father's brow and strokes his old, withered head.

"So tell me, Katy, do I look like I'm dying?"

She starts to sob. And I see Max coming back with Michael, who is also thirteen, and Jeffrey, who is nine. They remind me so much of Paul and me when we were kids. Michael is kind of geeky and really smart like his dad and Jeffrey is a cute little wild man who is constantly getting reprimanded for his inappropriate behavior.

"We wanna see the big bloody lugey Poppy made," he says. Immediately my brother says, "Jeffrey! Get out!"

"We just wanna see it," he says.

"No, you do, Jeffrey," Michael says. He looks at his dad. "I didn't care."

"Yes, you did. You wanted to see it," Jeffrey says.

"Shut up, Jeffrey," Michael says and he puts him in a headlock.

"Oh no," Poppy says. "Who is zis wrestling in za room?"

"Both of you, stop it!" Katy says. And Max winces with amused guilt as Paul separates them. How can I get mad? In fact I love him for it. And the nurse comes in, very concerned, telling us Poppy needs his rest, that the doctor is coming and for everybody to, "Please leave."

"Who cares what ze do? Rest. I'll rest enough when I'm dead."

But she ushers us out anyway.

"Sorry, Poppy."

"Yeah, sorry, Poppy."

"Bye, Poppy."

"See ya soon, Dad."

"Be back in a little while."

"Bye, Paul, I love you…"

22

Katy needs to fly back to San Francisco for some board meeting of her company. She refuses a ride to the airport from Paul and takes a taxi. "Just get the kids back by five on Sunday," she says. I'm glad she's gone, I always feel so dirty around her.

So we go to breakfast at the Coronado Loews Hotel on the bay just down the road from my father's condo. Paul and Margaret always stay there when they visit because it's close by and… well, they can afford it with the three hundred and fifty dollar a night suites, views of the bay, four star restaurant, massive adjoining swimming pools, spas, game rooms for the kids… *I seethe with jealousy and resentment. I hate them for it. No, I love them. I want it. I love them.*

Luxury love. Luxury love. Luxury love.

While the kids attack the mile-long buffet of eggs sunnyside up or over easy and any kind of omelette or breakfast burrito and pancakes and bacon and sausage and French toast and fresh fruits and multi-coloured, multi-flavoured muffins, Paul, Margaret and I sit outside on the patio.

Paul asks me how the writing is going, the commercials, same shit. Margaret asks without really caring unless I show a pay cheque. Then they talk business... stocks and bonds which just sounds like dribble to me while I concentrate on breaking off nice little even pieces of the eight extra sausages I pulled off the buffet platter to feed to Shnooky, who sits by my side.

"It's so cool they allow dogs at this hotel," I say.

Paul shoots me a look in the middle of his... I invested in this stock that went up and that stock that went down bullshit... like, who gives a shit about your dog? He actually does call her, "Dog." *Her name is not, Dog, it's Shnooky. Got it? Fucker. And I'd kill for her. Okay?*

Anyway, we get to talking about Poppy and we all agree he is impossible, even when he is dying. Margaret tells Paul there is absolutely no hope and starts talking about his will, getting him cremated and where to spread his ashes and getting a real estate agent to sell the condo and splitting it up three ways and it's all so detached and matter-of-fact and me and Paul just listen and agree because the truth is we're all there more out of obligation than love for old Poppy and I feel empty and sad and excited about getting some money at the same time. I mean when my mom died, I got nothin'...

"How about a fuckin' ring, Margaret, one measly little ring? How come you get all the damn jewellery and Paul gets all the fuckin'

*silverware? Mom said she was gonna leave me the whole house
when she died! I'm the only one that really loved her and you, Paul
and Dad fucked me over. You changed the will and fucked me over.
I know it!"*

"Dave, anything you get you're going to pawn it for drug money.
So we all decided you get nothing until you are off drugs."

And now I am and here we are.

"What about his girlfriend or whatever she is?" Paul asks.

"Jessica? He took her out of the will when they had their last
fight," Margaret says. "She doesn't know that, though. I'm sure
she is going to show up at some point and I'll just tell her. He has
no money left anyway. I've been supporting him for the past two
years."

"Jesus," Paul says. "I thought he would have at least a hundred
thousand left over from selling the house. He made easily two-fifty
on it and that was after buying the condo. What did he do with the
rest of the money?"

"He spent it, Paul."

"Wasn't he getting like thirty thousand a year from the government
too?"

"Spent it."

"On her?"

"I don't know, Paul, her, other women, I don't know."

We all look at each other for a second, registering what we all

198

do know about Poppy's lifelong obsession with prostitutes, then Margaret gets busy biting a nail, Paul stares at the table, while I apply a little acupressure to my temples almost pushing my thumbs through my skull.

What a moment of mirthful family reflection.

God, can we all just disappear... now?

Then the kids come over with their plates piled high and as Jeffrey holds out his and says, "Dad, look!" a muffin topples off, along with three pieces of bacon and Paul yells, "Jeffrey!" as Shnooky gobbles them up. I laugh and tell Paul to relax. He tells me to shut up. I call him an asshole and he motions to stab me with his fork and Margaret calls us both assholes and already we need a break from each other.

"I'm sorry, Paul," I say.

"Yeah..." he says and before he can say he's sorry too, he gets a business call and walks away from the table.

So before we head back to the hospital, Margaret and Paul go to their rooms for a rest, the kids go to the adjoining pools for a swim and Shnooky and I go to the beach for a run even though it's against the law to bring her. Fuck 'em, I'll take the ticket. She is worth way more than any ticket. And I have gotten those tickets. Dog on beach. Dog off leash. Dog in a national park. Dog in a wildlife reserve. Hundreds and hundreds of dollars. I got a ticket for

'No seeing eye dog harness' when I faked 'vision impaired', wearing black-lensed shades, shuffling through the sand behind her.

I did have her on a leash but... and then I got chased down at Point Dume beach by the police helicopter when we tried to make a getaway one time. And we added, 'disturbing the peace' and 'insulting an officer' to the list. He was a fucking moronic asswipe, dumbass cocksucker to chase after us and call out the helicopter but I guess I didn't have to tell him so... I think I'll just take the ticket this time.

And we run down the southern end of the long narrow silver strand with its broken shells of pink, white and brown mixed in with black specks of dried crude oil and washed-up seaweed strewn about the sand and I think maybe I'll devise a little, "My Dad is dying" excuse just in case I can get out of it that way.

"Look, I'm really sorry. I know I'm not supposed to have my dog on the beach, I know the law and I respect it. But let me just say she never chases any of the migratory birds, never and... okay, listen I didn't wanna say this... but my Dad... my Dad is dying... and I'm really torn up about it... and I need to take a run and clear my head before I go back to the hospital... and I just... I really just need my dog with me... please..."

And I watch her race down to the shoreline over the wet sand and prance through the sizzling sea foam as I keep my steady jog. And she races back towards me, stopping to scoop up an empty crab shell in her jaws and toss it in the air and I go over the excuse again and again until I feel it in my bones, until I believe my excuse, until it is incorporated in my breath and my being. *I'm really torn up. I'm really torn up. I'm really torn up...*

No you're not. No you're not. No you're not...

"Ahhh! You're full of shit!" I scream, just as Shnooky trots up and her perky ears and tail drop in terror as she slinks up beside me. *I didn't eat it, Daddy, I just picked it up and played with it because I was happy, happy running along the beach with you.*

"It's not you," I say. "I love you. Let's just keep running. Maybe I can outrun my fucking thoughts. Maybe we should run to fucking Mexico. Huh, Shnooky?"

Anything you want, Daddy, anything you want.

And what I want is to love my dad one tenth as much as I love her. One tenth as wide. One tenth as deep... but I don't. I just don't. All I can do is take loving actions. That is the spiritual way I've been taught. Even though I don't feel it. I don't fucking feel the love that I want, for my father, my sister or my brother. We don't hug and laugh and cry together. But I can show up.

"We can show up, right, Shnook?"

Sure, Daddy, sure.

So I don't fall in the sand and sob or scream, "Fuck!" into the wind and say, "Why? Why? Why!" I did that when my mom died when I was dry chewing her Vicodin, shooting her morphine, crawling to the hospital every day, narcotic baked, selling cocaine to one nurse and fucking another, all the while crying for my mother and causing havoc with my hatred for the rest of my family.

My mom's death was such a disaster, for all of us. She was the backbone of the family, loving us all unconditionally, blanketing my father's sordid ways with loyalty and decency even though I think the devastating inner pain beneath the front she put up brought the cancer into her body.

I'm proud of you, David. Look at you now.

"Are you, Mom?"

Yes, my love…

"Why do I still have hate?"

You have so much less, so much less…

And I drop to my knees in the sand for prayer and communication with the spirit of her love… love, again love.

And the wind blows and the waves churn and the high winter clouds float by the sun that sparkles and dances on the ocean and as the screams in my head quiet and quiet and quiet, I melt again, I melt into it all.

23

Steven is with Margaret to meet us in the hotel lobby and what a dashing, sophisticated, privileged couple they are. She has on a new outfit, white cashmere sweater, tan suede pants... costly casual wear and he, silver-haired with a robust complexion that defies his sixty years, complements her colours in his custom, tailor-made crisp white shirt, beige slacks and herringbone, double-breasted cashmere sports coat, the kind where you can actually unbutton the buttons on the cuffs which really means something in the class department.

It even has some name, which he explained but I forget, something that merits the three thousand dollar cost of the fucking jacket. He actually gave me one of his old ones. It doesn't really fit right or match any of my stuff so I just keep it in the closet, feel the soft cashmere, unbutton and re-button the cuffs occasionally. I did try to sell it once but was only offered a hundred bucks. "For a three thousand dollar fucking jacket?" I said, then they asked me to leave the store.

Anyway, now onto the jewellery to complement my sister's

glacier-sized rock on her hand, thumbnail-sized diamond stud earrings and thick as a chain-link fence gold necklace... and I'm not talkin' diamond pinky rings, I'm talkin' thirty to one hundred thousand dollar watches. He owns like fifteen of them.

Today it looks like he has on the eighty thousand dollar model that shows the whole gold and jewelled mechanism at work under the clear crystal face, the one that keeps the "best time in the world", the one that you can't even read what fuckin' time it is because you can't see where the hands are with all those mechanisms moving around. I'd hock that thing in a fucking second, buy a Timex and put a down payment on a house.

Steven has an impeccable doctor's bedside manner, which means he could not give a shit about you, but seems so genuinely caring you could never tell. I always go along with it because Margaret's new-found generosity does stem from his earnings. Does that mean I'm a sellout? For Max, yeah, I am.

"Hey, Maxy! Gee, you're gettin' bigger every time I look around. How are ya? Doin' okay?"

"Yeah, I'm okay."

"Good, and how's school?

"Good."

"Glad to hear it. Good kid, good kid, smart kid, too." Then he pats me on the back and says, "I don't know how ya do it, Dave. So how are ya? You feelin' okay?"

"Hey, Steven... yeah, I'm okay. How are you?"

"Pretty good for a man pushin' sixty-one that got up at 4:00am, performed major surgery then hopped on a plane out here. Pretty damn good. And what have ya been up to?"

"Well, ya know I have this commercial running on TV and I'm adapting this kind of novel that I ah, wrote with this guy, into a movie..."

"Yeah?" He says cutting me off with that false fucking bedside manner smile. "Tell me when it comes out. Love to see it."

That ends that. Now he's on to Shnooky.

"And how's the little Shnooky doin'? What a good girl, behavin' herself right here in the hotel. Couldn't get our dogs to do that, could we, Margaret? Come here, girl, say hi to your Uncle Stevie!"

Shnooky looks at me.

I don't buy it, Daddy, do I have to?

I almost have to kick her in the butt to get her over to him and she goes wagging her tail and everything just to make Uncle Stevie happy. He gives her a couple of empty pats on the head. Okay, that's done.

"Well, I guess it's time to go over to the hospital and check on your dad," he says. "Everybody ready?"

"Just rarin' to go, right guys?" Margaret says to me and Max as we walk out to the valet, and Steven doesn't really get it. He admires my dad even though Margaret reminds him over and over if he had to grow up with him, he wouldn't.

"Where is your car, Dave?' Steven says.

"I left it at Poppy's. We walked over."

"Well, leave that piece of crap over there and ride with us. I got a nice big town car; fit the whole family, including Shnooky, right, girl? Wanna ride in the front with Uncle Stevie?"

Even when he's calling me a loser he's charming, I think, as Margaret says, "Steven, Shnooky loves Dave and only Dave, can't you see that? She's not all goofy and drooly over anybody that walks by like our dogs."

"Well, I'm not anybody that walks by. Far from it."

"I know, honey," she says, hugging him and kissing his neck. "You're king Steven and every dog in the world loves you, even Shnooky, okay?"

God, she strokes his massive ego but it's love, their love... although while she's hugging him I see his eyes eat up the thin-wasted, tight-assed, local blonde teenage valet girl, whose perky little tits bounce in her Coronado Lowes t-shirt when she hops out of the Town Car.

"Here ya go, miss," he says as he hands her a crisp twenty, reading her name tag with a quick eye and adding, "Lily, what a sweet name." And Max looks at me like... whoa, Dad, that's sick!

"As long as it's not too sweet, right honey?" Margaret jokes as we all get in the car. And Steven gives her an appeasing smile as we drive off, and I feel bad for her because I see the pain on her face beyond the joke, but I'm not gonna meddle.

So instead of saying, "Hey Steven why didn't you just tell the valet girl, I have a lot of money and I want to fuck you when my wife's not around," I ask Margaret where Paul is, ya know, change the subject, ease things up a bit.

"Jeffrey used his cell phone to call Katy and left it on," she says, "something about ruining the battery so Paul had to go into Coronado and buy a new one. He's going to meet us at the hospital."

"Poor Jeffrey," I say. "Paul is so hard on him. I hope he doesn't screw him up like Dad screwed me up."

"Dad screwed us all up, Dave," she says. "You just took it a lot further than Paul and I."

"I happen to think your father is a good man," Steven says. "An intelligent man, a charming man…" and I wait for him to say, *"And a successful cheater like me, that's why I admire him."*

"Oh, Steven, shut up!" Margaret says, because now the stored up, jealous anger is transferring over. "He was a nightmare to grow up around and you'll never know because you weren't there. So stick your admiration, you know where!"

"Okay, dear I know, I know, whatever you say," he replies with a patronizing grin and I can sense him transferring his own thoughts into an image of the valet girl's teenage twat in his mouth. I lean forward, just about to ask him, "What are you thinking about Steven, like right now?" so I can prove it but Max grabs my arm because he senses what I'm thinking.

"No, Dad," he mouths. I take his insightful advice and settle back in the seat.

Take it easy. Breathe deeply. Look out the window. Pat Shnooky.

Yeah, Daddy, pat me, pat me. And you know I'd never sit in the front seat with Uncle Stevie, not when you're here Daddy, never.

24

Margaret and Steven confer with the doctor in ICU, Paul paces in the corridor on a heated business call and I file the kids into the tiny waiting room where this severe, snobbish woman, maybe seventy, is staring at some stupid daytime soap on the shitty little twelve-inch TV screen with the sound off. The kids stare at each other, holding back giggles while I look at a fake gold-framed painting of palm tress swaying in the breeze by a sea wall, and another of some sea scallop shell floral print piece of shit.

And I motion them to sit down and there are only eight cheap chairs locked into each other, arms and legs touching with the old frump and her friggin' suitcase-sized handbag taking up two, so we all have to sit crammed in under the fluorescent light with the institutional wall-clock ticking and I see one of those 'Desiderata' poem plaques tacked up so I take in a few stanzas…

You are a child of the universe
no less than the trees and the stars
you have a right to be here
and whether or not it is clear to you

the universe is unfolding as it should
be at peace with God even whatever you conceive him to be
with the shams and drudgery and broken dreams it is still a
beautiful world
Be cheerful. Strive to be happy.

I feel two distinct entities within me. One that wants to take the words in with acceptance and another that wants to rip the fucking Desiderata off the wall and put my fist through it. Anyway, Jeffrey breaks the silence.

"My grandfather is gonna die," he says to the lady. "Why are you here?"

Max puts his whole hand over his face and laughs into it as Michael hisses, "Jeffrey!" and looks to me for backup, but I'm not Paul. I think it was a legitimate question. I'm gonna give Jeffrey a chance. I wanna see where he's goin' with it.

"My mother has cirrhosis of the liver if you must know," the lady says. Oh yeah, I think, she was the ancient one writhing in pain in ICU last night. Bad way to go, cirrhosis, three of my aunts died that way. Could have been me if I kept hammerin' away at my liver with the drugs and the booze too.

"Is she gonna die?" Jeffrey says.

"Well, I never!" she huffs, then gets back to staring at the TV.

"Would you mind if I changed the channel?" Jeffrey says.

And I see his intentions; a little small talk, a little socialising, then a little channel changing. Why not? Right? I mean he is cute and quite charming in his own special way. A lot of women would have gone for it, easy... but not this old bag.

"Yes, I would mind," she says.

"But you don't even have the sound on."

She ignores him, stares straight ahead. Michael looks angry that no one has reprimanded his little brother but Max and I are having more fun watching him than any TV show.

"Come on, lady, please," he says.

"No."

"Why?"

"Because I find you quite an offensive young man."

"And I find you quite an old stuffy puss lady."

"Such language, how dare you?" she says.

And now I feel it's time, as a grown-up, for me to step in.

"Okay, Jeffrey take it easy," I say. "Let her just look at it, don't worry about it."

"It's not like I said pussy," he says. "I only said puss."

"Okay, okay."

"Max says fuck a lot, did you know that, Dave?"

"What?"

"I don't care, it's no big deal," he says. "My Dad makes a big deal out of it but I know you don't, do ya, Dave?"

And before I can answer he says, "I like to say fuck, too. Fuck, fuck fuck... fuck, fuck, fuck..."

Max just gets up and walks out because he can't contain himself anymore. Michael follows, saying, "Jeffrey, you're so messed up," on his way out and it's me, Jeffrey and the incensed old lady left.

"I'm sorry," I say to her.

"As you well should be," she says back, and I feel myself getting a little agitated so I say, "Come on, Jeffrey, let's just go," and we stand up.

"I'm sorry, too," Jeffrey says. "But not that sorry."

"Why don't you instill some manners into that boy!" she says.

"Why don't you... why don't read some of that poem on the wall?" I say. "Maybe it will help you."

"What an ass!" she says as I exit, proud, tall and justified with my arm around Jeffrey's shoulder and... well, you could say I agree with her on that count.

So me and the kids are standing outside the waiting room, laughing about the situation. Even Michael is laughing because he sees Jeffrey isn't getting scolded and he can admit to himself that it was funny. Paul sees us from down the corridor. "I'll get right back to ya," he says into his phone then snaps it shut and walks over.

"What happened?" he says.

"Nothing," I say. "It's just too cramped in there."

"Yeah, Dad," my new partner in crime chimes in. "It's too cramped in there. Didn't you think it was too cramped in there, Max?" Max is with us in a heartbeat.

"Yeah, pretty cramped," he says.

"Hey, Michael?" Jeffrey says, and the way he looks up at his big brother with all the hope in the world for some camaraderie hits me hard. It brings me back to my childhood with Paul and makes me wanna cry. "Did you think it was pretty cramped in there?" he says.

Michael hedges. Shit. And of course Paul suspects and waits for his loyal good son to drop the axe on his little bad one.

"So what happened, Michael?" he says. "And don't answer, Dave," he adds.

"Fine," I say, and Paul bears down on him and Michael looks up at his dad and Jeffrey and Max and I all look at Michael preparing for him to bust us... but, wait, he's not relishing the moment, he's tightening his lips, he's shifting his feet, he's dropping his eyes and then...

"I guess it was kinda cramped in there," he says and I wanna scream, "Yes! Michael!" but I laugh out loud instead.

"Okay, Dave, what kind of crap are you teaching to my kids? Somebody is going to tell me what happened."

"Nothin' happened," I say.

"Okay, I'm going to go in that waiting room and if you broke something Jeffrey, I swear...."

"I didn't break anything, Dad, but there is a crazy lady in there and I wouldn't talk to her..."

"What? What crazy lady?" But before he can interrogate any further Margaret comes out of the ICU door with a grave look on her face.

"Okay everybody," she says. "Poppy is getting worse, he's slipping in and out of consciousness, and Steven just had him sign a living will..." and off our blank looks she continues, "which means if his heart stops he requests no more medical attention to try and keep him alive so everyone... go in and say what you want to say, this is probably your last chance to do it."

"I don't know what to say," Max says.

"Me either," Michael says.

"Hey guys, how about saying this," Jeffrey says as he waves his hand around like one of the 'Little Rascals'.

"See ya around, old Poppy."

Everybody laughs except Paul who tells him, "How about no, Jeffrey."

"It doesn't matter," Margaret says. "Poppy is beyond caring anyway."

I don't know what to say either but I know I have to go in there.

25

My father's eyes seem clenched in terror as he twitches and trembles, and gasps out in inaudible German. It's like the inevitable purgatory of his own mind has finally reached him. That's how I see it anyway. Paul looks away. He doesn't want to see it and Margaret just sees it as body pain. She signals to Steven who respectfully waits at the nurses' station, small talking, bragging, I don't know, they all seem to be paying attention to him. So he comes in.

"Damnit!" Margaret says. "Didn't we just talk to the doctor about increasing the morphine drip?"

"They did increase it, dear."

"Well, tell them to increase it more."

"Any more would kill him."

"Good, why should he stay alive a minute longer like this?"

"I know," Steven says, "I know, this is tough. He's having a hard time passing." Then he rests his hand on my father's trembling shoulder.

"Oh, Steven, what have zey done to me?"

"It's okay, it's okay," he says as he wipes a tear from his eye and

I see this is no bedside manner. He genuinely cares but I judge it because Steven respects the characteristics that I hate. Fucking arrogant, domineering, know-it-all cheating assholes. *Why bother now, though? You can't change your dad on his deathbed... and does Steven even care what you think?*

"Better say somethin' to your dad," he says to me and Paul.

"Jesus," Paul says. "I don't know... does he..." and he steps in and blurts out... "I love you, Dad." My father's eyes open. He sees him but he can't face him.

"I did vhat I had to do," he says. "I vasn't wrong, I vasn't wrong... your mother understood... she understood everything... I did what I had to do..."

"Okay, Dad, okay..." Paul says and he has to walk out. Then my father sees me.

"Oh David, oh David, come here," he says in a determined voice and it's like he's willed himself back from death's door just to talk to me. As I move closer, I glance at Margaret. She looks disappointed. She just wants to get it over with, I'm sure of it.

"Yeah, Dad," I say and now I think this has to be it.

Something cathartic has to happen here. Even Steven feels it. He steps back out of the way, out of the way of the last words between a father and his son. I know I'm gonna tell him I love him, I have to tell him that but I wanna wait and see what he's gonna tell me. His green eyes are dull grey and clouded with death but focused with intent because since he has been so close to the other side, I believe, I believe he can tell me now, tell me something I need to know. He licks his cracked, paste-coloured lips stained with dried blood, takes in a shallow breath that rattles in his chest… and here, and here, and here it comes…

"You must," he says. "You must… get my lottery ticket off za kitchen table and see if I've won."

I can't even fucking believe it! I mean, I'm not gonna accept this. How can I? There has to be something more. There has to be. So I ask him…

"But, Dad, come on, please… isn't there anything you want to tell me… or anything else you can say, anything about life or death or something that you've seen or felt now that you're almost there…" and he groans and puts up a shaky hand to stop me and says…

"It's all nonsense."

Well… so much for a final spiritual breakthrough.

And I realize there is nothing more I can do. That's all he has to say, that's all he wants to see and that's all I'm going to get. So I let it go and I say, "Okay, Dad, I'll check your lottery ticket." And he smiles at me and says, "Thank you, you keep za money."

Wow. I don't know, I don't know what to do. I got so much and so little from him at the same time. *Tell him you love him, tell him you love him. Can you say it?* And just as I'm opening my mouth…

"Oh, dio! Oh dio! Oh dio!" and here she comes, his girlfriend-nurse-escort, young enough to be his granddaughter; Jessica, flying through the ICU and into the room, with her heaving boobs in her blinding magenta blouse, with black mascara tears streaming down her inch thick, caked on, made-up gorda face, pushing me out of the way to get to his bedside.

"Mi, Paul. Mi Paul. Mi Paul."

A tear squeezes out as he closes his eyes and moans, "Go away…"

Then he slips back into morphine-induced unconsciousness. Jessica looks at us in horror.

"He is dead?"

I swear I hear my sister say, "I wish," as she looks back at Jessica but she doesn't say that, she just looks at her like, no, you stupid whore.

"No, dear," Steven says to Jessica or more precisely to Jessica's tits. "But he's close, very close. Best to let him just go peacefully."

And she sobs and coughs a hacking cough, and I think, *fucking bitch gave my father the bronchitis then he coughed so hard he tore his fucking ninety-three-year-old aorta. She killed him and here she is sobbing, putting on the act. How many other old, desperate, sex-starved suckers does she have like this? Stay with them until they die and get a nice little sum. Stupid cunt, doesn't know he wrote her out of the will, though. Should I tell her? Should I tell her right here?*

Should I scream it out in the hospital room for everyone to hear?

"Wow, I think I need to go outside and smoke a cigarette," I tell myself but when Margaret says, "Well, go and smoke one," I realize I've said it out loud.

"Okay..." I say, swallowing down my embarrassment. "Okay," and I leave the room.

And as the kids play in the park with Shnooky, Paul makes more business phone calls and I smoke and hate myself for doing it, but rationalise that if I ever needed to, this is the time and I'll quit for good, as soon as it's over and all that bullshit, while I simultaneously fantasise how fitting it is that my father bequeathed me a multi-million dollar winning lottery ticket on his dying day and I go over my dialogue with the Network Newscasters...

Yeah, I mean I felt when he told me to get the ticket that it was a winner but 28 million dollars! I couldn't believe it! You ask were we close? Well, I'll tell you we had a very painful relationship but behind it I believe we wanted to be close... we just couldn't ever reach out and touch each other. But now, after this amazing act of fate, I mean him giving me this winning ticket like he knew... I just think it shows, I mean that it's a sign that me and my father always had this, well, this kind of connection, bond if you will, that...

I'm interrupted by Jessica, running out of the hospital, screaming at us, "You can think what you want about me. So I'm a bad girl.

So what! I loved your Daddy. I stayed with him! I loved him!"

And as she jumps into her car and peels away, I figure Margaret must have told her she was cut out of the will and I promise myself I'll throw her a million from the lottery ticket if I win.

Paul comes over.

"Did he die?"

"I don't think so," I say.

"So what do we do now?"

"I guess we wait."

26

You checked the lotto numbers?

   Yes, sir.

   And I didn't win?

   No, sir.

   Nothing?

   Nothing.

   You sure?

   Sorry, sir.

   Yeah, me too… me too… me too.

Shnooky's barking wakes me up. It's 2:37 am. Someone is banging on the door. I look at Max on the couch next to me so cute, hair in his angel face, snoring like a little buzz-saw. Then I hear Paul calling out my name, yelling out my name.

"Dave! Open the door! Dave!"

I get up off the couch and answer it. Paul smells like liquor and his eyes are full of tears.

"Dad died," he says. "He's dead. He's dead, Dave."

And even though I was prepared for it, I feel stunned by a cold, heavy wave of my father's death passing through me.

"When...?" I say, getting my breath back.

"About an hour ago the hospital called..."

"Oh, man... why didn't you call me?"

"I wanted to come over, I wanted to tell you..." Then he throws his arms around me and blurts out, "I'm sorry..."

And he hugs me so tight I can barely get my arms loose to hug him back.

"I'm sorry too," I say and Shnooky looks up, concerned that I'm getting the life squeezed out of me.

What do I do? What do I do, Daddy?

It's okay, Shnook.

He's really, really upset.

I know. I know.

Paul looks at me, sniffles and wipes his eyes. "And I'm sorry that we were never close... and I'm sorry because a lot of it was my fault."

"It was my fault, too."

"No. I was a shitty big brother."

"And I was a shitty little brother."

"No. Listen... when we were kids, little kids... I used to blame you for things I did, like the time I broke Mom's fancy china platter and the lamp in the living room when we were jumping on the couch and a lot of other stuff too."

I want to tell him to shut up with his drunken confessions that he'll probably forget he said in the morning... but I realize it's the only way he can confess. I used to get drunk and confess all the time and never mean it. Maybe he means it. Maybe I should give him a break.

"Don't worry about it. It's okay," I say.

"No, it's not, it's not okay," he says. "And Dad used to call you a stupid little idiot... and when you said you didn't do it, I called you a liar and he believed me... and then we both called you stupid and laughed at you... and then you'd start crying and Dad would call you a little baby and punish you... and then you started doing bad in school... and getting all messed up on drugs... and I feel, I feel like a lot of it was my fault... because I helped Dad make you feel like you were... like you were a fuck-up..."

And now I'm going back in my own mind and I'm hearing them both laugh at me and I'm hearing my father calling me a stupid little boy... and I feel the pain and the hate and I clench my fist ready to punch my brother in the fucking mouth.

God help me. God help me. God help me.

"And one thing I did that I really feel bad about," he says, "...is when I cut a hole in the mattress... and you know, I put Vaseline in it and I... I fucked the mattress and Mom found the hole and freaked out and I blamed it on you... and Dad took away your allowance and made you work in the garden for the whole summer to help pay for a new one."

And Paul is sobbing over this and all of a sudden it just seems so funny.

"How old was I then?"

"You were ten and I was thirteen."

"And you fucked the mattress?" Now I'm laughing and Shnooky is circling around us, wagging her tail. *Good. Good. Good. Love. Love. Love.*

"Shut up, it's not funny," Paul says. "And I had to bend the springs out of the way with pliers so I wouldn't, ya know, scrape myself. I actually did scrape my dick the first time."

"The first time? How many times did you fuck it?"

"A lot. It was months until Mom found the hole, because I used to put the mattress stuffing back in after every time so when she changed the sheets… and then I just forgot to do it."

"Lost respect for the mattress, huh?" I say, and he looks at me like, 'what the hell?' and I'm laughing again then he gets it and starts laughing and Max calls out from the couch.

"Dad…"

"Yeah…"

"What are you doing?"

"Nothing, Paul came over."

"What happened?"

"Poppy died."

"Then why are you laughing?"

"I'll tell ya later, go back to sleep."

"Fine." And he's back asleep as fast as he woke up. Then silence.

"Good kid, good kid," Paul says. "You really straightened out and took care of him." Then he drifts off into intoxicated reflection with a couple of long blinks and head-nods and says, "I never hated you, Dave... ya know... I was just... I didn't know what to do... I mean you were so crazy... I didn't know if you were gonna live or not... I... I was scared for you... I was scared for you, Dave."

Wow, I think, drunk or not, it wasn't easy for him to get that out.

"Thanks for saying that, Paul," I say. "I guess I was kinda scared myself."

"You think we can get a little closer, stay in touch more?" he says.

"Yeah, that sounds good."

"I want you to know... that I love ya, Dave... I do."

"I love you too," I say. And as we stand together in the dark, two brothers, our father now gone, we are closer.

There was no funeral. Old Poppy had it in the will that he didn't want one. Paul went to the hospital and made the arrangements with the crematorium on his way to the airport. Steven went back to New York to perform some more major surgeries and infidelities while Margaret stayed in Coronado to deal with a real estate agent. She asked me to stay, pick up the ashes and spread them on the lawn in front of our father's house, which he also requested in the will.

"No way I'm going to spread them, Dave. You do it."

"But he has no lawn, only bushes and a walkway in front…"

"Dave, just handle it, okay? There's a big lawn in front of the complex and while you're waiting to pick up the ashes you can clean his place out so the real estate agent can show it."

"I have to clean it out?"

"Dave, I'm not stepping foot in there. I'll pay you five hundred dollars to do it or I'll hire someone else. Your decision. I just want it done. The sooner it's cleaned out, the sooner we can sell it and the sooner we can split up the money."

"What do I do with all his stuff?"

"Keep what you want and throw the rest out. I don't want any of that old crap. Call the Salvation Army for the furniture, the beds, whatever. I don't really care, just get it out of there."

After many sad and painful trips to the dumpster, the place is cleaned out. Detach and dump. Detach and dump. Detach and dump.

"Max, Shnook, help me, just help me."

"Okay, Dad."

Okay, Daddy.

Most of it is old crap like Margaret said, because she and Paul already took all the valuables after my mom died; jewellery, good furniture, rugs, lamps, silver... I was all fucked up then so nothin' I could do about that. I tell Max to take what he wants...

"Purple Heart! Purple heart! I want Poppy's Purple Heart!"

"Okay, anything else?"

"Dad, look at all these Playboys and Penthouse magazines."

And I wanna grab an issue and take it into the bathroom and flip through the pages and get lost in all the pictures of beautiful tits and ass and pussy and stroke my cock and...

"Throw 'em out," I say. "What else?"

"I'll find somethin'."

"Good, okay."

And I salvage a few things for myself; some tarnished silverware of my mom's, including spoons I used to bend and cook dope in... *sorry Mom, again...* a chipped antique china serving platter, her favourite silver-handled cheese slicer, a couple of family photo albums, an old Nikon camera, a few tools and an Ivory Buddha from Cambodia that my father promised me if I stayed off drugs (that was in the will, "If Dave stays off drugs he gets the Buddha woman statue"). And I realize, because of the way I have been living my life, I am going to get an inheritance of enough money to put a down-payment on a house for me, my son and my dog. My dream come true and I feel grateful, almost giddy... and I get a burst of excitement...

Holy shit! Holy shit! Holy shit! Calm down. Calm down. Calm down. Smoke a cigarette. No. Breathe. Breathe. Breathe. Take it easy. Breathe. Clean. Breathe. Clean. Be happy. Be grateful. Okay. Happy? Yeah, happy is okay. Not too happy, though. Not too happy. More grateful than happy, that's better, better, safer for you...

And I get the Salvation Army to come for the old couches, chairs, tables and beds. Margaret barely steps foot in the place, does a thirty-second inspection, says it's, "Not very clean but it will do." She tells us to pick up the ashes and meet her by the front lawn of the complex in an hour. She has to see the probate lawyer first and has an evening flight home, but she wants to witness the ash spreading. Hurried, high-strung and very serious. Max repeats the words, ash spreading, in an inquisitive, studied manner then looks right at Margaret, holds his tongue with his thumb and forefinger and says them again so they come out, "Ass spueading."

"Not funny," Margaret says, but I'm laughing.

228

27

They're heavy. You hear about that but you don't know until you experience it yourself. I hold the thick plastic bag full of them with one hand as I sift through with the other, squeezing, feeling little pieces of bone, letting them drop between my fingers. Human ashes. My father's remains. So strange.

Max stands next to me in the centre of the close-cropped lawn while Shnooky sniffs around a cluster of baby palms off to the side, and Margaret stands on the curb, chewing on a nail, watching. There is a calm breeze. The sun is going down. I guess it's as perfect a time as ever for our ceremony.

"Is this good here?" I yell out to Margaret.

"Whatever you think, Dave."

I grab a handful of ashes, toss them into the air... they fall and just lay there on the lawn. Oh, so fucking weird, this is!

"The grass is really short," I say.

"Just spread 'em around, Dave."

"Dad, give me some," Max says.

I open the bag wide and he takes two handfuls.

"I wonder what part of Poppy these are?"

"I don't know Max, I'm... ah... feeling a little dazed here, a little weak."

"Dad, relax, its just ashes." And he runs off towards the palm trees to spread them as I stand motionless and stare into the bag.

Margaret yells out, "Come on, gotta catch a plane, Dave."

"All right," I say, hearing my high-pitched, quivering voice that sounds like a man who is just about to lose his mind. I mean come on, I'm standing here fertilizing the lawn with my fucking father.

This is what he wanted and you're the one chosen. You can do it. You're the one.

Okay. Okay. Okay. I take another handful, walk a few steps, toss them in the air, take another handful, walk a few steps, toss them in the air. Oh, it's so hard to do this.

Max runs over.

"More, I need more, Dad," and he digs in and runs off again.

"Almost done, Margaret," I say and as I look over, I see her wipe a tear from her eye.

"Just the wind," she'd answer if I asked, "Are you crying?" So I don't. I don't ask.

"Okay," she says, and I can tell she's holding back the floods, probably let it all go in private on the plane, maybe in the bathroom. I'd run over and hug her but she'd push me away.

"Dad, come here," Max says and he grabs my arm.

"What? Let me empty the bag."

And the remainder of the ashes trails out behind us as Max drags me towards the palms. Shnooky trots over to greet us.

"Out of the way, Shnooky, don't mess 'em up."

"Mess what up, Max?"

Then he points to the ground about ten feet in front of us and gives me a proud smile.

"Dad, look."

I look and I'm about to say, "Look at what?"... and then I see it, spelled on the green lawn in big letters of grey ashes...

P O P P Y

And I call Margaret over. "Please, please, please, you have to." And she begrudgingly comes.

"What is the big deal?" And she sees it. "Oh my God!" And she laughs and laughs, then she cries and cries, then she hugs me and I hug her and she hugs Max and Max hugs her and Shnooky circles around us, singing into the air with gleeful barks as our ceremony ends.

28

We cross over the Coronado bridge in the twilight, me, Max and Shnooky, all staring out the window at the boats and the buildings and the bay for the last time and I let out a long sigh as we get onto the 5 north back to Los Angeles.

"Dad, how about if I read to you from the Clunky book," Max says.

"What?"

And I glance over and see Max, pulling an old, faded, frayed college binder out of his backpack.

"The Clunky book, Dad. I took it from Poppy's."

And he shows me the cover that has, 'Clunky's Adventures' scribbled on it in ink. I know the book. My father wrote it about me when I was a year old. I was Clunky.

And Max opens the cover and there, on the first cardboard page, is a glued-on water-colour painting of a fat, little, rosy-cheeked, baby boy in blue denim overalls standing under a traffic light, in the middle of a street block, directing cars as a few surprised pedestrians look on. On the opposite page is a taped-on, handwritten piece of paper. And Max reads...

The other day, Paul and Margaret went to the village and at the main intersection they believed they saw little Clunky directing the traffic just like a policeman. Quick, quick, Margaret took Paul by the hand and ran home to see if it really was Clunky in the village.

Then he turns the page and shows me the next watercolor painting of little Clunky sitting in a big cardboard box, staring out the window at some trees. He grins at me and says, "Dad, you were so fat," then he continues reading...

All out of breath they arrived home and saw old Clunky sitting in a box, looking out of the window. Who was it standing in the street?

Then he flips the page to a watercolour of a big green truck with, 'Clunky Bakery' on it in orange letters, and Clunky at the wheel. And he reads...

A few days later, Margaret and Paul went for a walk and they saw a bakery truck pass by and the driver looked exactly like little Clunky. Margaret did not believe it and ran home as fast as she could.

Max flips the page. "Dad, look," he says and he starts laughing as he shows me the painting of a beet red-faced little Clunky, sitting in a high-chair, banging a couple of building blocks together.

"I'm driving here!" I say but I start laughing too as Max reads on...

And there he was, fat little Clunkhead, screaming his head off, sitting at his own table.

"Clunkhead! He called you Clunkhead, Dad?"

"Yeah, I guess so. God, I was a little screamer!"

And we're both laughing so hard that Shnooky throws her paws up on the seat and barks in our ears like she's laughing too and Max flips through the remaining few pages, showing Clunky riding a horse, flying an airplane with Clunky airlines written on it and engineering a train with Clunky R.R. written on the side. And in the narrative, every time Margaret or Paul think they see Clunky, they race home and there is little Clunky, crawling on the rug or playing with a toy and finally sitting like a little angel in his crib, so it's all a big mystery that no one can find out because Clunky can't speak yet. And Max reads the last line of the book...

Therefore Margaret and Paul will have to wait a little bit longer until Clunky can talk. Maybe then he will let them know all about his great adventures.

And as Max closes the book he says, "Dad, Poppy really loved you when you were a baby, huh?"

"Yeah, I guess he did."

"So what happened?"

"I started to talk," I say, and I try to laugh again but I can't. I try to reassure Max that I'm okay, so I give him a smile, but it's cracked and weak so I look back at the road and we drive in silence. I take deep breaths to try to breathe away the inevitable but I can't so I just give in, I give in to all the love that was misguided or misunderstood or just plain lost between me and my father throughout our lives, and I begin to sob, and Max begins to sob for me, and we just drive and sob and drive and sob and Shnooky jumps in the front seat and whimpers and leans in to each of us, and licks the tears from our eyes.

29

Weeks have passed. I've tried to stay in touch with my brother and sister but everybody is back to their life. Paul is too busy to talk and Margaret has nothing to say. And Poppy is free at last or karma has him starting his next life as a girl, or he's wherever I think he might be at any given moment. Who really knows? I did feel his spirit wrap its arms around me like a warm breeze when I was running up Bronson, and hear his voice tell me he loved me. Then it was gone in a second and a few days later I heard him telling me I was an idiot. I know I can't trust his voice like Keri's or my mom's. I think he's gonna fuck with me until the day I die.

Anyway, I got some of the money and I wanna surprise Max when I pick him up from school, so I'm out here at this Toyota dealership in Buena Vista or Buena Park or Buena something, trying to get a deal on a new 4Runner so I can be a legitimate, respected carpool dad/mom. My friend Eddie drives one and he's a good family man. He says they have a lot of room for skate-boards and surf-boards and boogie boards and dogs and kids, and they run great and he leases one every three years and that's what I should do and what the fuck do I know? I test drive one and it's great. I mean, of course it's great, I never owned a new car in my life, let alone leased one. So embarrassed isn't the word, being forty-three years old doing this for the first time and I don't have bad credit, I just have no credit.

I've only had a bank account since Keri died. She was the responsible one with the bank account and the credit cards. I just gave her the cash when I worked and before that, I just bounced around the world taking money out of whatever model agency account I was with at the time, like a kid getting an allowance, and they took care of the bills. When I was a drug dealer, I just paid whoever I was living with in cash. I mean, I had pockets full of cash and cash hidden in shoes and drawers, under the fucking bed and I never thought I was even gonna live this long to be responsible and have required credit history.

So I look at all the fucking contracts and terms I have to read through, and sign as I sit hunched over a desk in the Toyota salesman's snake-pit, feeling like I'm back in high school failing a test, and the young crisp-shirt, slicked-back sales dude almost makes me vomit from the overdose of cheap Calvin Klein cologne he's slapped on his neck as he yaps over my shoulder how they're bending over backwards to help me out with just this much down-payment, and that much per month, and they'll throw in a big favour by taking a couple of hundred off for the Scamp, even though it's just scrap metal inconvenience. I know he sees how desperate I am just to have a new car and then the vampish sales manager, with a name tag that reads, Veronica, sashays over and purrs and flirts and repeats all the terms again and says, for just this much more per month I can have the limited version in millennium silver with CD changer, electric seats, moon-roof and leather interior. I know the game but I play it anyway because I want the car for my kid. So I agree and hand her the thirty-five hundred cash down-payment and she checks the contracts and tells me in an oh-so-sexy way that I have one more little signature to make before they bring up the 4Runner. Then she glides away, and as I stare out the window, pen in hand, a poem passes though my head...

Puffs of cotton clouds float by

in the powder blue California sky

sun shines down on the pastel green

swaying leaves of palms

while I sit inside the dealer

Ship

I'm on their ship

cruising to destination take your money

handing the cash while holding my breath

swayed by

Raven-haired, captain, sales manager Veronica,

who's deep dark brown eyes

that smile and hypnotize all in the same moment
draw me in for the sale,
all the time knowing her swelling breasts
heaving with each honeyed breath she takes
helped tremendously to close the deal.
and all the time knowing
her smile
will fade to icy indifference after my last trembling signature
and all the time knowing I will be cast ashore.
owing and owing and owing
while the sun, the sky, the clouds, the palm trees
will just be
Not knowing
Not caring

And I sign and walk outside, kiss my hand and place it on the hood of the Scamp.

"Bye, Scamp. Thanks."

And I get in my new car and drive away.

I blend right into the carpool line at school with all the moms in their Range Rovers, Mercedes and BMWs. Max is expecting the Scamp to come chugging up with his maniac dad at the wheel, so he doesn't notice me in my brand new, millennium silver, limited

Toyota 4Runner, lookin' all nice and normal. He's hanging out on the sidewalk amongst all the kids with his friends, Leo, Darrel and Matthew, all geeky-cute and gangly with long hair and vintage wear, talkin' and laughin' and carrying on. Leo is an artist like Max, Darrel is a great little guitar player and Matthew can build his own fucking computer already.

They're good smart kids and good friends. My friends at his age were all drug addict delinquents. I remember my friend Eric Carlson's nickname was 'Caveman' because he would get so stoned he couldn't even talk. All he could do was grunt and mumble. And what was my nickname? Oh yeah, 'Narcotics' but that wasn't until tenth grade. Right. I worked hard to get up to that status. Jesus God, why?

Oh, there's Carla with her wavy, strawberry blonde hair, dressed in a short denim skirt and tank top with sneakers and suede jacket. God, she looks so much older than Max, she's almost a head taller. She's called before and when she does, he grabs the phone away from me and goes outside. Look, he's flirting with her, more like teasing, making wild eyes and crazy faces. And she laughs… Oh! She kisses him. Aw, he has a girl that likes him. That's so sweet. Fuck, Leo sees me watching.

I shake my head and mouth the words, "It's not me, Leo." Oh, shit, he nudges Max and points. It takes Max a couple of seconds to register that it really is me then he comes marching up to the car.

No more leaning over to roll down the window. Electric. The whole panel right at my finger tips. Yeah! The window glides down. Max leans in.

"Dad, what the hell? Pervert!"

"I didn't see anything. I didn't."

He gives me a little hateful, disgusted look then he starts checking out the car.

"This is it, our new car," I say.

Now he's getting excited, I see it.

"When?"

"Today. I got it today."

"What happened to the Scamp?"

"Scamp is history. I'm hangin' with the carpool moms now."

Then a mom behind me honks her horn and I turn around to see her motioning at me to move forward. Then she honks again as she's looking at me... and I snap.

"Take it easy, damnit! Fucking relax!" I say.

And her look turns to shock and fright and Max shakes his head as he gets in and says, "Dad, you will never be able to hang with the carpool moms."

"So fucking what?" I say, but then I say, "Okay I'm sorry," and I shout back to the woman, "Sorry, I'm sorry," and I wave good-bye to his friends, who are all laughing because they think I'm crazy and Max doesn't care anymore because he's busy with the car stereo settings; adjusting the bass and treble and speaker balance and his favourite radio stations.

"When are we getting the house?" he says.

"Max, we just got the fucking car, okay?"

"Dad, okay."

"Do you like the car?"

"Dad, yes… but we need the house too," he says as he leaves the radio on the classic rock station where John Lennon's 'The Ballad of John and Yoko' is playing and I scream out singing along to the line, "The way things are goin' they're gonna crucify me," but I switch it to, "You're gonna crucify me," as I look at Max all crazed, like it has some deep meaning he is supposed to get, but it's all displaced and ridiculous and he just laughs at me and pats my leg, like he's reassuring the insane.

"Dad, I like the car," he says.

"You like the colour?"

"Yes, Dad, I like the colour too."

30

I'm chewing my fourth piece of Nicorette and it's only nine in the morning. Anything to stay off cigarettes... but this fucking gum is expensive plus you gotta stick it (or park as they say in the directions) between your teeth and gums to let the nicotine flow into your system and I'm just suckin' the living shit out of it for every last drop so I know I'm looking at tooth loss, gum surgery or mouth cancer down the line if I get hooked on it. If? I am hooked on it, damnit, and I'm telling Shnooky as she lies on the floor next to me and watches me stare at the computer, "One month with this gum crap and I'm done." And I stare at the computer... stare at the computer... stare at the computer.

"Fuck!" I say, then I stand up and pace around the apartment, adjusting the wad of nicorette with my tongue so I can suck on it some more. Where are those ideas? I told Tony's father I'd get back to work on the screenplay without him while he was at rehab but the truth is I can't write it alone. Even though Tony is an illiterate, moronic crack addict, I can't write it without him, not this story anyway. So I say, "Fuck it, Shnooky, he's gonna be there for six months, I'm gonna work on my own stuff."

Okay, Daddy, good idea, good idea. Lets start writing.

I think maybe I'll re-write the script I wrote about what happened to Max and me after Keri died. It almost got made, that one. Got a big agent representing me, not as a real client but as a 'pocket client', which meant it was only for that movie or 'project' as they call them. Project this. Project that. Fuck you, I hate that word, project.

Everybody is always talking about the project they're working on and dropping names of whatever fucking actor or director is going to be attached... hate that fucking word too. Attached. I remember when I was getting a bunch of heat from one of my plays and I was telling some snotty-ass, phony literary agent I was being interviewed by that I was thinking of turning the play into a movie and he asked me if anyone was attached yet. I had the play with me so I slapped it down on his desk, grabbed one of his post-its, wrote, De Niro on it, slapped it on the play and said, "Yeah, I have fuckin' De Niro attached." Then I wrote Penn, on another post-it, slapped that on and said, "I have fuckin' Sean Penn attached too! Who else do you want attached? Can I write the fuckin' movie first?"

Okay, so that didn't work out. Where was I? Oh yeah, the agent that had me as a pocket client. They said they loved the story but it was too dark, that the father character seemed a little too crazy to even be near a five-year-old boy, let alone bring him up.

They said they just didn't see it working as a feature film.

They asked me to lighten it up so they could attach one of their TV star actors (who was on some series that I hated) and make it into a movie of the week. I wanted to say, "It's about an ex-junkie, porn actor that's suicidal after the death of his kid's mom and has to bring him up on his own without a clue how to live himself. How the fuck can that not be dark and crazy? Do you see that as a TV movie? That vapid piece of shit actor could never play the part. You cocksucking idiot!"

…But I needed representation, didn't want to make the mistakes I made with other agents so I tried to write it for TV. Their first note was to move the car accident back at least five pages because it didn't happen soon enough. So I choked that down and did it. Then I took out all the swearing, took out the scene that the agent said made them retch, the one where the dad was crying while jerking off to his old porno movies as his son slept on their shared single bed in his body cast, and any scene like the agent said, that made them think the dad was just too crazy to even be around his son, let alone bring him up. So I changed the whole movie; homogenized it over and over and over until it sucked… but the agent liked it and it was ready to go to the network. Then they wanted an 'approved writer' to do another draft.

They wanted me to take a cheque and get lost… yes, so then I did tell them to fuck themselves and lost that agent and now every time I think about working on it, I feel ill and don't know where to start. So I sit back down at the computer thinking I'll just come up with something new, come up with a new idea, write it down, start an outline and get going. So I sit there waiting for the words to magically appear. No, they don't. More gum. Fresh nicotine juice to give me ideas. As I tear another piece out of the package, and pop it in my mouth, the phone rings. It's Frank, the Real Estate agent.

"Yeah, Frank, I'm, ah… pretty busy working here but we can talk. What's up? You found a house?"

I met Frank when I was driving around the Hollywood Hills up from Beechwood checking out houses for sale. I was getting the rest of the money and the time had come to seriously look. No more dreaming, I was gonna get one. Why not? Why can't we have a house in the hills? Maybe not a big one but at least a two-bedroom Spanish style with a little lawn in front for Shnooky to romp around on and lie in the sun, or maybe even a modest deck in the back with a view. I did some figuring (not research, just figuring) that a house like that couldn't be more than four hundred thousand and if I put ten percent down, the payments would be about two grand a month, plus the five hundred and thirty for the car and Max's school (now that my sister was making me pay), even with the scholarship was seven hundred a month, plus throw in another four hundred for food and utilities… that would be about thirty something thousand a year and I had enough to last, say, three or four months if I didn't work... but something would come up... another commercial, screenplay something... so with that possibility of say, forty thousand dollars more, I could last a year... then do some more figuring after that.

Not that I put any of this down on paper. I just figured it out in my head because I knew if I put it down on paper, I would see I couldn't do it. I did call Margaret.

"Dave, if you don't think you can do it, don't do it."

"Okay, thanks, Margaret."

And I didn't ask anybody else because they would tell me I couldn't do it either. Maybe they'd tell me to look for a cheap condo in the valley, deep in the valley. But fuck that, I wanted the house. I wanted the house. I wanted the house in the hills for me and my son and my dog. And with this money I was getting, it was now or never, and I had to have faith...

Even though the thought did cross my mind to invest my money in a nice kilo of heroin (white if I could find it) cut it up, sell it and have more than enough for the house. Fuck, shit, fuck. Can't do it. Can't do it. Can't do it... But I'm not getting high anymore so I could sell it fast and efficiently and make huge profits... no, you'll use it, eventually, maybe not until the last ounce or gram is left but you'll use and use and use, then all the money will be gone and you'll be strung out hopeless and the state will take Max, and Shnooky will be back on the street... but if you don't use... with heroin being so cheap these days maybe you could get two kilos and easily turn that into a few hundred thousand profit... then you'd have money to put down on a bigger house, a much bigger house. Yes! Do it! No. No. No. Yes. Yes. Yes. No, you will use and die.

Okay, so anyway, I had to have faith and I remembered a story someone told me about how these Welsh lads of old would run through the countryside and come up against these huge stone walls, seemingly impossible to climb, and they would throw their hats over first to give them the incentive, that once the hat was over, they had to climb over, some story like that. So I decided I was throwin' my hat over the fuckin' wall here.

And Frank was setting up one of those 'Open Houses' where you get to go in and check out the place. I checked it out; two bedroom, two bath, hardwood floors, new kitchen with granite top counters and six burner iron stove, big living room, a den, and deck with view all the way to the ocean. It was nice. Three quarters of a million nice.

So I told him a little of my story and my current situation and asked him if there was anything around in the low four hundreds, thinking I sounded kinda savvy even though going one dollar over four hundred thousand was already a far stretch for me. He saw I had no idea about real estate and I saw that he saw I had no idea, but he didn't jump down my throat.

He was very casual, not all frothing at the mouth and hungry to sell like I imagined most real estate agents to be, not that I personally ever met any but I saw their pictures on bus stop benches with those refrigerator teethed, phoney smiles and I hated 'em... didn't trust 'em. Frank seemed somewhat honest. Perhaps he just used the opposite approach and he was more full of shit, I don't know, but somehow I felt reassured when he talked to me, somehow I trusted him.

He told me for that price he couldn't find much in the area but he'd look around and try to find me the right house for the right price, so I gave him my number and told him to look.

"You find one in the hills, Frank?" I say.

And I hear his laid back laughter on the other end.

"You find another forty thousand to put down, Dave?"

Again, the thought of selling that heroin.

"No."

"Don't worry, I found something right for you. Meet me on the corner of Willoughby and Gardner."

And I know that area. It's not the Hills but it's a cool area. Max hangs out at a skateboard shop nearby on Melrose sometimes. We could walk to restaurants and it's closer to car pool and it's not too far to drive with Shnooky for our run up Bronson. The way Frank says it's right for us, sounds so perfect, like our dream house has arrived just like he said it would... so I get off the phone, jump up out of the chair, dance around and sing to Shnooky...

Meet me on the corner of Willoughby and Gardner

Meet me on the corner of Willoughby and Gardner

Meet me on the corner of Willoughby and Gardner...

I meet Frank and we go to the house and it has that Spanish-style look; the white stucco with the red clay tiled roof and everything... by the way, I don't really know what the fuck I'm looking at, I'm just going by what Frank says... then we get inside and it has the floors, the hardwood floors that seem to be a big selling point.

"See, hardwood floors throughout, Dave."

"Yeah, Frank, I see, I see."

But it's no bigger than our apartment with an extra bedroom slapped on... a cute little shack with a ten foot cement patio at the back, and the sidewalk for the front yard... and Frank is telling me this is a good deal for the price and I'm thinking'...

No. No. No. This is it? This is supposed to be our dream house? What the fuck, Frank, you rippin' me off here? Four hundred and thirty grand? Ya know, when I was a kid ya coulda bought every house in the neighborhood, I mean all of 'em together for that price. And what are you making off of this, huh? You're like all the rest of em', aren't ya? Rip-off cocksucker... think I'm stupid?

Now my faith is gone (funny how it goes so quickly) and I'm goin' straight to hell thinkin' I'll never find our dream house, never.

The cold reality is, I have to take this one because that's all there is for what I can spend… and every time I ever did try on a pair of pants I always felt like I had to buy 'em. Shit. It's even more than I can afford. This house is gonna tap me out completely. I'll have to give back the car and Max is gonna be so devastated…

Frank, seeing the panic in my eyes, clues me into another reality that I didn't seem to grasp.

"Dave, you don't have to take it."

"Huh?"

"There are other houses, buddy, don't worry. I know this is a big deal for you. I'll look around, find another one and call you, okay?"

And he gives me a wink and a smile and I wanna hug him and cry.

31

So Frank got back to me with what he called a great choice idea for us, to buy a duplex.

"What's a duplex, Frank?"

"You're kidding me."

"No, I'm not, Frank. Sorry."

And he told me how a duplex was like a two-family house separated by a common wall or ceiling and that I could own the building, live in one half and rent the other half out.

"You mean, there would be people living right next to us or under us?"

"Yeah, and paying half the mortgage, at least."

I remember how the manager of our apartment building, a bitter old bag who used to live underneath us, would bang on the ceiling with a broomstick and scream out, "Cut it out, God damnit!" when Max rode his skateboard on the floor or wrestled with me and Shnooky on the floor, or when she thought the TV or stereo was too loud or when I screamed out in bloody murderous writing frustration... the manager that got lung cancer and died fifteen years after she quit smoking, which I'm sure was caused by her consistent, unrelenting anger.

And I think I don't wanna buy a place, have to live that close to someone and be in charge. But the idea of paying half the mortgage sounds excellent and we could get someone like the gay flight attendant that lives underneath us now and is never there… but maybe not.

"I like the sound of getting help with the mortgage, Frank, but I don't know about the duplex idea."

"We can also look for a place with a small guest house."

"Separate from ours?"

"Well, it will be close, Dave, I mean we're talking a two bedroom with a one bedroom guest house but yeah, it is separate."

"And nobody can bang on the walls or the ceilings?"

"Ah, no Dave, I would think not."

"Find it. Find it and I'll buy it."

So I'm celebrating with Max, not that we even found a house yet, but I'm celebrating over the idea because now that I have a renter paying half the mortgage we can splurge on a nice Ahi tuna dinner, not that Albacore isn't good, but sushi grade Ahi is just better. A half pound steak each, seared, thirty seconds on each side with some green beans simmered in garlic, ginger and soy sauce and some rice…

"Dad, why can't we just have our own house?"

"Because I need the rent from the guest house to help pay the mortgage."

"I want our own house without a guest house."

"It will be a separate house… I thought you'd be happy about this. Ya know I don't have money like your friends' parents, okay. Jesus Christ! I'm doin' what I can do here!"

"Don't start yelling, Dad."

"Okay, don't give me grief, then. I'm doing the best I can."

"Fine," he says.

"I thought you'd be happy that we were getting a house at least," I say.

"I am."

"Okay."

"Dad?"

"What?"

"Don't get mad, but where is this house gonna be?"

"I don't know yet but we'll find it, okay? Eat your dinner."

"Why did you take the bigger piece of tuna, Dad?"

"Fine, then you take it."

And I give him my piece and we eat and watch a Simpson's rerun and laugh at an episode we've both seen twice before as we toss Shnooky little scraps of tuna.

The phone rings. It's my commercial agent, Kim, who has an audition for me. Some other Sam Shepard type, this time as a farmer for some satellite radio company or something and I could give a shit, but she tells me that it's the same casting director that cast me in my last commercial and she specifically requested me. So I take down the info and tell Max, "Well, that's pretty cool. Maybe I'll get this commercial too and we'll have more money."

"It would be cooler if you were directing the commercial, Dad," he says.

And I take a breath as we watch Homer, who in this episode is touring with the Lollapalooza rock festival as a sideshow act, dressed in tights and a cape, touting his iron stomach by taking cannonballs to the gut. The kids at the festival think he is so wild and crazy and his son, Bart, thinks he is the coolest but his wife, Marge, is concerned because the doctor told him if he takes one more cannonball he's going to die.

So we're watching the climax as Homer stands in front of the cannon deciding whether to be cool and die and all the kids are cheering and Marge is yelling, "Homer don't do it!" but he doesn't wanna let Bart down and he's sweating and belching and the camera cuts back and forth from him to the cannon, him to the cannon, him to the cannon... then the cannon goes off, the ball shoots out... and Homer steps aside. And the crowd boos and Homer is no longer cool but he's alive and he has his family and Bart hugs him and doesn't care if his dad isn't cool and I feel like this is one of those moments, one of those realizations.

"See that, see what's happening there?" I say. "The fact that we're watching this episode and having this conversation. Don't you think it's some kind of sign?"

Max scratches his head like he's really pondering my cosmic lesson, really listening to me and letting it sink in. Then he looks at me with earnest eyes and says, "Yeah, Dad, I do... it's the sign of an idiot."

He gets up, pats me on the head and says, "But I still love you. I'm goin' to do my homework now." And he walks to the bedroom, smooth strides; no giggling, no turning around and I just watch him in awe. What the hell, I love the little monster so much.

32

So I'm at the audition. More Sam Shepard types but not many of the good-looking, leading man Sam Shepards here, thank God, I feel so fucking ugly around them. There are more Sam Shepard character types on this one; everybody is a little older, a little rougher, more weathered looking. I'm not as rugged as these guys either.

That's how it is, I usually get sent out for both types and end up falling between the cracks but I'm committed today; unshaven, got on my dirt-stained boots, Levis and long-sleeved undershirt from the Vedanta gardening days and I'm lookin' the part. And besides I got Pam, the casting director, who gets my sense of humour and knows a lot of my history, on my side. So I'm laid back, hangin' out and waving, "Hey, y'all" to the other fuckin' farmer hopefuls.

Pam calls me in. She's a jovial, smart, sassy black chick. She is tall, lean and stacked… and married, and I respect that. But she loves to kid around.

"Hey, Dave, when are you going to bring me in a tape of one of those movies you used to do?"

I kinda pop my eyes at her and motion to the young hip-hop

257

type assistant she has running the camera.

"Maybe next time, Pam. Come on, don't embarrass me like that."

"Embarrass you? How can a guy like you be embarrassed?" Then she turns to her assistant and says, "Ya know what he did at the first call I had him in on? And I didn't even know him then."

"I booked that commercial," I say.

"Yes, he did," she says. "But that first audition cracked me right up."

And she tells the story of how I had to do this routine of a guy in one of those TV network trucks, monitoring all the screens at some major sporting event and the team I like wins and I'm supposed to continue working but I can't contain myself and I leap out of the truck and act all crazy excited about it (it had nothing to do with the actual commercial it was just to show exhilarated excitement). So I did the monitoring routine, saw my team win then leapt out of the imaginary truck, screamed, "Yes!" into the air then dropped to my knees and started simulating wild masturbation.

"And he was going like this," she says as she clenches her fist and jerks it up and down and makes a contorted face. "It was crazy funny." She laughs again as the assistant winces and looks at me like I'm some old perv but he laughs a little because, I mean, he is her assistant.

"Okay, Dave," she says. "Nuff a dat shit. This here is a big spot. The advertisement agency is in negotiations with a handful of famous musicians and you're going to be paired up with one of them. The deal is you're out on your farm doin' what farmers do then this big-ass satellite crashes through your barn and you look around like…"

"Like, what the fuck was that?" I say

"Exactly," she says. "So you pick the farmer stuff. Whatever you'd be doin' out there in the fields, diggin' holes, plantin' seeds… whatever."

"Does this director have a sense of humour?"

"You know he does if he's workin' with me, baby," she says.

So I slate my name, agency, into camera with the profile horseshit they make you do; look to the left, look to the right, then she says, "When you're ready, Dave," and I turn around and simply act like I'm pissing… just a farmer pissin' in his field. Then I hear the crash, spin around as I'm zippin' up my fly and hobble off towards my imaginary barn.

I do it so serious that I guess it looked even more ridiculous on camera because the assistant is cracking up too.

"You're a hoot, Dave, that's all I needed," she says. "See ya on the callback."

And I'm walking out, head somewhat in the clouds (my fucking little baby ego all stroked and happy) and I hear, "Dude, how'd it go?" And sittin' amongst some other Sam Shepard farmer types is Corey, this forty-year-old, has-been-before-he-ever-was actor I know who is a complete surfer dude from Santa Cruz, I mean the whole lingo and everything and he's not joking.

Max gets a kick out of him and we have all gone to the beach together a bunch of times. He actually gave Max some tips on surfing and tried to get me back into it. I used to surf but I kinda lost it in the drug years and couldn't really get it back so I picked up boogey boarding because, well it's just easier. Corey puts up with it but he is embarrassed to be in the water with me when I'm on the fucking boogey board.

"Dude, you gotta learn to surf again or I can't hang with you. I mean, dude..."

All he does is surf and act... that is when he gets a job. He is a handsome guy but something is a little off, something about his ears and teeth. He's like a cross between Sam Shepard, Elvis and Goofy.

"So, dude, tell me, how'd it go?"

"You just asked me that, Corey."

"Dude, but did you answer?"

"It went fine. Pam is cool. So what's up with you, Corey? Been surfing?"

"North west north swell is in, dude. Broad Beach is goin' off, shoulder to head high just peelin' off the point."

"Wanna go out there after this?" I say. "I'll go out."

"Dude, I was out this morning. I got some like gnarly play I'm in that I gotta rehearse for after this. I'm like nude in it, dude. I like play this crazy husband of this babe and I like just walk around nude and go off on her. Kinda like Brando did in 'Streetcar Named Desire'. That's why I took the part."

And he looks so serious about it… and he is a nice guy, good to my kid too… so instead of saying, "Hang it up, you buck-toothed loser," which regretfully enough I am capable of saying, I just say, "Corey Brando, huh?"

"Dude, you know it. So, like, what have you been up to?"

"Nothin', tryin' to write, taking care of Max, same old shit. Oh… and my Dad died."

"Dude, I'm sorry but, like, seriously I wish mine would check out. I hate his guts and he's got like a shitload of money. And that fucker owes me man, it sucked growin' up with him."

"Yeah…" I say, "I actually got a little money from mine."

"Dude, I thought you were less tense than usual. Got some dough, huh?"

"Some…"

"Dude, you should take Max to Bali, go surfin'."

"I'm just layin' low. I'm tryin' to buy a house."

"But, Dude, you gotta celebrate a little. You still seein' that Spanish babe?"

"Argentinian, Corey."

"Whatever... are ya?"

"No, I'm not."

"Dude, she was so hot... but fuck it... let's hit a strip club then."

"Not my style, Corey."

"Dude, you were a porn actor!"

And he says it loud enough to turn a few heads. Something about that word, Porn.

"Come on, keep it down, Corey," I say.

"What's the big deal, dude? Ya know what I always wanted to do, was like make a surf porn movie with rad surfers and huge waves and hot babes and all they do is like surf and fuck... that would be so cool."

"Stop being a fucking idiot," I say.

"Dude, you're the idiot. You have like all this dough and you're not doing anything. Just come to the strip club. It will be good for you. The babes are so fine plus when you're loaded with cash they treat you like a fucking king. They ride ya into lap dance heaven."

"Lap dance heaven, huh?"

"Dude, you know what I'm talkin' about."

"Not really but I'll think about it."

And the casting assistant calls Corey into the room.

"Dude, stay in touch."

"Alright."

"And, dude… be careful on those waves with your little boogey board."

33

I cruise up the Pacific Coast Highway with the Shnook under the pale turquoise sky mixed with tones of silver and green. The sky is always special when the swell is big and there is no wind so the waves just roll through the glassy surface of the ocean. I look out at them every chance I get and I look out at the surfers as we pass the major spots on the way up the coast, Sunset, Topanga Point and Malibu Pier.

I get surf fever. Even though I was never really good at it and gave it up, I still get the fever. I wish I was good, believe me, I wish I was riding fifteen foot tubes at pipeline with the pros on the north shore of Hawaii, not a middle-aged, mediocre boogey boarder who can't even get out in five foot waves at Malibu with the locals. I mean, Corey wouldn't be caught dead with me out there so I longingly watch them as I drive up the coast... but in my mind, I could have been... I could have been... I could have been rad and rippin' and ridin' those waves with the best of 'em.

I had the chance, too, I had the chance to get better at least way back when I was living with Keri. She had been renting the bottom of a house at Point Dume, right on the cliffs over Westward beach

264

for seven hundred bucks a month. She had it since she was a senior at UCLA. A little beach bungalow pad and I moved in with her to clean myself up and have a good life.

Two surfboards sat right outside on the patio. There was a pathway down to Westward and the walk to Big Dume beach was five minutes. Coulda gone surfing every day. But I couldn't even get it together to do that. What a miserable, drunken, bullshitting bastard I was.

One night fuelled with mushrooms and tequila, I told Keri I had a vision of us in the house as a happy, old, grey couple. And I saw Max visiting us with his children; I even said he would have three, a boy and two girls. I cried with joy and told her I was gonna straighten out for good, work hard and buy the entire house for her and then someday we would sell it for millions and travel the world together in our golden years. And she ended up throwin' me out of that one over and over and over again.

Someone else finally bought it. And as I drive past the crashing, closed out waves of Zuma, I look back towards the point and say, "What a fucking idiot I was, Keri. I'm so sorry."

Oh Dave, don't get all dramatic. Just find the house for you and Max, okay? I'm fine. I'm golden. I'm perfect.

God, whenever she wants to, she's just there.

"Thanks, Keri," I say and as I think of something else to add, I feel she's gone again.

I walk down Broad Beach in my wetsuit, holding my boogey board and fins with Shnook trotting next to me. Since it's a private beach lined with houses and most of the owners have dogs, they never really enforce the dog laws. Sometimes in the summer they have these imbecile cops in shorts and polo shirts, riding little Honda ATV's up and down but only on weekends or the fourth of July, Labor Day… days we make sure not to show up.

The tide is halfway out which is the best time for waves here. At high tide they roll right through the point and break too close to the beach and at low tide the rides are too short and there's just too many rocks to manoeuvre around. The waves are maybe shoulder high, not as big as Corey said because most surfers just exaggerate the size of the waves. Hey, me too, when I get Max at school I'll tell him it was eight foot, no seven, he'll call me a liar if I say eight. Maybe I'll stick to five… or four to five sounds better, about shoulder-high which is what it fuckin' is! The truth takes a lot less work, doesn't it?

So I step into the water. Shit… is it cold! One of the big disappointments of southern California is the ocean temperature. No gulf stream in the Pacific. Go down to Laguna, San Diego… still cold. Ya gotta go hundreds of miles down into friggin' Mexico before it starts warming up. I mean, why can't the water be warm here? Southern California just implies warm, same as Southern Florida. Water is fucking warm there, hovers around seventy degrees in the winter and it's like a bathtub in summer. I used to just lie out in the sand bar at Key Biscayne and bake... but out here, it rarely reaches seventy and that's in August. This time of year, late winter, early spring, the air temperature can hit eighty degrees and the water stays between fifty-two and sixty. Tops. Every time I go in, it fools me. I always expect it to be warm. I know that says something about me.

So as I wade into the swirling white foam, I wanna piss in my wetsuit right away. It does warm you up but I hold off, better to wait until you're fully submerged. And Shnooky, who is already up to her neck in it, wades in with me, more out of concern than want.

You sure you'll be all right, Daddy? The waves look big to me. Don't stay out too long.

"Stop it," I say. "I'll be fine. Go wait on the beach."

I'll just wait here for a little bit. I won't go in. I'll just wait here and watch.

"Fine. Stay. No further."

I pounce on my board, start kicking, paddling and duck-diving my way through a good-sized set of waves. And I piss in the wetsuit, but not to worry, the ocean water passes through and washes it out.

I make it through the set pretty easily. There have been times when the ocean was so turbulent and the waves were breaking so strong, I just never made it out, got thrashed around and spit back, over and over and over until I had to give up, sit on the shore, out of breath, gagging on choked down sea water, watching all the guys that made it past the break. Talk about feeling like a beaten down loser…

Take a breath of relief, Dave, you're out beyond the break now, feeling the next swell roll under you. And the sun's out stronger, bringing new shades of blue to the sky and hues of glowing orange to the green and silver outline of the clouds.

Look at those pelicans flying past with their enormous wings and their huge, smirky beaks with deep gullets. Woah! One just dive-bombed into the water and scooped up some fish. Oh, and there's some dolphins swimming by, all smooth, dark grey and soft black and a seal just popped his head up. He's checkin' me out. Look at his little grey whiskers. What a beautiful day.

I see six guys out at the point and they're gonna come barreling across when they catch a wave so I figure I'll stay where I am about fifty yards down, wait my turn. The bigger waves are all breaking off the point. I'll catch a smaller one. Corey usually passes on the first wave in the set because he says they build in size. The second, third, fourth waves are the ones he goes for so I'll wait this set out, watch a few of them ride then catch the first wave of the next set.

I see a few of 'em paddling like crazy. One guy gets it. He takes off, drops into the wave and rips across, cutting up to the lip and back as he barrels right past me and kicks out over the top, his board soaring into the air on its leash as he does a summersault dive into the water. Fuckin' balls, balance and style.

Then I watch the next guy take off. Here he comes swinging his arms back and forth as he cuts up the wave. These guys are good surfers. The first one comes towards me as he paddles his way back to the point. He's about twenty years old, looks like an ad right out of a surf magazine.

"Nice ride," I say, and he nods like he's used to it as he glides past. He doesn't even look at me. I'm a boogey boarder, practically invisible.

That's okay. I'm cool with it. I get a little adrenaline circulating but I don't call him a fuckin' thimble dick punk or anything. I respect his talent and I'm out here to have fun. The last wave of the set comes in. It looks smaller than the rest. Maybe I'll take it. I start paddling and kickin' my fins. Oh, someone else is on it. I back off, watch him rip by. No problem. I'm patient. I look back at the sun, feel the warmth on my face, look at the beach, wave to Shnooky. I can wait my turn.

And I see the next set coming in. The three guys from the last set are paddling back so if I take the first wave on this one, there's plenty left for the other three at the point. Here it comes. I start paddling and kicking, looking over my shoulder. I'm in a good position.

I glance over to the point, see a surfer paddling. Is he gonna take it? No. Yes. No. It's mine. I keep ferociously paddling then I feel it taking me. Wow, it's bigger than I thought. And I drop down and cut right, leaning into the wave, feeling the spray from the curl over me, and the thrill of the ride. My hands are clasped around the edges of my little boogey board, my chest glued to the centre with my legs flyin' out behind me and I'm yellin' out like a kid on a rollercoaster ride. Then I feel a smack to the side of my left thigh. What the hell? Was that a rock? A shark? Then I feel the hands yanking me off my board and I wipe out, get sucked under and pummelled by the wave, come up for air just in time to get thrashed by the next one and go under again.

I surface, gasping for breath in knee-high water close to the shore. And there is the surfer, the one I didn't think was gonna take the wave, standing a few yards away from me, cradling his board in one arm with the other stuck straight out, forefinger pointing towards the beach.

"Get the fuck out of the water, dude. Now!"

He couldn't be more than sixteen, his wet sun-bleached locks in his smooth bronzed face all gnarled up and ready for combat.

"Sorry, I didn't see you coming," I say. "But ya didn't have to punch me."

"Are you talking to me? Do I know you?" he says.

"Did you even see 'Taxi Driver'?" I say.

"Huh?"

"I mean come on, are you kidding me? I'm old enough to be

your father. I'm just trying to have some fun here."

And when he realizes there is nowhere he can take it, that it's not going to escalate into a surf brawl on the beach, he drops his board back in the water and says, "This isn't a place for you, old man!" then he jumps on and paddles back towards the point. And I see Shnooky doin' her own doggy paddling towards me, coming out to the rescue.

Daddy, Daddy, what's happening, what did he do to you? Are you okay?

"Take it easy, I'm fine."

But I don't feel fine. I don't feel angry. I feel confused and sad. I could go back out in the water. I mean, I'm not afraid to, but the beauty is gone from the day. Old man.

34

Wake Max. Make breakfast. Pack a lunch. Yell at him to hurry the fuck up. Take him to car pool. Run Bronson Canyon with Shnooky. Come home. Time to write. Ideas. Ideas. Ideas. Nothing. Nothing. Nothing. So I pick up one of my many old, frayed college ruled notebooks, all of which are filled with an array of messy, handwritten scribbles. And I flip through the pages.

Fuck you garlic

Fuck you peppers

Waiting for what, more olive oil

Talking to each other about the great meal you both made

before

So much sauce

So much cheese

So much great, great pasta

Forgive me please

You lying fucking vegetable assholes

But I was there and the dinner sucked

Big time

Vegetables are just like people

What a drag that they're so full of shit too…

Just an angry little drunken cooking poem I wrote a while back. Flip. Flip. Flip. There has to be something on one of these pages to spark a new idea. What's this here with the asterisk next to it?

Nitrous oxide. Dentist. If bomb dropped. Brazil

Bad crown - espionage - big big deal - Undercover

Abused by beyond

Therapist between patient and hygienist stressed up her arms into her body.

Out past Mars somewhere.

Probably had a complete vision of some movie when I jotted that down… yep…

And I'm sucking on another piece of Nicorette. God damnit!

What's this?

Drunk and naked

With a rock hard erection

I lay on the bed dizzy and grinning

As you sit there fuming with my cock in your hand

Yelling in my face

This is the last time

this is the last time

this is the last time…

Sure baby sure, sure baby sure, sure baby sure…

Must have felt so cool when I jotted that down. Now I feel like an idiot for writing it. Turn some pages here. Wait. Oh, this one…

My little boy looks like a golden angel

As the sunset's rays bathe him in slumber

My sweet, sweet son

My sweet…

God, that was a long time ago. I remember that moment too, when Max was a baby, sleeping in his little window bed that Keri made. Now I just want to lie down and take a nap.

Okay, okay, movie idea, movie idea. Oh, this looks like a great one, well thought out.

The scene opens with… and the rest of the page is blank. Fuck. All right, here's an essay or maybe some attempt at a stand-up routine about… *the difference between shitting in the privacy of your home or in the public toilet stalls where all you think about is if the guy next to you heard you fart and that you always seem to drop the embarrassingly loud plopping bombs in the toilet water?* What's this here? – *(to audience)* - in parenthesis, so I guess it was some stand-up attempt and it goes on about this for a couple of pages. *How many of you are the quiet type shitters who wriggle around the edge of the seat trying to drop one on the porcelain?*

Talk about shit, how did I write this? And the pages and pages of desperate love poems I don't even wanna look at, but I glance over a couple.

Nothing I do ever matters to you
Nothing I say ever means anything
I pour out my heart and fill up your glass
Then you pick up the glass and you throw it...

And I stopped. Must have got a call from her or the dealer or something. Okay, one more.

The storm is now behind the tower
There are no trees there are no flowers
It would have been better if you treated me better
Then I wouldn't have gone and blown my head off
Lessons from a dead man that loved you so much
But you'll do it again, you'll do it again
You know who you are
So what's for you to learn...

That was that waify, little English witch-model in Tokyo. Can't even remember her name now. Okay, that's it. I can't look at these anymore. Oh, here... humiliating commercial auditions.

Be Serpent in garden of Eden wearing fluorescent green Mexican wrestling mask, coaxing teenage Lolita Eve with stinky dog breath tennis ball as apple for Investment Company ad.

Act like sheep boy and eat Skittles off wooden stool.

Dress up like Amish and wear triangular shaped Styrofoam head of cheese...

What? God help me. Don't sweep me back. I just wanna get started on something new here. Why can't I think of anything? Why am I so blocked? And I remember hearing Robert McKnee or McKee, the pompous, know-it-all, Humphrey Bogart wannabe, chain smoking, writing seminar teacher, master, guru or whatever, (I took the course and day-dreamed through half of it and hated him through the other half) saying some shit about writers' block meaning lack of research. What if you don't have a fucking idea to research? Why is my mind so dead?

And I find myself wanting to call Patti to see how Tony is so maybe I can get an idea from him at rehab. Maybe the idea is rehab. A movie about Tony in rehab? My mind swirls with images of all the crazy shit he must be causing up there. So I call.

"Hey, Patti, how's it going?"

"Good…"

She always says, "Good," even when Tony is smoking crack in her garage under a tarp behind some old lawn chairs.

"How's Tony?"

"He's fine. You know Tony, always up to something."

"So he's doing okay in rehab?"

"Oh, yeah. He met some fellow crack addict from CAA there."

"A crack addict from CAA?"

"Yeah, I guess they're everywhere these days, anyway he's some big writer or producer that Tony says wants to do his life story."

"Really?"

"That's what he said anyway. But you know Tony. Anything is possible. So how are you doing? How's Max?"

And I don't know why I feel sunk and empty and pissed off that even in fucking rehab this guy can bullshit anybody. Some fuck from CAA, some Harvard grad wannabe cool crack addict asshole writer that Tony is gonna scam and have him write his story, his fucking story... fucking CAA. Jesus, now he'll probably get hooked up with CAA as a co-writer and he can't even spell... and they'll make a movie out of it and both get rich and I can't even come up with one fucking idea to write anything...

"Dave, are you there?"

"Huh? Yeah... um... I'm here, we're okay, ya know, getting by. Tell Tony to call me if he wants... just wanted to, ah, bounce some ideas around."

"You want the number up there?"

"No... he can call me if he wants."

"Okay, take care, say hi to Max."

I hang up and immediately start staring at the computer screen. Come on. Come on. Come on! Please, God, give me something!

The phone rings again. I look at Shnooky and say, "If this is bad news, I'm gonna kill somebody!"

Daddy, stop, please...

I pick up and answer with a deep unhappy, death greeting.

"Hello…"

"Dave, it's Frank. You okay?"

"Frank?"

"Your real estate agent, Frank."

"Oh, sorry Frank…"

"Listen, I found it. Nice two bedroom with a little guesthouse and a renter already in there paying twelve hundred a month. It's perfect for you and it's not even on the market yet. Better bring your son on this one."

"And my dog?"

"Sure, bring the dog, bring the dog."

35

"Do you like it?"

"I don't know, Dad, we haven't even gone in yet."

"Looks nice, though, doesn't it?"

We get out of the car and stand across from the house on Waring Street.

"You like the red walls? It's kind of a mixed stucco Spanish-style I think and the yellow around the window frames or sills. No, the window sills are inside the house, right?"

"Dad, it's not yellow, it's mustard."

"Okay, mustard. It goes with those black shingles pretty nice, though. The Spanish-style house I saw on Willoughby had those red shingles made out of brick."

"How could shingles be made out of brick, Dad?"

"Maybe they were tile, then, or clay, yeah, red clay, that's a Spanish style. So this isn't like real Spanish-style but I like it better."

"Dad, I don't think you know what you're talking about."

"Yes, I do. Hey, I like the fence for Shnooky so she can play in the yard and it's got that cool purple door, and see those lemon trees and the big cactus?"

"We'll have to change the colour of that door, Dad."

"Okay, we'll paint it any colour you like."

And we cross the street.

"Come on, Shnooky."

"Dad, you should have put her on a leash."

"Take it easy," I say as I snap my fingers and she follows right next to me. I turn the knob on the fence door.

"Hey, it's open."

"Dad, we should wait for that real estate guy."

And I know he is right.

"Fine," I say, and I walk down the sidewalk a few yards to see a little gate door in front of a garage with matching red brick and mustard colours.

"Look, this says 7112½. It must be the guest house."

And I hear some dreamy music coming from inside... sounds like an old Nick Drake song called 'Place To Be.'

And Frank pulls up.

"What do ya think? Looks good, huh? This your kid?"

And Frank and Max shake hands and he pats Shnooky.

"She okay off the leash?"

"See, Dad!"

"Quiet, she's fine." And we follow Frank through the gate and walk up the short stone slab path to the front door.

"Nice little yard, huh, Dave? Needs some work but you got your citrus trees, some nice Cactus plants."

And we go through the front door into the living room that is small… but it does have those nice hardwood floors, and a fireplace.

"Cosy, isn't it, Dave? And don't forget you have the guest house attached so this is considered a three bedroom unit."

And we look around and there is a little bathroom in the hall with a shiny new porcelain toilet and sink.

"Nice remodelled half-bath here," Frank says, even though there is no bath and we go into the kitchen that has a good gas stove and deep indigo tiled floor and granite counters and a back door to a little patio that Shnooky goes out while we check the bedrooms and Max already picks the bigger one, of course, that has the full bathroom attached with the bath and shower.

"I'm coming in whenever I want," I say.

"You'll come in when I let you come in, Dad."

And he starts shoving me out and I put him in a headlock then he breaks loose and we laugh and slap at each other and I chase him back into the living room, through the kitchen like it's already our house and we hear a lyrical woman's voice from outside say, "Who is this cute doggy?"

"That's the tenant," Frank says to me. "She's not obligated to show you the guest house but feel free to say hello."

And his cell phone rings.

"This is Frank," he says as I whisper, "just gonna get the dog," and we go out the back door towards the garage across the weathered, wood patio that Max tells me needs refinishing.

"Okay, Max, we'll do it." And then we see this tawny brown-haired, green-eyed, angel-faced, bare-footed hippie chick, maybe twenty-five, dressed in flowered, bell-bottom jeans, faded red t-shirt under an orange, Indian wool, woven vest, sitting outside the guest house on a sun-bleached blue cushioned lawn chair.

She has a baby girl dressed in powdered denim, Oshkosh overalls on her lap, that she spoon feeds raspberry yogurt to while she hums along to what sounds like Neil Young's 'Heart Of Gold' playing from inside the open door while Shnooky helps with the feeding by licking the excess yoghurt off the baby's face.

"We just love your dog," she says.

"Thanks. That's Shnooky."

"Oh, Shnooky, we love Shnooky, don't we, darlin'?" And her baby coos and puts her little hand over Shnooky's nose while she licks away.

"Is that song from the Harvest Album?" I say.

"That's right. Very good, very cool," she says.

And I feel myself wanting to tell her a little anecdote of when, 'The Needle and The Damage Done' song would play on that album and Neil Young sang the line, 'Every Junkie's like a setting sun,' I would spit back at the record, all teenage nasally narcotic, "Not me, man, I'm never goin' down." But Max senses my twisted mind calculating some charred cool response I'll regret and just says, "Dad…" in a way I know means… please don't do it…

So I just smile like an old bore and say, "Yeah, I used to listen to that album a lot when I was… a… well, when I was just a few years older than my son, here… ah… Max is now."

"Okay, Dad," he says which could easily be translated as, "Shut up."

And hippie-chick mom laughs, and says, "I'm April and this is Daisy."

"I'm Dave and this is Max."

"You already said my name, Dad."

And April spoons some more yoghurt into her baby's mouth and says, "You guys are cute together. What music are you into, Max? Not mainstream, I bet."

"Not really," he says.

"Let me guess. I have Beck, The Pixies, The Shins, Radiohead…"

"Radiohead is cool," he says. "I like old bands too, like from my dad's time."

Little Bastard, I think as she says, "You dig Zeppelin? I never get sick of Zeppelin."

"Yeah, Zeppelin is cool too," he says and she gives him a little 'thumbs-up' and smiles and Shnooky licks more yoghurt off the baby who giggles and I don't interfere with my vast knowledge of Led Zeppelin, knowing every album and song with an escapade to go with each one, because I am daydreaming about all of us together, laughing, listening to music, playing with the baby, fixing up the house and whether April could be like Max's older sister or my younger sister or maybe we could get married and Daisy could be Max's younger sister and we could have more kids…

"So you guys might be moving in, huh?"

"Yeah, I mean we like it so far."

"I love it here. I hope Daisy and I can stay if you do."

"Um, it looks like you take care of the place."

"Dad, we haven't even looked inside yet."

And April laughs and picks up Daisy and says, "Come on," and we follow her into her world of flowers and posters and beads and little stuffed bears and donkeys and lambs for Daisy and all the stacks of CD's and cassettes and old record albums and a couple of guitars… and there's all kinds of candles everywhere in the garage transformed into a one bedroom loft with mahogany stained wood floor leading into the bronze tiled kitchen.

"And here's the bathroom," she says. "The owner put in a new toilet and shower. Be nice to have a bath, though, for Daisy." And as I'm thinking if I can afford to put a bath in and lower her rent, Frank sticks his head in the door.

"Gotta show another house, Dave."

"Okay. Hope we see you again, April, if we get to live here… I guess."

"Cool, good luck. Bye, Max. Bye, Shnooky."

Outside on Waring Street, Frank tells me that if I want the house, all we have to do is put in an offer because fortunately his relationship with the seller enables us to bypass getting a pre-approval letter from a mortgage broker. There is no one else to bid against so all we have to do is fill out a one page offer form, sign it and write a cheque for three percent of the total cost, that will be refunded if the deal doesn't go through, or used towards the purchase price if it does go through. I just say, "Do it, Frank, do it. I'll sign, I'll sign, I'll write the cheque."

Dad, promise me if we move in you won't…

Won't what?

Dad, you know what I mean just promise…

Okay, I promise.

36

I call Frank every few days about the house and he reassures me that he is in touch with the seller, not to worry, that things are being worked out. Meanwhile I get the callback on the Sam Shepard farmer audition. I do the same routine; act like I'm peeing in the field, everyone laughs then the director tells me to just turn around and stare at a spot on the wall. He has me do that three times, says, "Thanks, see ya later," and now I am up for the job. It's so easy when they want you and impossible when they don't.

So I'm "on avail" as they say in the business, which means for the days they have slated to shoot this commercial, they have first dibs on me just in case a slew of other commercial offers come rollin' in. Yeah, super commercial star Dave, that's me. No, not the case. But that is why they do that avail shit because some commercial actors actually do work all the time. I've overheard 'em yapping and braggin'.

I did fifteen national spots last year! I booked three last month! I can't believe how busy I've been...

Fuck you, not my case... never was.

But, hey, I'm grateful I might get this one. As a matter of fact, I'm counting on it so I'm figuring the money I need to put down on the house, less the bid payment and subtracting April's rent (which I'll drop to a thousand) off the monthly mortgage payment. And it will be close, I'll be tapped out in a couple of months but when the commercial starts running and the residual dollars flow in, I'll be covered.

And another hopeful thing is that Bernie, this fledgling writer/ director/producer who loved my plays back in the day, called me. Five years ago he had given me a few thousand, along with a shabby memo-deal, promising twenty thousand more (if it went into production) to do a re-write on some adaptation he wrote of this 1890's Joseph Conrad story, 'Outcast of The Islands.'

He got very intense about how Conrad's theme of the white man, who's drawn towards the darkness then swallowed up by it, intrigued him and compelled him to write the script and that he felt I was the guy who could make it better and keep it raw and keep it real. He told me not to read the original story because it might ruin my vision that needed to be in sync with his vision which wasn't exactly Conrad's vision. Anyway, Bernie's vision could have brought Conrad back from the grave to slit his throat.

It was some modernized half-assed cop story about a crazed white detective and a hot black chick that I couldn't take seriously and wanted to name it, 'Bernie wants to Fuck a Fine Black Actress' but I needed the dough and I wanted to put my mark on it so I made it very sick and sexy and twisted and dark-as-dark-could-be with everybody going straight to hell in the end.

I thought it was pretty funny, although I guess no investors did. So I never heard back from Bernie. But as I was saying, he called out of the blue and told me he re-circulated it and has a couple of new, really hip, investors interested. He thinks they might be major crack dealers but still, they're investors and I could be looking at my balance of twenty along with a second re-write fee.

And we're drivin' down Sunset Boulevard through Beverly Hills to drop Max at his friend Leo's in Bel-Air for a Friday night sleepover and he's sifting through his CD's he's gonna take to Leo's and Shnook is loungin' on the leather in the back and I'm taking glances at the tops of all the luxurious mansions, hidden by massive hedges and iron gates, one after the next after the next, thinkin' it's not such a big deal if those few good things happen for us; the house, the commercial, the screenplay.

I mean, look at these people, what do the people who own these monstrosities do? What do these people do? Hollywood Sellouts. Weapons Runners. Evil Cocksuckers.

No. No. No. That's what I used to think just to make me feel better and maybe a few of those types do live here, but I can't think of them like that. No. These mansions and the people in them have to be inspiration to me. Anything is possible. Personally, I'd rather live at the beach or further up in the hills when we get rich, but we'll start small on Waring Street.

Who knows? Bernie's movie could go, it could be a hit and I could be writing scripts for millions while simultaneously being the TV spokesman for some major product and we could get a huge mansion with an Olympic-sized swimming pool set on a sprawling landscape, overlooking the Pacific and we could put April and Daisy up in a big guesthouse, unless we get married… no, I promised Max.

Doesn't matter, she's not attracted to me anyway, just thinks I'm a nice older guy, but she did say I was cute, no she said that Max and I were cute together. So, that's okay, I like her anyway. She can live rent-free in the guesthouse. I bet she's in a band. I wonder what kind of band? What if we built her a recording studio and she recorded an album, a multi–platinum, fucking album? Why not? I'm sure she's a singer, probably can sing all across the board. The music she listens to goes all across the board. Great influences.

And Max could help produce the album. He loves music. Maybe he could be one of the youngest producers in Hollywood. They are all so young anyway. I mean, this wouldn't happen for a few years. He'd be sixteen then, almost seventeen. I bet there are music producers that young…

"Dad, you missed the turn."

"What?"

"You missed the turn to Leo's house."

"You wanna be a music producer?"

"Sure, Dad, whatever, turn around."

Leo's house is a big, beautiful, stone mansion, set on a couple of wooded acres. There is a pool and tennis courts in the back and Leo and his younger brother, Sammy, have their own skateboard park set up there, with half-pipes and ramps and rails, and a row of big plywood boards that they do spray-paint graffiti art-work on.

The only reason I know, is that the maid tells me they're back there sometimes when I come to pick up Max and I go around the side path to get him. Otherwise, I wait at the door as a maid calls him on the intercom to come down. It's not that Leo's parents aren't friendly; I just never really see them. I've seen his father, Richard, twice, walking by the inside hallway as I wait at the door with the maid.

"Hey, Dave, how's it going?"

"Okay, Richard, how are you?"

"Good, good."

And he's gone into another room. I've only seen Leo's mom, Laurie, by chance when she is either coming out or driving into the garage in her vintage Jensen-Healy convertible. She doesn't even say hello, she just smiles and gives a little wave, like perhaps I'm just Max's driver. She has told me over the phone though, "We just love your son," so that's enough for me.

No, it's not. I want them to fucking accept me as an equal and invite me over for cocktails and a swim but maybe that will happen, when I'm rich, too. Then they can respect me enough to become their so-called friend which is what most of the friendship is based on in this bullshit fucking town, riches and fame and all that crap... but don't let me digress. Max has a great time there and I'm not gonna ruin it.

So we come up the wide, smooth, rose-coloured cement driveway to see Leo, head down, hair flying back and forth and arms flailing as he practises kick turns on his skateboard. Max honks the horn. Leo looks up, all wild-eyed and sweaty. "Dudes, what the hell is happening!"

Max laughs and says, "Leo is so crazy," as he skateboards up to the car and hangs on the front window.

"Dave, drive up a little."

"Okay," I say as I give it a little gas and drive another ten yards with him hanging on, grinning across at Max.

"There's Shnooky! Hey Shnooky!" he says as she gets up and wags her tail. I stop the car and he boards around to Max's side.

"Dave is so cool," he says to Max as he swings open the door and Max gets out with his CD's, backpack and skateboard.

"My dad would like, ground me if I asked him to do that."

And as I smile wide from the compliment, Max turns to me

and says, "Dad, don't let it get to your head, you're not that cool." Then he throws me a mock kiss, drops his skateboard down on the driveway and hops on.

"Bye, Dad."

"Bye."

Then Leo races back around to my side and hangs on as I back down the driveway.

"Hey, Max tells me you're getting a new house."

"Yeah, soon you can come spend weekends with us."

"Ya know what would be really cool, Dave?"

"What?"

"If you bought the house across the street. It's for sale, ya know."

And I look over at the fancy black and gold realtor sign in front of a massive three-storey mansion and instead of getting pissed off and saying, "What are you, fucking nuts? You rich, naïve little cocksucker! I could never buy that house, not in a million fucking years!" I smile and say, "That would be cool, Leo, maybe our next house," because I feel anything is possible for us right now.

"See ya later. Have fun."

"Bye, Dave. Bye, little Shnooky Shnook."

37

So I'm back in the apartment fishing around for the old Bernie
script. I wanna look it over and start comin' up with ideas for the
re-write and I think there might be a copy of Conrad's 'Lord Jim' in
my mess of a bookshelf because Max had to read that in school,
but I really should pick up 'Outcast of the Islands' if I can find it
and get 'Heart Of Darkness' too, just so I have Conrad in my mind.
Maybe if I'm saturated with him, I can attempt to weave some kind
of genuine thread through the hacked out, piece o' shit script I
wrote. I know I'm getting way ahead of myself but I'm excited to get
on it. After I do the commercial of course. Maybe in our new house.
Yeah, that's where I'll write it.

Then I get the calls, one after the next after the next.

Frank tells me the owner is changing her mind and giving the
house to her daughter.

"What daughter? What the fuck, Frank?"

"Sorry, Dave, her daughter was excluded from the contract and
she can do what she wants."

Kim tells me I've been taken off hold for the job.

"But the director loved me... they all laughed. What the fuck, Kim?"

"Sorry, Dave, they decided to go another way."

And Bernie tells me the investors just got busted for ten kilos of heroin.

"Why did you have them as investors? What the fuck, Bernie!"

"Sorry, Dave, and I thought they were crack dealers."

And I hear the same consolation from all of them.

"Don't worry, Dave, you'll get another house."

"Don't worry, Dave you'll get another job."

"Don't worry, Dave, we'll wait 'til they post bail and see what happens."

So it's bad news and my expectations are squashed again but I've been knocked down so many times that I'm used to it. Well, not that used to it. I'm still stamping around the apartment, hyperventilating and screaming, "No! No! No!" while Shnooky trembles in the corner... but I feel like I'm gonna get over it. Not now but soon. Maybe. I don't know. Maybe not. Why couldn't things have just worked out for once? Well, I guess I can get another house. Not like that one, though. Selfish bitch owner, giving it to her daughter. She could have gotten any house. I needed that one. I should burn it to the ground so nobody lives there... but April, poor April and little Daisy... what would they do? I wonder if she is gonna miss us? I'm gonna miss her. It would have been so great over there. Ah, fuck April, she probably thought I was a creep and told the owner not to sell the house to me. That cunty, phony, hippie wannabe...

Stop. Please. Stop. Please.

No. Wait. Shut up. I have more...

And that cocksucker commercial director, how could he just change his mind? Bastard. The advertising people probably forced him to. I knew I shouldn't have done that pissing routine. They all laughed. Wait... the snotty, stuffed shirt on the cell phone, he didn't laugh that much. Yeah, he was the one. Bet he was the boss. Damnit! And Bernie, Bernie's just a moron... fuck that stupid script, I hated it anyway. And I scream out, "You happy now, Joseph Conrad, wherever you are?"

Fuck it. I should just blow all this bad news off and go out somewhere. Just go out. But I don't even know where to go anymore. Out where? I was out. I had my time. I was out on a twenty-year summer vacation; out in New York, out in Miami, out in LA, out in Honofuckinlulu, out in Paris, out in Berlin, out in Madrid, out in Milan, out in Tokyo and Sydney friggin' Australia. All I have to show for it is a bad liver, a bunch of stamps on my passport and some wild fuck stories. Now I'm just an old, boring, balding, teetotaler that stays with his kid all the time and doesn't know what the fuck to do when he's not taking care of him!

I've tried to go out before when Max was spending the night

somewhere. I've called up some of my beyond 'Big Lebowski' burn-out friends that are still hittin' the clubs and bars and parties, trying to impress little, hottie girls half their age with TV and film credits from decades ago.

"Oh, you were that guy? I saw that when I was three."

"But I still look good, don't I, baby?"

"Kinda…"

And all I do is stand in the corner and judge people so I don't feel so horribly insecure. That was a line I remember from, Dostoyevsky's, 'Notes From Underground'…

'I for instance am horribly insecure.'

"And all the rest of the crap stems from that," I say to Shnooky, as I yank my little Dostoyevsky paperback off the shelf with 'Notes…' and 'The Dream of A Ridiculous Man' and selections from 'The House of The Dead'. Not that I finished any of them, twenty pages into his stories always put me in a tailspin.

Maybe I should stay in and read Dostoyevsky until I'm so bug-eyed disillusioned and despicably despairing, that I tear the pages out of the book with my teeth and gnaw on them while I throw myself on the floor and writhe around, grovelling, snivelling, swallowing down his inked words, spitting out the chewed up pieces of saliva-soaked paper all over myself until I burst into hopeless hilarity.

Who am I kidding? Like I'm some expert on Dostoyevsky. Did I read 'Crime And Punishment'? Did I read 'The Idiot'? I'm the idiot. I'm the fucking idiot here, aren't I? I feel like some delusional, sad sack he would have written about. No, he wouldn't have even bothered. How could I have counted on those things to happen? Again, I got caught up in it. Again!

Oh shit, the self-hatred is seeping in. Oh, damn, I am feeling this. Here it comes. Oh, no. I have to put my hand over my face and close my eyes. Please go away. Please go away.

The phone rings. I couldn't get any worse news so I pick it up.

"Yeah..."

"Dude, ready to hit a strip club?"

"Corey, no, I'm havin' a little meltdown here."

"Dude, let's celebrate. I booked that job!"

"What job?"

And I know what job but I just want to hear him say it so I can feel the dagger of despair plunging in deeper.

"That farmer job. I booked it!"

"Good... good for you, Corey, I gotta go."

"Dude, stop bummin' and come to the Star Strip on La Cienega, you need to get out."

"Fuck you."

I hang up on him.

So it did get worse. Great. I'm really revelling in it now. What other pain can I gather? I punch in Carolina's number. No longer in service. Her mother's number. No longer in service. The whole family lives with that guy now. Yep. He made his move. He made his commitment. I couldn't do it. I blew it with her. I just kept thinking, it's not gonna work, it's not gonna work, it's not gonna work… and it didn't.

Am I ever gonna find the right woman for Max and me? Have I tried? Have I really tried to find someone to be with since Keri died? No, just a few months with this one here, a few months with that one there and in-between… nothing. So there, I have more pain now. I am so deep in the shit of pain, there is no escape. What do I do? What do I do? What do I do?

I know what to do. I know how to get through this. I know the solution…

Get quiet and pray. Yes.

And I open my little prayer book and read the daily meditation…

This is the time for my spirit to touch the spirit of God. I know that the feeling of the spirit-touch is more important than all the sensations of material things. I must seek a silence of spirit touching with God. Just a moment's contact and all the fever of life leaves me. Then I am well, whole, calm…

And as I'm reading this I drop to my knees, feeling in my soul that this is right, this is what I needed, this is perfect. And my eyes drift to an old LA weekly on the floor. Maybe I'll just go to a movie, I think, as Shnooky snuggles up to me and licks my face.

Maybe you should just stay on your knees and pray a little longer, Daddy.

"Stop it, I'm fine," I say as I set the meditation book back on the shelf and pick up the paper.

And as soon as I stand up, I feel like I'm on my way to some sort of hell but it's just a tiny little glimmer of a flame, nothing to pay attention to. So I flip to the movie section like I'm really gonna go see one then I realize I can't go to a movie because this paper is a month old. Who knows which ones are playing anymore? Right? Then I laugh a sick, helpless laugh like... Who are you kidding? And I look at Shnooky and say, "Did I laugh like that?" As I keep flipping through to the theatre section. She looks at me very concerned.

Oh, boy, Daddy. Put the paper down.

I wave her off and stop on the page where they have 'Pick Of The Week' and other recommended plays. Stupid 'Pick Of The Week'. I remember when my play was pick of the week. *Big fuckin' deal, keep flippin' the pages. You know where you wanna go.*

I rip through the music section with page after page of concerts and clubs and bands and bands and bands. "Jesus, this is a hard business," I say. "Ian Hunter from 'Mott The Hoople'? He's still playin'? Joe Cocker? Holy shit, and they're playin' little clubs now. They used to be huge in my day. How do any of these bands make it? So many. So many, Shnooky. Let's see... what's on the next page? Shall we?"

Daddy, you're in trouble.

But I'm already there, in the back pages, staring at all the strippers in all the ads for all the clubs. Full nude, live nude, totally nude, lap dance, couch dance... cock rub... Well, I don't read that but I imagine it and I imagine this is how I'm gonna get fixed. Fuck it. Do it. Get it over with and call it a night.

Don't meet Corey, though? No. I'll go where nobody knows me. Yeah, I'll go to a club in the Valley, deep in the Valley. And now my mind is just immersed in perversion. Deep in the Valley of her pussy, her sweet little shaved pussy, I push my tongue in further and further and further until I feel the rivers of cum running down then I take out my big throbbing cock and...

"Ah, fuck, I am in trouble, Shnook!" I say. "But it's too late. So don't bug me. Lie down and shut up."

When did I breathe last? Oh, my head is getting full, fillin' up with it. Maybe I'll just call in some young slut to give me a half-assed back rub and jerk me off. I got at least three hundred cash in the drawer and money in the bank and a bank card in case I need extra for a blow job or a fuck and as I'm saying, "This is bad, this is bad, this is bad," I'm already looking through those ads...

Horny Redhead, Busty Blonde, Brown Sugar, Asian babe, Latin Lolita... Hotties, hotties, hotties, all dripping wet and ready to go. In call/out call 24/7...

And then onto the pages with all the mini headshots and sexy names and one-line enticements and I focus on a pouting purse-lipped brunette with wicked, fuck-me eyes... 'Tia. Exotic Eurasian with a tight little package for your big one. Outcall only.' Oh, Christ, I already feel so inundated with smut sick... but I have the phone in my hand and I'm calling.

38

"Whaddya need, pal?"

"Pack of Lucky Strikes and some matches, please."

And I'm staring at all the liquor bottles on the shelf, thinking, not yet but I could be back for one as I pay for the smokes and rip open the pack right there on the counter.

"You... ah, got a trash can for the wrapper?"

"I'll take it, pal, you look like you're in a serious hurry."

"Yeah... thanks," I say, and I stick a cigarette in my mouth, light it on the way out of the liquor mart, taking deep drags to make up for lost time. Then I just leave it dangling between my lips like I never quit and hop in the car. *What am I doing? What am I doing? What am I doing?* And that's my mantra all the way to the bank machine where I draw out three more hundred and head back to the apartment to get ready for Tia. And what a stupid John I was on the phone.

"Can she give a good massage, too? I mean, if I want one?"

"Of course she can, honey. What's your address?"

"And she's the girl in the picture?"

"Yeah, honey, of course. What's your address?"

I get home and clean up, chain smoking, ignoring Shnooky's pleading looks to come to my senses. I vacuum the bedroom like a madman, rip the sheets off my mattress, put on new ones, straighten Max's blankets out on his bed, hide Keri's pictures in the drawers... No. I can't do it in here. I rip the sheets off the mattress and bring 'em into the living room to toss over the crusty couch pillows. The place is a mess. *So... ah, yeah, Tia, I'm back and forth from my new house in the hills I'm rebuilding and I kinda let my kid live here on his own... and I can't believe the goddamn maid didn't clean this week...*

Shut up. Who cares? Tia is a whore, coming over to get you off, get paid and leave or get paid, get you off and leave. They always get paid first. You know that. You whored yourself. Didn't you? Remember the ménage with that porn actress you were working with, Kelly I think it was, and the wife of the ex-police captain of Greenwich Connecticut, while he watched nude with his captain's hat on and smoked free-base? He paid five hundred up front for both of you. And then he took his billy club out and tried to handcuff you to the iron bedpost? Too much cocaine for the old captain. He was scary high. Good thing Kelly talked him down. That would have been a real mess. You were a real mess back then. Why are you doing this now? Shut up. Sweep the floor. Take out the trash. Make the place decent. It will all be over in an hour. Man, smoking these Luckies is making me sick. Sure, light another one.

I get the place decent enough, take the trash around to the dumpster behind the building and as I'm walkin' back up to the street, I see this girl get out of the passenger side of a black Chevy Impala with tinted windows that's double-parked in front of my car. When she looks up at the building, I can see from the streetlight that she has long, frizzy brown hair, really bad skin and sloppy balloon-sized boobs under some flimsy, cheap, pink lingerie top. She leans back into the car to say something to the driver. I see the short, black skirt hike up over her thick, fleshy legs in torn fishnets with black garters going up to her huge ass cheeks, separated by a stretched-out red thong. Are those pimples on her ass? Oh, no, this can't be her! Oh, come on, I don't want to hurt her feelings but I can't do this. Good. I'm over it now. It was meant to be like this so I wouldn't have to do it. I'm just going to tell her before the driver pulls away.

"Excuse me," I say as I walk up to her. "Are you supposed to be Tia?"

"What do ya mean, supposed to be?" she says. The accent is street harsh and hateful. "I am Tia. You Dave or David or whatever from number three?"

"Yeah, yeah, that's me, but…"

"Well, you wanna go upstairs?"

"Ah… wait… I mean, you don't look anything like the picture."

"Haven't you heard of advertising, mothafucka?"

And I hear a deep voice from inside the Impala say, "What's wrong, Maria?"

"I thought you said you were Tia?" I say.

"Tia. Maria. Do you really give a shit what my name is? Now are we gonna go upstairs or what? Because if not, I want you to pay me. I didn't come all the way up here for nothin'."

I can tell behind it all her feelings are hurt and she knows I think she's ugly but I'm not gonna have a heart to heart honest share about it. No. It's not gonna work like that. And now I see some neighbours looking out of their windows.

"Listen, I'll give you twenty dollars for your trouble."

"Twenty?"

"Okay, forty. Look I'll give you sixty bucks, okay?"

"I want my three hundred dollars."

"I don't have three hundred dollars."

"Then you can talk to Gus," and she hits the side of my car as she yanks her door open, gets in and slams it shut.

"Hey, that's my car," I say as this enormous kinda White/Black/Mexican looking mix of a monster in a purple sweat-suit gets out of the Impala and strolls over to me.

"Nice ride, new Four-Runner limited," he says. "And you tellin' me you ain't got three hundred dollars?"

I'm thinkin', he's gonna put his fist through the window or

through my head so I say, "Look, I have the three hundred, it's just that…"

Then he smiles, puts his tree trunk arm around me and leans into my ear. "Listen, man, I know your situation. You called for Tia and you got Maria."

"Yeah, exactly," I say.

"And Maria ain't exactly no Tia," he says.

"Exactly…"

"Well," he says, "because most dudes don't give a shit. The girl shows up, they ready to go… know what I'm sayin'? Now you, you're picky. I can respect that. So exactly what do you want?"

I can't say that I want him to get his big, purple sweat-suit ass back in the car and drive the fuck away, so I just say, "Um…" and he says, "Now you ain't gonna get nothin' that looks like Tia for three hundred, I mean that's like saying you're gonna get Angelina Jolie for three hundred. Understand? Tia is hot. Tia is fine. Tia is two thousand dollars, my friend."

"Yeah, that's… I can't do that," I say.

"Okay then, brother, we understand each other. Now this is what I can do. I can get you a girl a step up from Maria, a big step up for the same three hundred, which I am going to have to take from you now…"

And I see I'm gettin' ripped off here in a nice way by a big guy that wouldn't hesitate to just snap my arm like a twig if I didn't play along… so I play along.

"Okay, send another girl."

"And you like 'em more on the slender side, right?" he says as he holds out his hand as big as a plate. I put the three hundred in it.

"Yeah, slender will be cool," I say.

"Yo, those Lucky Strikes you smokin'?"

"Ah, yeah…"

"Give me one of those, brother," he says. So I give him one and he holds it between his sausage-sized fingers and looks at it admiringly. "My old man used to smoke Luckies," he says. Then he pops it in his mouth. "Give me a light." I light it. He takes a deep drag and coughs out half of it.

"Damn, that's a real man's cigarette," he says, and he gives me a wink before he gets back in the car. Maria flips me the finger as they drive away.

39

Although it was meant to be, I can't accept it anyway and have to take it further down, down, down.

"So you're doin' okay, then?"

"Yeah, Dad of course I'm okay," and I hear Leo's and some other kids' excited conversation and laughter in the background and music playing.

"What have you guys been doing?"

"Dad…"

"Just tell me, please."

"Ya know, skateboarding, some artwork…"

"Leo's mom make you dinner?"

"She doesn't make dinner Dad, the cook makes dinner."

"But she eats with you."

"Yes, Dad…"

"What did you have?"

"Dad, Jesus, we had some pasta."

"What kind?"

"I don't know, meat-sauce…"

"Better than mine?"

"Come on Dad, no, okay? Can I go now?"

And I hear a girl giggling right next to the phone.

"Is that Carla next to you?"

"Dad, stop being a pervert."

"Don't call me that! Ever again!"

"Dad, calm down."

"Just don't call me that."

"Okay, Dad. I'm sorry. I gotta go, okay…"

And it's just my heavy breathing into the phone and silence on his end with music and laughter in the background and I know he's waiting for me to let him go back to his fun, back to his life, back to not worrying about me.

"Okay," I say, "I'm sorry too. I'm glad you're having a good time over there. I love you."

"Love you too, Dad. Bye."

I hang up the phone and now, in my wretched rationalization, it's all right for me to take the other three hundred from the drawer and head to a strip club. And as I grab the dough and the car keys, Shnooky sits by the door and gives me a last pleading look. *Why do you have to go? Why?*

"I can't talk. I can't talk," I say. "Don't even look at me." And I walk out.

I'm on the 170 North into the Valley before I'm even conscious of it. Just get it done. Just get it done. Just get it done. *Just get what done?* Can't hear that voice, sorry. Here, off the Sherman way exit. West? Yeah, the little map on the ad showed it was west. Good. I remembered the directions. Don't wanna get lost and freak out. I'm that close, I feel it. Tense and hell bent.

It's fuckin' ugly out here, dank and foggy, nothin' but crap fast food joints and salvaged auto parts. Better that way. I feel ugly too. And I see the big, grey, cement warehouse on the corner with neon pink, green and black on the walls. Totally Nude. Video tapes. Talk Booths. Show Girls. Pussy, ass and tittie parts. Where do I park? They got a drive-in garage with free valet parking. No thanks. Better I park down the street for a quick getaway. Get away from what? *Get away from yourself.* Shut up.

I park halfway down the dark, dismal street with fences and barbed wire on either side. I walk up to the strip club, with the name 'Déjà vu' in big black letters on the entrance marquee. Now if that isn't perversely profound, as if it's screaming at me... *you've already been here in your life, Dave, understand? Already been, get it? Go home.*

But it blows by with the stank night breeze as I walk up, pay the pink-haired, pimple-faced girl at the door with the pin-head, muscle-bound bouncer next to her, twenty for the cover and two drink minimum.

'Comfortably Numb' by Pink Floyd is soaring out of the sound system as I see past the DJ booth and revolving disco balls hanging down to the floodlit, mirrored stage where a tall, tanned skinny girl with stringy, bleached blonde hair and fake, softball-sized tits slinks around on six-inch platform heels, caressing the three shiny dance poles like they are all huge cocks under her control.

She looks as stoned as the song suggests. The black fluorescent lights shine down from the ceiling so her tiny, white thong glows purple as she glides it down over her tight, tattooed ass cheeks like she could care less about the guys sitting around the edge of stage, leering and jeering and tossing dollar bills down. I feel a lump in my throat. Run or be sucked in. Run or be sucked in. Run or be sucked in. And I just stand there as she squats down, legs spread, on the edge of the stage and idly fondles with her shaved pussy. *I'm so bored and stoned. I bet Dave is the only one that could really fuck me, really fuck me long and hard...*

And now I'm sitting down at one of the cheap, fake wood tables on a fake, red velvet chair, my eyes fixed on her, mesmerized with all the other desperate horn dogs in the dark as she licks her fingers, draws them across her nipples, gives her ass a soft slap then crawls around scooping up the bills.

And the wannabe radio DJ barks out from the booth, "Let's hear it for Samantha!" as she slinks off the stage and I stay for the next dancer and the next song and the flat club soda in the orange fluorescent drink cup that the waitress brings over, looking odd just because she has clothes on. I slap down a ten-dollar tip from my roll of three hundred in her palm like I'm some big shot with all my lap dance moola while my head is screaming, *I'm so sick of you, you stupid motherfucker!* And I remember someone once told me if you don't think you are supposed to be somewhere, ask God to come with you and if God says, "No," then you aren't supposed to be there. So God is not here... and who the fuck do I think I'm listening to?

So I sit there sucked in and girls come and go and dance and strip to rock and rap and rave and trip hop as the DJ calls them out; Summer, Honey, Ikira and Fiona who tweaks around to some crazed, computerized outer space beat with a Satanic background female vocal repeating, "Do you know how I feel when I fuck on cocaine?" over and over and over and it's so intense it scares me but makes me wanna go there too and lap dances are offered but I'm not ready, not ready to be humiliated and cum in my pants or not get hard at all or whatever the fuck I think might happen back in the forbidden fantasy rooms. Definitely not just a good time, a fun time, a lusty happy few minutes with a young sexy stripper. No, no, no, for me it's way more serious. I'm on a mission run by the monster that has taken over, leaving me way, way, way in the back seat.

"Put your hands together for Holly!" the DJ says and I come

back to focus to see a gymnast's figure with a gangster snarl in a schoolgirl outfit, skipping out to a song by the band 'Sublime' and I know it's one of Max's favourites but I can't remember the name and I think of calling him up while Holly grabs a dance pole and swings around it then locks her hard brown thighs on, shimmies up and hangs upside down while her plaid skirt flops over her tight stomach and shows her bare ass that has hot red and lime DayGlo streaks painted on each cheek and I'm staring, eyes hooded and biting my lip feeling like Agualung, feeling like Steppenwolf, feeling like a dirty old man, feeling like...

And I go off in my head again when I'm sixteen, in my old house at two in the morning and I'm in my bedroom peaking on chocolate mescaline and I have a black light buzzing deep florescent purple on the ceiling painted with DayGlo stars and spaceships. And I'm with my girlfriend, Holly. Her name was Holly and we're listening to 'Good Morning Little Schoolgirl' by the band 'Ten Years After.' We're sixty-nining and as she's giving me a long, slow psychedelic blow-job, I'm licking her pussy and finger-painting her ass cheeks with red and lime DayGlo. Red and lime DayGlo. And everything is throbbing and throbbing and throbbing. Then I start to cum and as I feel myself cuming and melting and melting and cuming, I lift my head because I think my eyes are rolling completely around in circles. Then I see that the bedroom door is cracked open and my father is standing there with his hand stuck in his plaid pyjamas, biting his lip, watching with hooded eyes, the same hooded eyes that I'm watching with my hand on my…

"Wanna dance?

"Huh?"

"A lap dance?"

And I get up, destined to my own doom.

"No, I need a lot more than a lap dance," I say, and as I walk out she calls behind me, "Fine, I hope you find it, ya old freak."

I'm in the car and it's started to rain. I'm headed downtown to push the sick blood passed on to me from my father out of my veins, the only way I ever knew how. It's a done deal now. What was I waiting for, anyway? And that demon voice in my head says, *Come on, Dave, we knew it would come to this…*

And I'm off the ramp at Alvarado like a 'Skinner's Rat' finding his way back through the maze even though it's been years and years, the behaviour is still ingrained, etched so deep and yeah, I have a cigarette dangling from my lips and my 'Coltrane Plays The Blues' CD on because it makes everything feel so much more perfectly desperate with the rain coming down harder and the lights reflecting on the wet slick, black, garbage-strewn street.

I feel a nauseous comfort like I'm coming home to hell again as I drive past the Hollywood Express Inn, over Beverly Boulevard, past the Winchell's Doughnuts and the Royal Viking Hotel where my friend Bobbie overdosed. I cross over Third Street and come on down the hill towards the infamous drug haven of downtown, MacArthur Park, which I only knew from a song by the actor Richard Harris when I was a kid growing up in New York.

It was some drippy acid love poem he was reciting to orchestra music, some Hippie shit, and I scream out over the wailing saxophone, "MacAuthur Park is melting in the rain..." and I know there are tears in my eyes because the emotions have to build and build and build until I stick the needle in my vein... right, I mean that's how it is supposed to go and I look through my tears, through the smoke, through the windshield wipers fending off the pelting torrents as I come up on Sixth Street.

I'm lookin' for a dealer to buy some bags or balloons or foil or whatever the fuck they're selling the heroin in these days but the park seems vacant and the sidewalks are empty and it looks like nobody is out on the filthy street, save a drenched bum or two pushing a shopping cart. Why can't I find one? Maybe they won't come up to the new Toyota 4-Runner as quick as they did to my beater Plymouths and Dodges in the old days. If I was in the Scamp they'd be racing up to me, coming out of the building stairwells or wherever they hide in the fucking rain, I think, and I'm pissed off that I'm in a new car and it doesn't even seem odd that I am because all I want is the dope, the dope, the dope.

I pull over and sit and watch and wait, desperate, crying and smoking and the jazz playing and me knowing this is really it, I'm really gonna do it, I'm gonna cop as many bags as I can and go back to the Royal Viking and get loaded and maybe I'm gonna stop and maybe I'm gonna blow through all that money in the bank for weeks on end until I hear Bobbie callin' my name and I hear a cool whisper in the back of my head... *Max will be fine. He can live with Leo's family. They love him, Laurie said they did. He'll be better off without you...*

I shut Shnooky completely out like she never even existed. I have to. Shnooky. No! Don't think of her. Shnooky. No! Don't think of her. There is no Shnooky. There is no Shnooky. There never was...

And the rain plummets down as I sit and wait in desperation for my destiny with demise. Oblivion. Obliteration. Blot it all out. Better for me to die...

It feels so intense and so dramatic that it makes me think of a scene, a scene I wrote in the movie about Max and me.

Keri's friends have gotten together and decided I'm not fit to bring him up by myself because I'm just too crazy to cope and they call in the child welfare department and put pressure on me. I have to give Max to Keri's friend, Barbara, until I get a job, a place to live and get it together or I will loose him for good. I can't get it together and I can't cope. So in the scene, I drive down to Alvarado and Sixth Street to buy some heroin and fucking show them with an overdose. It's afternoon. It's not raining and I don't have Coltrane on. I have the Rolling Stones' 'Monkey Man' blasting out of a cheap cassette deck. I'm not crying, I'm in a furious rage, tearing through traffic, honking my horn…

And now I start to think, this is so much more heart-wrenching and painful, the way it's happening now, with the rain and the jazz in the wee hours on the empty street. And there is no dope to be found. Much more dramatic! I should go home and re-write that scene. It would make it a much better movie.

Then it hits me. How fucking absurd is that? I'm ready to die and I'm thinking of how to re-write that scene.

"God help me… please! God help me. And I sit there hopeless, waiting to die, just waiting for it to be over when I feel a surge come over me, a surge of warmth through my body, stronger and more pure than any drug, followed by laughter and tears and more laughter and more tears because now I hear a chorus of voices; my mom, Keri and even my father saying…

Go home, go home, Dave, go home…"

And tapping on my window is a bug-eyed Mexican kid, in a soaked black bandanna, LA Raider's jersey and baggy jeans, holding an umbrella in one hand and some of what I know is dope clenched in the other. But I'm safe now.

"Hurry up, hurry up, whadddya need?" he says, looking up and down the street with frantic jerks of the neck. I hand him the rest of my pack of Luckies and say, "Nothing, nothing man, take these…"

I'm back home like it was all a bad dream, walking through

the door. Shnooky is jumping up with her paws on my legs and I'm bending down and holding them with my hands as she whimpers and kisses my face...

Oh Daddy, oh Daddy, oh Daddy...

"It's okay, Shnooky, it's okay... I'm okay now."

Early the next morning we go for a run up Bronson Canyon. The stream is rushing with white water and the dirt trail is a deeper brown from the last night's rainfall, and the wild grass and plants on either side are covered with thousands of tiny, diamond droplets with rainbow colours shooting through them as they glisten under the warming sun and the hills are every shade of green with dots of yellow daisies and mustard flowers blooming, and as Shnooky stops to sniff and pee, I reach out and wipe my hand over some tall, sweet fennel...

May I please, Mother Nature?

Of course, my son, of course...

And I bring my hand to my face and christen it with the water from the heavens and take in deep breaths of the cleansed air and I know, I know, I know deep into my soul that I have been granted another reprieve as we continue up the trail, and the birds sing and the bunnies hop and the lizards scurry and it is a glorious spring day.

40

So I go up for more commercials and get close but don't get 'em; too old, not old enough, too edgy, not edgy enough, too quirky, not quirky enough, too handsome, not handsome enough... and that's how it goes and so what? And I keep writing bits and pieces and get started and think it's a movie then find out it's only an idea and I start on something else and I hear Tony made a deal with his story and so what? And I go on a few dates here and there but I'm not for her or she's not for me and I don't know if I'll ever find another woman to be with and so what? And we look for houses everywhere from Silverlake to Mar Vista and they're too expensive or too shabby and we can't find the right one and so what?

We go on, our little family goes on and I tell Max that maybe we should move up to northern Maine near my cousin Cindy's farm where we could get a house with more than twenty acres for less than fifty thousand and I could get a job as a carpenter's helper and write at night and he could learn pottery or sculpturing after school from the local artists and we could live off the land and dig our own clams in the bay and get fresh lobsters, and live relaxed in nature with no pressure, and Max tells me that half-way through the first winter it would turn into 'The Shining' and I'd be chasing him around in the snow with an axe.

I tell him I've changed and he says, "Yeah, Dad, but not that much," and I laugh because he's right and I don't know what's gonna happen but I have faith, I have faith, I keep the faith.

You are changing, Dave…

Then one morning when I'm in the Mayfair market buying a hunk of the eighteen-dollar-a-pound Parmesan cheese that I used to steal, which is the best amends I can do without actually confessing to the crimes, I hear this woman's deep, sexy voice with a thick Long Island, New York accent over my shoulder say, "Oh, buying the expensive cheese, you must be doing all right for yourself."

I turn around to see Marni, this svelte, busty real dame of a woman in her fifties, with cat-like hazel eyes and tousled eggplant hair, dressed in a tight Versace suit.

Marni used to be a Playboy Bunny in the early seventies. She married and divorced some millionaire record company magnate, who was beating the shit out of her. Then she moved to Hollywood and got interested in producing TV. Couldn't deal with the prime-time network jerk-offs, so she started putting together these soft porn vignettes for late night cable when I met her as a possible writer for hire. Even with my experience in that field, so to speak, I could not write a passable script. Couldn't get the formula, kept going off on my own tangent.

She gave me more than a few chances, too. "I love your writing," she would say, "it's edgy, it's funny, it's dirty... but it just doesn't fit with what I'm doing here."

"I'll show ya what fits," I'd say back and she'd answer, "Try it, big shot," and we'd go on that way, flirting, but it never amounted to anything and she said if she was ten years younger I'd be all over her and maybe she was right. But we became friends and she had Max, me and Shnooky over for dinner a few times and I helped her son Gary with his cocaine problem... then we lost touch like people do when one wants a relationship and the other doesn't.

"Last time I saw you, you couldn't rub two nickels together," she says as I stand there with the cheese in my hand. "You really gonna buy that or are ya gonna stick it in your pocket?"

"I'm buyin' it."

"Then give me a hug, tell me about yourself. How's Maxy? How's the puppy?"

We hug and I tell her Max is doing well in school, Shnooky is all grown up and beautiful, waiting in the car and I tell her about my dad dying, that I got a little money.

"Any money from the writing?"

"A little, not much."

"Don't worry, it will happen. The way you're gonna make it is by doin' your own thing."

"Yeah, I guess..."

"You guess? I'm tellin' ya it's gonna happen. Remarried yet?"

"No."

And she confesses she had big designs on me back in the day but now she's with a much handsomer, younger... and richer man.

"Thanks, Marni."

"What can I say, Dave, you blew it! Me and him are producing game shows now, a lot of money in game shows."

Then I ask about Gary and she tells me he is doing great, no drugs, and working as a real estate agent.

"I've been trying to buy a house for months," I say. And I tell her what I've been looking for and how much I have to spend and she whips out her cell phone.

"You have to talk to Gary, I mean right away," she says. "He just found a place yesterday... you're gonna love it... he dragged me over there, wanted me to buy it as an investment..."

"And it has a guest house?" I say.

"It has a great guest house with the most charming couple already in... I can't believe I ran into you like this, Dave, I'm tellin' ya, this is your lucky day."

"Where is it?"

"Right over the hill in Studio City."

"In the Valley?"

"Hey, don't knock the Valley. This is the deal of the century we're talkin' here. But you have to act on it, right away."

"Okay, okay, I'll talk to him," I say as she makes the call.

"Gary, honey, you're not gonna believe who I have next to me," she says, and she fills him in on the info and hands me the phone and the first thing he says to me is, "Dave, I have the house you are gonna buy."

41

I follow Gary's directions to meet him in front of Jerry's Deli on Ventura Boulevard because excluding late night hell rides to strip clubs (that I don't plan on revisiting) I don't know the Valley. "You will, because this is gonna be your new neighbourhood, Dave," is what Gary says and I have my cheque-book that I picked up at home because he also tells me we are gonna put in an offer on the spot.

"Dress nice, okay?"

So I put on some khakis and a button-down blue shirt. 'Nice casual', as they say in the stupid fucking commercial business. Anyway, I don't know what to expect.

Gary used to be a petty criminal con-artist; collecting money for bookies, shoplifting designer suits and re-selling them, ripping people off in Pyramid scams, dealing fake ecstasy in nightclubs... anything to keep his own game going, but he seemed he was already at the end of that game when I told him my story. He seemed ready to give up. Funny how sometimes you can help someone younger by telling them how bad it got for you. It can save them years of

324

added misery… if they're ready. So I'm glad he's using his con artist personality now, legally as a real estate agent, and I know Marni would never fuck me over. And when I pull up to Gary's and see him standing outside holding a briefcase, dressed sharp in a grey pin-stripe suit, looking handsome, tan and healthy I'm reassured all the more… but I have to kid around just a bit.

"You buy that suit?" I say out of the window. He flashes a big grin and points his finger at me.

"Funny, funny, I like that," he says. "Thank God those days are over… right?" And he struts up to the car.

"Nice. Limited version, huh? Like the colour."

"Yeah, I came into a little money…"

"Just at the right time, too," he says as he gets in, puts his briefcase between his knees and shakes my hand. "You look good, younger than last time I saw ya. You doin' somethin'? Botox? Chemical peel around the eyes or somethin'?"

"You must sell a lot of houses, Gary," I say, and we both laugh.

"Come on, let's go," he says. "I'll leave my car here in the parking lot, we'll ride over together." Then he pulls a white paper take-out bag from his jacket pocket and opens it.

"Want one? Jerry's chocolate Rugala, the best. Jay loves these. That's the guy you're buyin' the house from." And as I take one from the bag and say, "So you're sure I'm buyin' this house, aren't you?" Shnooky, who has been lounging in the back seat, sniffs out the Rugala and sticks her head between us.

"You brought the dog?" he says.

"Gary, this dog is like my wife, I bring her everywhere."

"Dave, don't say that in front of the guy, okay?"

"Don't worry," I say, and I bite off one half of the Rugala and feed the other half to Shnooky.

"Hey, you do treat her like your wife. She is very cute, I gotta say. Nice eyes, looks like she's wearin' makeup on 'em."

"You're too much, Gary," I say. "Where are we goin'?"

And we go back down Ventura to Whitsett Avenue and take a left past the little public golf club.

"You'll be playin' here soon."

"I don't play golf."

"You might take it up."

And he tells me to take a left down Woodbridge Avenue. I look at the houses. They just look like regular houses, nice, decent with well-kept lawns and little flower gardens and picket fences and as I'm thinking this may be boring but at least safe and peaceful, Gary fills me in on the perks.

"Ya got Ventura just a few blocks up with Ralph's market and Starbucks or Coffee Bean, whatever ya like. Sushi restaurants up the ass. I know you like Sushi. And then down a few blocks on Riverside you got Whole Foods market. You go for that health food shit, right? Where is your kid in school now?"

"Santa Monica,"

"Santa Monica?"

"He's in a private school."

"You're rollin' in it, huh?"

"He's on a scholarship, Gary…"

"That's cool, that's cool, I always knew he was smart. So ya got the 101, two seconds away to the 405 or ya can jump over Coldwater Canyon right to Beverly Hill in ten minutes, maybe fifteen and take Olympic down to Santa Monica. I mean, this house is perfectly situated for you and ya can practically skip to Hollywood for your auditions. You still doin' those?"

"Sometimes."

"Book anything lately?"

"No."

"You will, you will because once you get the house, the work is gonna come, trust me, and get this, the house is a pocket-listing which means it's not on the market and Jay, who trusts me completely because I've gained the respect from always seeing him on the Holidays, is relying on me to find the right buyer."

"Holidays?" I say.

"Come on, Dave, you know, the holidays. Rosh Hashanah, Yom Kippur…"

"I know what they are but I'm not Jewish, Gary."

"With a beak like yours?"

"My Dad was a half Jew. He had the nose. My Mom was Scottish, so I'm like a quarter Jew."

"Well, now you're a full Jew, okay? I already called him and said you were an old friend of the family. Just follow my lead and this will be a slam-dunk."

"I haven't even seen the place, Gary."

"I'm tellin' you, you'll love it. Two bedroom, two bath, gleaming hardwood floors, fireplace in the living room with a den and a nice guest house in the back already rented, and I'm gonna talk him down from the four hundred and fifty asking price… Come on, what's not to love? You got your cheque book?"

"Yeah…"

"How much in the bank?"

"Forty-six, forty-seven thousand…"

"Perfect. Good credit? You're payin' off the car, right? Finance or leasing?"

"Leasing."

"Great. Got a financial lender?"

"Ah, no…"

"I got the guy, best financial lender around. I can hook you up with him this afternoon after Jay takes the offer. Make a right on this street. This is it."

And I pull over next to a fat Magnolia tree in the sidewalk and he points to a sweet little sage-coloured, wood and stucco house with a white picket fence in front and a freshly cut lawn with lavender and rosemary bushes under the windows.

"Nice, right?"

"Yeah, it looks nice," I say, and I feel my heart beat a bit faster.

"Let's go inside, I got the key. Jay will be here in a few minutes... but no dog, please, until the deal is a lock."

"Shnooky, you gotta stay," I say to her. "But you can come in soon, okay! Look at the lawn while I'm inside, that could be yours." And she wags her tail. *Okay, Daddy, okay. I like it.*

"How much do you talk to her?" Gary says.

"A lot," I say, and we get out of the car and walk up to the house.

And it's nice inside, too, better than any other house I've seen for the price by far. I don't know where the fuck Gary got the term, gleaming, but the hardwood floors are newly stained and clean. The kitchen is small but has tile floors and granite counters and Gary says Jay is gonna leave the stove, the refrigerator and the dishwasher. The living room has a high A-frame wood ceiling with two small skylights and a red brick fireplace with a maple-wood mantle. The two bedrooms are of equal size and I already know Max will want the one with the bathroom attached. I'll be fine with the one in the hall because it has a nice big bathtub. Then we go to a little den area.

"Perfect office or TV room," Gary says. And he slides the glass door open to a small cement back patio with a couple of flowerbeds full of weeds.

"Needs a little work back here," Gary says as we walk out. "You could make this all lawn or a new deck or whatever." Then I see a cute, rustic-type cabin.

"There's the guest house. Got a couple in, payin' a thousand a month and they love it. Nice big bedroom loft upstairs, living room, kitchen and bathroom downstairs with their own back patio. Jay says they're beggin' to stay. You could probably raise the rent to twelve hundred. And get this, they're both school teachers so they could probably help your kid with his homework." Then he shows me the garage with the sinking roof and old wood doors from when the house was first built inside along with a funky old splintered-wood desk and fat, cracked, brown leather chair.

"It could use a little work but you got a lot of storage room here. Jay is gonna leave this desk and chair here, too. They could be antiques. Who knows?" Then he shows me the dusty cement and drywall laundry room with a run-down washer and dryer.

"Get another year out of these babies, easy." And as we walk back to the main house, he says, "It needs some touch-up work here and there. I mean, of course it's not perfect…"

"I want it," I say as we go inside.

"I knew you would," he says. "And I'm happy that you're the guy that's gonna get it because I owe ya a big solid from when you helped me back in the day."

"Thanks, Gary."

"Hey, I was goin' down a bad road and ya helped me."

And I follow him into the kitchen where he slaps his briefcase on the counter, pops it open and pulls out a purchase agreement.

"I got it all filled out, deposit, first loan amount, balance and total. We're offerin' four thirty-five down from the four fifty so you'll have to write the offer cheque for twelve grand, okay?"

"Okay."

"You got it in the bank, right? I mean you can't bullshit me now. This is it."

"I got it, Gary…"

"Okay," he says as he hands me a pen. "Sign it and put your initials there on the bottom where it says, Buyers Initials."

And I sign and initial just as a pudgy, very conservative no-nonsense looking guy in Levi's Dockers and a polo shirt comes in. Gary strides up to him.

"Jay, my man, he loves it!" he says as he hands Jay the Rugala. "Don't tell the wife I gave you these." And Jay smiles as he digs a hand in the bag and fishes one out.

"Dave meet Jay. Jay, Dave," Gary says, and Jay pops a whole Rugala cookie into his mouth, wipes his hand on his pants and shakes mine. *God, don't let him see I'm a crazed freak,* I pray to myself as I look him in the eye, honest, humble, sincere and say, "I really like the house…"

Jay nods as he chews and I can't tell if he gets where I'm coming from or if he's just enjoying his Rugala so I say, and I honestly do feel it from the bottom of my heart, I say, "And I'd love to live here with my son…"

Jay stops chewing and meets my gaze. I don't know if he gets me or hates me. He is studying me, though. I don't blink, I don't look away. I have nothing to hide. I am telling the truth. I see something register on his face. He has made his decision but I can't tell what it is. I don't want the tears to come down but I have them there, right at the edge of my eyelids. Real tears, ready to go. Is he going to say something? Should I say something more?

Then Gary puts up both his hands and says, "Listen, let's cut to the chase. Dave is a great guy, he's perfect for the house, and we got the offer already filled out… I mean, come on, Jay, you're a Jew, I'm a Jew, he's a Jew… we're all Jews here, let's do some business!"

And as I'm thinking, I hope he doesn't ask me any questions about Temple or the holidays, and making a mental note not to get a Christmas tree for at least two years, Jay picks up the purchase agreement and pops another Rugala in his mouth. And as he studies the offer, he chews and chews and looks up at me and nods again, and Gary nudges me and winks as I stand there with a frozen half-smile, thinking… try to be normal, try to be normal, try to be normal. Then Jay says, "I have to talk to my wife, I'll let you know this afternoon."

42

The excitement and fear are battling it out in my body. I'm trembling when I pick up Max from school. But beyond it all I have a sense of calm and faith that all will work out as it should… but I am trembling and Max sees it as he gets in the car.

"Dad, what's up?"

"Oh, nothing… just ah…" and I let out an involuntary laugh.

"Dad, are you losin' it?"

"No, I'm cool…" And I wanna tell him everything from meeting Marni to Gary to the house to Jay, and if I didn't shoplift Parmesan cheese from the Mayfair back when, none of this would have happened. None of what, though? What if it doesn't happen? How many times have I waited and waited and waited… and lost? So I have to keep quiet. I can't let Max down again, not after losing the house on Willoughby. Even though Gary told me it was a great sign that Jay wanted to speak to his wife.

"If he didn't say that, then I woulda been worried," he said. "He wants to do it, Dave, trust me. Jay is just one of those guys that has to check in with his wife on everything. He has to check in on how much toilet paper he uses, ya know what I'm sayin'? Six sheets, seven sheets, he tells her. You think he told her about the Rugala? Every fuckin' cookie. If he didn't, it would be like cheating for him. Believe me I know this guy… and I gotta hand it to ya, when you got all emotional and said how you would love to be there with your son, you choked him up. He stopped chewin'. Did ya see him? I thought he was gonna cry but that would have been bad if he did, he would have been embarrassed and the deal would have been off. That's why I cut in and did the Jew routine. I'm tellin' ya it worked. Together we got him. So here's what you do, ya pick up your kid from school, play catch or something, watch TV, relax and get ready for my call tellin' ya that you're a new homeowner…"

And I laugh a soft, high-pitched laugh again as Gary's voice rings in my head while I drive up Olympic Boulevard in the afternoon traffic, almost by the Braille method.

"Dad, you're on drugs again," Max says.

"No, I'm not."

"Then what's going on?"

He looks back at Shnooky like she's gonna give him some inside information and I hear her tail thumping on the seat like she's not allowed to say.

"I'll tell you soon."

"Tell me what?"

"Please…" and I'm picturing him in my mind, walking into his new bedroom, his new bedroom, his new bedroom…

"Dad…"

"Just… don't worry, don't worry, okay? Let's just go home, play catch or something, watch TV, relax…"

"Dad, we never play catch…"

"Okay, okay, so we'll go home and we'll skateboard or you'll skateboard and I'll watch or we'll just take it easy… take it easy… take it easy…"

"Dad, you sound really strange. I think you should just tell me…"

"I know. Play some music. Put something nice on."

"Okay, Dad." And he takes out 'My War', an old 'Black Flagg' album from his CD case, slips it in and cranks it to torture level trying to get the information out of me, but I don't give in.

"Tell me, Dad!"

"No!"

"Tell me!"

"No!"

"Tell me!"

"No!"

And that's how it goes with Max demanding and me protesting and Henry Rollins ranting and screaming all the way home.

I'm exhausted, on my knees in the bedroom. Max has hit the fridge and is gobbling up last night's rib roast, even though I asked him not to. There is no co-operation. No deal. He has me over a barrel but I can't tell until I know. I can't.

"I wanted to save the rest of that for tonight."

"Only if you tell me…"

"Fine. Take it."

"And I'm eating a big hunk of this Parmesan cheese, too."

"No. It's too expensive…"

"Dad, all you gotta do is say…"

"Take it. Eat it. I don't care."

And Max eats as I pray and the voices in my head, of heaven and hell, battle out my fate.

Too good to be true. Too good to be true. Too good to be true.

No it's not. No it's not. No it's not.

Don't deserve it. Don't deserve it. Don't deserve it.

Yes you do. Yes you do. Yes you do.

"Dad, what are you doing in there?"

"Just cleaning up…"

The phone rings.

"I got it Max…" And believe me, I don't get off my knees, not for this one. I pick up the phone.

"Hello…"

"Dave, Gary here."

"Yeah, Gary."

"I talked to Jay."

"Yeah… and?"

"And he didn't accept the offer." And I grab the pillow and I scream into it.

"Dave… are ya with me?"

"Yeah… he didn't accept the offer."

"But…" Gary says, "he put in a counter offer for four hundred and forty so if ya wanna sign off on it, I'll call him back and we'll do the deal."

"Do the deal?"

"Yeah, Dave, if ya want it for that price, which I'm tellin' ya, is still the best deal in town, the house is yours."

"Mine?"

"Goin' into escrow, my man, all I need is your signature of acceptance and the deposit cheque and you'll be a new homeowner in thirty days. Are you in?"

"Yeah… I'm in, I'm in!"

"Can you meet me?"

"Where?"

"Back at the house."

"When?"

"Right away."

"I'll be there," I say and I hang up the phone, get up off my knees and walk into the living room where Shnooky is gnawing on a fresh rib bone that Max has dropped on the floor.

"Dad, sorry, don't get mad."

And I just stare at him, breathing easy, staying calm.

"Was it bad news?" he says.

"You wanna come for a ride?" I say.

"What for?"

"So I can tell you."

"Why don't you tell me here?"

"Because I can't."

"Why not?"

"Because I have to show you."

"Because you have to show me what, Dad?"

"Because I have to show you... our new house!"

43

Of course Max, being used to Hollywood, said the Valley looked stupid, ugly and boring and that he didn't know what he could do there. He said he was never going to hang out on Ventura Boulevard so I better be prepared to drive him to Melrose a lot, but the look on his face when he saw his good-sized bedroom with his own bathroom told me he was willing to make the sacrifice.

He scoured the whole house with a keen eye, pointing out which light fixtures we should replace, how the kitchen should be remodelled, what colour he wanted to paint his bedroom walls and how his bathroom tiles should be changed. Then we went through the den and he mused over whether I should use it as an office to write in or whether it would be the TV room. And we stepped out to the back patio where he told me I better get busy weeding the flower beds and planting something cool like cactus plants or Birds of Paradise, which he remembered as his mom's favourite. And as soon as he saw the garage, he decided he was going to turn it into his own art studio, and that we better get to work on fixing up the roof and putting in a bathroom because he would be spending a lot of time in there.

"And a heater for the winter, Dad."

"Can we just move in first?"

"Okay, Dad."

"So you're sure you like it?"

"Yeah…"

"What?"

"Yes, Dad, I like it."

"Love it?"

"Dad, I like it, come on."

Then the tenants came back to the guest house, both in their early twenties, a black guy and white girl, dressed cool, in Max's opinion, with long Rasta hairdos, and they were very polite to me, expressing their wish to stay. And they had a dog, a shaggy Golden Retriever, named Carrie. I had to ask, "Do you spell that with a C or K?" and it was a C, but an interesting omen just the same, so we let Shnooky come back and meet her. They barked and played and rolled around on the ground like sisters, so it looked like an okay deal for all of us.

I got the loan from Gary's lender guy with what they told me was a great interest rate with no points attached (whatever the fuck that meant).

I signed and initialled page after page of contracts I couldn't begin to understand, with blind trust that I wasn't getting fucked over (not recommended to all) and Gary assured me, swearing on his mother and her mother that I was the luckiest guy in the world for getting such a great deal. We did the appraisal, the inspection, got insurance, all that stuff. My cheque for the ten percent cleared, the escrow went through and thirty-four days later Gary handed me the keys.

"Congratulations, Dave!"

And we moved in with the help of these two tweakers that must have been up on crystal meth for a month that I hired from an ad I saw, tacked onto a telephone pole on Beechwood. 'Movers, fast and cheap' was what it said and they had everything packed in boxes, taped and in their old graffiti-covered truck, with every piece of furniture from the apartment, before I could even point it out.

"You guys would make great robbers."

"Yeah, you know any place?"

"Ah, no... but maybe I should ride in the truck with you."

"Don't worry, man, you got nothin' here worth stealin'."

And they both gave toothless cackles and picked at their faces and pushed back their mullets. Yeah, ha, ha, ha, here's your hundred each... and we got the job done.

They slapped everything down in the house and left me with a promise to come back in a few months or so to see if I upgraded to anything worth their while, since I got a "New house and all," they figured I'd be, "redecoratin' soon enough." Funny guys. I took down the license plate number of their truck, just in case, and we settled in, organizing the house the best we could with all our old stuff.

So we needed new furniture. I was the first to admit it but we got into the house on a wing and a prayer and with what I had left in the bank, I was more concerned about eating than redecorating. At least I had Keri's couch re-upholstered, got Max a new dresser and new bed. His other remodelling plans had to wait, including the designer couches, tables, chairs, six-burner steel stove and double glass door refrigerator, that he picked out on his internet research.

"I hope you make a lot of money to satisfy your taste when you get older, Max. I hope you do better than me."

"Dad, don't worry, I will."

"And I hope you take care of me."

"Dad, I'm gonna throw you out on the curb and drive away... just kidding, I'll put you in some home or something."

"You better kill me before you put me in a home. I get sick, you pull the fucking plug!"

"Dad, take it easy! Pull the couch over here for now."

We arranged everything the best we could. It looked decent mainly because Max was the arranger and he got his way turning the den into the TV room and I set up my little desk for writing in my bedroom.

"I need a desk in my bedroom, Dad."

"You have that old one in the garage. Gary said it was an antique."

"That's for my art studio. I need one in my bedroom."

"I know, but for now you use your Mom's desk."

"That's gonna be our dinner table."

"It's our dinner table too, okay? It was in the apartment."

"I don't want this to be like the apartment."

"It won't be. Shut up. Go to your room."

"Fine. You go to your room."

"Fine."

And we both march to our separate rooms, slam our individual doors and Max is laughing and banging on his wall, while I'm laughing and banging on my wall.

"What are you doing in there?"

"What are you doing in there?"

And we both yank our doors open, race into the hall, and chase each other around the living room with Shnooky following, as we run out of the den door, around the back yard, up the driveway, to the front yard and tackle each other and wrestle around on the grass.

Our house!

Our house!

Our house!

44

So our new kitchen is stocked up with Whole Foods goodies. I make Max applewood smoked bacon, scrambled eggs with fresh thyme and sourdough toast for breakfast before we head out on our new car pool route to his friend Simon's house. Since it's 6:45 a.m. we beat the traffic up Coldwater Canyon. We pass a deer crossing sign towards the top.

"Wow, check that out," I say. And as we pass a big cluster of tall shaggy Eucalyptus trees at the top, I say, "Cool, look at those." And we make a sharp right turn onto Mulholland Drive west.

"You know this is called a hairpin turn, don't ya?"

"Sure, Dad, you're a race car driver. Just take it easy, this thing could tip over on this road."

And Mulholland does wind and curve around as we pass more Eucalyptus and pines and palms and driveways that disappear up or down into hidden estates of the rich and famous.

"There was a guy named Mulholland that owned all this property once," I say.

"That's nice, Dad." And if I knew the rest of the story, I'd elaborate but no matter, I feel exuberant on this fresh morning in my new surroundings so I just drive and take in the view of the valleys and the hills and mountains far away. Then Max tells me to take a left into a gated community entrance that looks very ritzy with lush green manicured lawns and flower gardens on either side and a European-style security guard house in the centre.

"Do we need a passport to get in here?"

"Dad, just say you're here to drop me off for car pool."

"Have you been here before?"

"Yes, Dad."

"With who?"

"With Leo."

"Why didn't you tell me?"

"What's the big deal, Dad, you don't have to know everything! Just pull up, I'll do the talking."

"Okay, you talk, Max," I say.

And he does in a calm, mature and friendly fashion to this pit-bull looking security guy with untrusting beady eyes and a shaved head who smiles back at him and says, "Hey, I remember you, kid," and he steps back in the office to call down to Simon's, all the time keeping an eye on me, waiting for me to make one wrong move. I know the type. Stop it. Be grateful for your son's social skills. Learn from him. All you have to do is smile at the guy, and I do.

"Thanks for waiting, sir, you can go down now," he says.

And Max sits back in his seat, relieved I'm behaving as we drive through the massive iron gates into the secluded community of private palaces.

"What does Simon's dad do?" I say.

"I don't know, but he's like one of the richest guys in the world or something."

"Wow…" I say and I'm impressed but I also feel somewhat small and insecure and Max, like he was rehearsing for this moment, just spits out every word I want to hear.

"Dad, Simon is just my friend, okay? It's not that big a deal. The house is way too huge and ugly inside, okay? I like our house better. And Simon never sees his dad because he's away working all the time and you're the best and I love you so much."

"Do it with more feeling," I say.

"No," he says, and he points to a call box under a surveillance camera to the side of another set of iron gates in-between a two-block-long, high stone wall.

"I feel like I'm entering a foreign embassy," I say.

"Dad, just press the buzzer, you crazy person!"

I press it and when I hear, "Security, can we help you?" I say with cheerful vigour, "Hello! Good morning! Max's Dad here to drop him off for car pool."

"Thanks, Dad, you still sound crazy," Max says as the gates open to this enormous compound where we have to drive over a bridge with a revolving water wheel to the side and stream running under it, stocked with multi-coloured carp that flows into a pasture with wild deer lazing around in the early morning dew.

I do feel daunted and dwarfed just getting my little house, and I don't know why some people have so little and some people have so much. But so what? I'm grateful for what I have and I'm here for Max to drop him off at his friend's, that's all.

So I enjoy the enormity of their wealth like I'm on some mini-vacation and we drive up to a big squirting fountain in front of the main house that looks like a fucking fortress. Then this other security guard, some ex-Israeli commando type with a holstered Magnum, walks out to greet Max with a show-dog type female Boxer prancing next to him.

"Dad, hold Shnooky." But she's up and barking.

You rich bitch! You think you're better than me! I come from the streets. I'll kick your coiffed, groomed ass! You prancy, pussy bitch.

"Shnooky, stop. She can't help it if she's rich," I say.

"Okay, Dad keep that to yourself," Max says as he grabs his backpack and jumps out of the car. And as I wave good-bye, this sweet-looking kid, with curly long hair, dressed in jeans, vintage t-shirt and Vans runs out of the house, up to my window.

"Hey, I'm Simon," he says as he offers me his hand and shakes it like a gentleman. "Nice to meet you."

"Hey, Simon, nice to meet you too."

"My Dad said you can just drop Max off every day and we'll take him."

"That sounds cool, thanks."

"And we can bring him back after school, too."

"Wow, that sounds great."

"Well… see ya," he says and he runs over to Max, slaps him on his back like a pal then the Commando points me to another exit of the compound before escorting the boys to a waiting Lincoln Town car. And I drive away feeling an odd sense of ease…

45

Shnooky and I have been running up Bronson Canyon almost every morning for the past six years. It has been our exercise routine, our solace, and our meditation with Mother Nature. We are known there. Two Stone and Purple Tongue. So we miss it, more than anything else, but it just takes too long to make the daily drive there in the morning traffic, run and come back home, especially when I am forcing myself to write or at least try to write, to fucking sit at the desk and scream for five hours if I have to.

But we need to run in the morning after we drop off Max, and being the social butterfly that I am, I don't ask anyone where to go. I just look around. So we find Fryman Canyon off Laurel but it's crowded with too many people in the latest jogging fashion wear, gossiping showbiz, and you need a dog-shit bag and there's a firm leash law so Shnooky is restricted from freely sniffing and old Two Stone can't use his rocks. Too civilized for us. So we try running the streets, up Coldwater, across Ventura and up Valley Vista road which is a nice little hill, only it's in a pristine, stuck-up Beverly Hills wannabe neighbourhood. We get the occasional, nasty, bitchy, better-than-you, yells out of the windows. Put that dog on a leash! Get your dog off my lawn! Clean up that mess! Clean up that Poop! Clean up that Crap!

They never call it shit. Sometimes I yell back, "Call it shit and I'll clean it up!" as I huff up the hill but I don't really intend to because I have my rocks in my hands and no bags. I try to gear it so Shnooky shits in this pachysandra patch between two houses under construction but it doesn't always work that way.

I know I'm gonna have to start cleaning it up soon. These people do call the police and no matter how hard I pray to get along with them, I still know that with me, a dog off leash or pooping on a lawn violation can escalate into a misdemeanor or even a felony. I can easily picture myself flinging a handful of Shnooky's shit into the face of the law, and getting an assault with a stinky weapon charge.

So day by day, we get more organized even though one corner of the living room is still furnished with unpacked boxes. I tell myself I'm gonna get to them, then I tell Max to get to them but neither of us ever gets to them. And sometimes the blame has to fall on the dog.

"Why haven't you unpacked those boxes yet, Shnooky? What do you do around here? Just lie around and eat and sleep. You have to do some work!"

I love you, Daddy, that's a lot of work. Full time.

"Okay, okay. You're right, you're right…"

And I lay down on the floor with her, kiss her nose and scratch her soft, furry tummy and say, "Love, love, love. Love, love, love."

Then I get up and empty out a box myself. And I plant those Birds of Paradise in the back with some purple iris's and I plant some wandering white rose bushes along the picket fence and put some jasmine under the kitchen window by the front door so when they bloom, we'll get the sweet smell as we walk in and out of our house.

I call my brother and sister to give them the good news and our new number.

"When did you buy a house?"

"Couple of months ago, Paul. I tried to call you but you never got back to me."

"I'm on a plane practically every minute of every day, Dave."

"Okay, I'm not mad, just wanted to tell you…"

"I know, I know… listen, Dave, I'm proud of you. Really."

"Thanks…"

"I've been meaning to stay in touch with you but work has been so crazy."

"I know."

"Maybe when things slow down, I'll come visit you at… shit, that's my other line…" Click.

"Okay, Paul, just wanted to give you the number."

And I call Margaret.

"You're in the house?"

"Yeah, we're in."

"Well, congratulations. I never thought you'd pull it off."

"Thanks…"

"Although I hope you know what you're doing. I hope you can afford to stay there."

"I have enough for a couple of months…"

"A couple of months?"

"Something will happen, I have faith."

"It takes a lot more than faith to cover a house mortgage and bills, Dave."

"Well, I need faith first."

"Okay, it's your life. I hope it works out."

"Me too."

And two weeks later I book a commercial for some cell phone company. Not even expecting it, not even knowing why I got the job because that is really how they work out. I went on the first call and they lined me up with a bunch of other middle-aged guys, told us to take our shirts off and asked us if we knew how to swim.

"Yes, I've been swimming my whole life."

"Thank you."

Then on the callback there was the director and the producer and the clients all sitting behind a long table, on cell phones, sipping coffee, eating off their gourmet appetizer platter.

"Just look out into the distance and laugh naturally," says the director.

"Shirt off?"

"No, you can keep your shirt on this time."

"But I just got a body wax..."

And they all laughed and I laughed along with them and they gave me the job, well me and about fifteen other people. I was one of many vignettes in the massive, stressed-out commercial shoot that took place all over LA. And after waiting from six in the morning until six at night, being driven from location to location, bouncing around in the back of the wardrobe truck, dressed up in a Priest's uniform without a clue why, they finally put me on a street corner and handed me a cell phone and some rosary beads.

"Talk into the phone, look off into the distance and smile," says the director.

"Talk to who?"

"Who cares? Talk to God. You're a priest."

"Ya know, it's funny, ten years ago if I put on this uniform, it would have burst into flames," I say, but now nothing is funny, no laughs, just... "We have twenty minutes before the sun sets. Talk into the phone, look off into the distance and fucking smile."

"Okay, okay..."

And I got the thankless job done before the sun went down with overtime for the day, and am hoping for the residuals to come. I mean that's all commercials are about anyway. Residual money.

Meanwhile I get an unexpected letter from Margaret that reads, 'Good Luck. I suggest you try to find a woman to share your life with now,' along with a ten thousand dollar, 'Happy Housewarming' cheque enclosed. And when I call her back to thank her for the money and the suggestion, she tells me she's divorcing Steven, she just caught him cheating on her.

"I still think you should find someone, though," she says. "A good woman for you and Max."

"But what just happened to you?"

"Dave, there's more good women than good men out there. Find one."

"Do you think I'm a good man?"

"Yes, Dave, I do."

46

So I'm driving the kids down Melrose Avenue on a Saturday afternoon to drop them off at the skateboard shop. Max is in the front seat working his CD's like a deejay, while Leo and Simon sit in the back, boppin' their heads to his tunes, both with a hand resting on Shnooky who is sprawled out between them.

As we pass Fairfax High School, I remember the time Max almost got mugged there. He used to skate in the back of the school on weekends with other little skaters and one day he stayed behind to work on some moves while the rest of them went back to the skateboard shop. When I came to pick him up at the shop, they told me he was still at Fairfax High so I drove over there to find him surrounded by five nasty little teenage street punks. So I say in the rearview to Simon and Leo, "Not a good place to skateboard alone, guys. Did Max tell you the story?"

"Yeah, that was so cool, Dave," Leo says. "When you told those kids you were gonna kill them."

"It wasn't right to say that. I lost my temper when I saw them hassling Max. And I didn't say I was gonna kill 'em."

"Oh yeah, Dad, you said, I'll kill any one of you that fucks with my son."

"Okay..." I say and Max looks back at his friends, wide-eyed and excited as I feel a flush of embarrassment.

"He jumped out of the car like a maniac. That's when we had the Scamp. Those fuckers ran so fast. My Dad looked really scary in that car."

"Don't say fucker."

"Sure Dad, you say it all the time."

"Well not as much anymore... and I wasn't that scary."

"Dad, you were. You still are sometimes."

"Well, I don't wanna be. Do you guys think I'm scary?"

And I look in the rearview and see Leo and Simon giving each other nervous looks.

"Dave, I always thought you were cool," Leo says. "But you were kinda scary."

"I thought you were kinda scary too when you used to drive up to school," says Simon. "But I think you're a nice guy now."

And I see in the rearview that he has an earnest look on his face and I see Leo nodding along with him in agreement.

"Definitely one of my favourite dads."

Wow. I'm proud and humbled. All I can say is, "Thanks."

Then Max leans into me with his own exaggerated earnest look and says, "My Dad, the nice guy," but I know he is proud too and happy his friends feel comfortable around me.

I pull up in front of the skateboard shop where I have to double-park because Melrose is mobbed with weekend traffic, and this tricked-out, fire-engine red, pick-up truck with five-foot high monster wheels, pulls right up behind me and blares its row of shiny chrome foghorns it has attached to the top of the cab. I clench the steering wheel like I'm gonna tear it off.

"Dad, don't blow it by screaming at him," Max says and he grabs his skateboard. "Come on, you guys, hurry up. Let's get out."

The kids grab their boards and scramble to get out of the car as the horns blare again and I see this redneck skinhead screaming out of his window.

"Move! Motherfucker!"

Take it easy. Take it easy. Breathe in and out. Don't get crazy. You're past that now. It's in the past.

Then I see Sal, the owner of the skate shop come marching out to the street, and even though he's young and hip, dressed in baggy skate wear with shoulder-length hair, his six-foot-two, two hundred pound plus Brooklyn-born body and wise-guy mug is not something to mess with. He ushers the kids to the sidewalk with one sweep of his arm then points at me and says, "Don't move." Then he walks right up to the guy in the truck. I can't hear what he says to him but the guy doesn't say much back and as Sal walks over to my car, the truck pulls out and goes around.

"How ya doin', Dave?" he says as he leans into the window and shakes my hand. "Where's the dog?"

"In the back," I say and he looks over my shoulder to see Shnooky lounging on the leather like a Queen.

"Oh, yeah, there she is. So friggin' mellow with all this commotion, right?"

"What did you say to him, Sal?"

"Ah, nothin', don't worry about it," he says as he waves traffic around me with a huge hand.

"Thanks."

"Hey, the guy was a moron, swearin' at ya like that when you're with the kids. And you stayed calm, that was the right thing to do." And as I say, "Thanks, Sal," we see the kids standing on the sidewalk, staring at us.

"Maxy, go in the store with your friends," Sal says. "Pick out some decals or somethin', I'm talking to your father." And as Max nods and walks in the store with Leo and Simon, Sal shakes my hand again.

"You doin' a good job, he's a good kid."

"Thanks."

"So what are ya gonna do today?"

"I don't know. I was just droppin' them off. I was gonna go home and clean the house…"

"Clean the house? It's Saturday, dude!" he says, and I laugh a little because hearing Sal say, dude, with his Brooklyn accent always gets me. "Go out and have some fun. Pick up a chick somewhere," he says.

"I don't know where to do that."

"The friggin' Coffee Bean is three blocks down. They got plenty of chicks there."

"Not my age."

"You're as young as you feel, dude!"

"Okay, I'll think about it. I'll be back for the kids around six."

"You got it, Dave. I'll look out for 'em."

"I know, Sal."

And he shakes my hand for the third time then walks back into his store.

Just for the hell of it I drive down Melrose towards the Coffee Bean so at least I can tell Sal I checked it out. And I see a melting pot of girls on both sides of the street. They're everywhere in every size, shape and colour. But they're girls. Kids. Most of them are closer to Max's age than mine. Sixteen, eighteen, maybe I see one twenty-three years old, if that. I look at myself in the rearview. Middle age. You're middle-aged. No big deal. You were young once. I can appreciate their beauty and drive home. Sal says you're only as young as you feel because he's twenty-six years old. I feel fine. I'm healthy. Damn. I'm too old for these girls and I know it.

It's a blessing and a curse. I don't need to just get laid on some bullshit rap with some young hottie; I need a woman in my life. And I stop at the light on Gardner Street, look over at the Coffee Bean. Sure, there's plenty of chicks there just like Sal said, and I wonder what Max would do if he was skateboarding down the block and he saw me trying to pick one up. Embarrassing. Fucking ridiculous.

Then I see a woman in a sleek, black pants suit, strut out with two coffees. Good thing they got lids on 'em, I mean she's really shakin' it, her ass, her tits, her long, raven hair all bouncing as she crosses the street in front of me. She looks Mediterranean or something. She has that dark olive skin and intense face. Shit, she sees me staring at her. Oh, no, she's coming right up to the car, probably gonna tell me to stop gawking or go fuck myself. Why doesn't the light change? Wait, she's smiling. Is she gonna try to pick me up?

"Dave, it's me, Sophie."

"Sophie... holy shit, Sophie!"

"How ya been?"

"Good..."

"You look good."

"You too, I mean I was staring at you..." And she beams a beautiful smile at me.

"I'm off the drugs. Five years."

"Yeah, it's been a little longer for me."

"That's why we look good. What are you doing right now?"

"I, ah, just dropped my kid off and…" Then the light turns green and the horns start honking.

"Take it easy!" Sophie yells at the cars backed up behind me then she points to a little beauty shop on the other side of Gardner.

"That's my store, come over and say hi."

And as I see the wedding ring on her finger, I'm more relieved than disappointed. I mean I'm happy for her. Sophie and I used to just smoke freebase together, anyway. We were just get-high buddies. Maybe we flirted some, but we were never really attracted to each other. So I'm happy for her, but it's been a long time and I wonder why I'm seeing her like this. Maybe I owe her an amends of some sort. So as I stare off trying to remember, I hesitate with my answer.

"Ah…"

"Come on," she says. "And guess what? Vivian is there."

"Vivian? Wow." And as the horns honk again, Sophie steps out into the street, stops the cars coming in the opposite direction and waves me through like a traffic cop, coffees in hand and all.

"Come on, park up the block and I'll meet you over there."

So I make the left on Gardner and drive up the block. And as I park the car, I get a flood of memories about Vivian, one of the first women I dated in Los Angeles over fifteen years ago.

I met her through this model friend of mine I knew from Tokyo, Lisa, who was a crazy live-wire so full of energy, so chatty, so fuelled by cocaine. She ended up a junkie hooker in Vegas, eventually. Poor Lisa. Anyway, she introduced us at some club up on Sunset Boulevard, me as a model and Vivian as a photographer.

Vivian looked like such a precious Asian beauty when I first saw her, so cute, so adorable, short, jet-black hair with long bangs, pouty red lips, wearing a red silk Chinese dress… and I asked her if she was Chinese.

"No, I'm Korean," she said, and she looked at me so bored, like I was just some other stupid model Lisa picked up to fuck and dump, that I choked and walked away.

The next time I met her was by accident in a bar on Santa Monica Boulevard I used to go with my friend Eddie. Vivian was at the bar with some Russian model I guessed she had just photographed, who was all made up and looking ravishing. And she knew it. Krista, Liza… something, I forget. But I kept looking at Vivian instead, not even listening to the Russian rambling about herself and her fabulous career. So she got pissed off and sought attention with some poseur a few barstools down. Then I remember asking Vivian for her number and her answering something like, "What for? I don't do test shoots with models." And I said something like, "I don't want a test shot. I don't even model anymore, I gave it up."

"Oh, so you're an actor now?" And I'm trying to remember how the conversation went and how I even got her number but I did. I think I told her I liked foreign films or something and she quizzed me and I answered correctly, naming Kurosawa, Fellini, Herzog, Truffaut and she agreed to go to a movie with me. Then I brought her to see Bertolluci's classic, 'Last Tango In Paris', thinking not a great choice for a first date, but she loved it and we both cried and after the movie I made some silly butter jokes that made her laugh.

Then we made love and she said I was a very sweet man. And I guess I was because I was only drinking occasionally at that time. Vivian drank too and snorted cocaine but only a bit here and there. Socially. I told her I was trying to stay off it but one night she took me to see Sophie. The pipe and the free base came out.

Vivian ended up taking two hits, went to sleep and left the next morning for work while Sophie and I stayed up for two days. I think I disappointed her because she was available less and less after that. And I got into the drugs more and more. I'd call her high in the middle of the night and she'd let me come over sometimes because I guess she did see the sweetness in me. She always used to ask me why I was so lost. I'd get defensive because I didn't know why. So we'd argue and I'd leave.

And I had met Keri since then at some art gallery. Her boyfriend's actually. Jesus, this is getting complicated. We were all so crazy back then. Anyway, Keri was intoxicated and flirtatious, we had some laughs, she argued with her boyfriend and we left together. Had some more drinks, went out dancing, to an after-hours club where Keri bought some ecstasy for us. I didn't know what it was. I took it. Then Vivian walked into the club. I forgot I told her I was going to meet her there. She walked in and saw Keri and me practically fucking in the corner. So she walked out. Then I never saw her. I moved in with Keri up at Point Dume, tried to get my act together again.

Meanwhile I heard Vivian had opened up some cool downtown nightclub and was the toast of the town. I was trying to play house with Keri because she was pregnant with Max. Keri wanted it to work. She saw something in me too. She said I had great light within me. But I was more filled with darkness. I wanted to be good, I was trying to be good but it didn't work. I couldn't do it. I couldn't face up to it. I wanted to run. But I wanted to do the right thing, too.

I wanted to be in love like the way Keri wanted me to be. So we decided to get married. And the night before the wedding, I called Vivian and went over to her place, strung-out, wired and petrified. She sat with me, patient, listening as I rambled on and on. Then she got upset because she felt so bad for Keri and the unborn baby. She said something like, "You better get your shit together. Get married and grow up…"

God, all this stuff I'm remembering. I wonder if she remembers? I think I saw her only a few times since then. Yeah, I remember seeing her in some store parking lot, Fred Segal's maybe, I don't know, and I told her Keri and I were happy and we had Max. I was stoned and grinning. I think she said, "Good," and drove away.

Then one night after Keri threw me out, I was holed up with Bobbie shooting dope at the Royal Viking on Alvarado, and I stumbled over to Vivian's club. There was a packed crowd outside waiting to get in. I saw Vivian at the door, dressed in her silk with wild black, gold and blue eye make-up that made her look like a beautiful little Dragon Lady. But she didn't notice me. So many people. I was way in back, looked like shit. I tried to get her attention with a limp wave or two then I figured she was ignoring me or too embarrassed to acknowledge my presence. Why would she let me in? I went back to the motel.

Then there was the time after that when I told her Keri died and I had straightened out and had Max. She was sitting with some guy at an outdoor café I had walked into for a muffin or something. Blueberry muffin, I think. I was gonna eat it there but when I saw her...

It was awkward and embarrassing. I talked a mile a minute. Bombarded her with hard and depressing information. I think she said she was sorry and wished me good luck. I walked away.

Didn't say hello to the guy or shake his hand. She didn't introduce us. He was younger than me and very handsome. I remember that. Maybe she's still with him. Jesus Christ, I can't go into Sophie's shop! What the hell am I doing? Hey, I'm not any of those things I used to be. Why not? Maybe I owe Vivian an amends. That's the least I can do.

"Come on, Shnooky, let's go," I say, and as we get out of the car, I feel a flutter in my heart so I get down on my knees to do my check the tyre routine and say a little prayer.

God help me be patient, kind, humble and mature.

47

There is a 3x3 foot sized headshot in the window of Sophie's shop of a beautiful, strong, intelligent looking blonde woman. I know she's some celebrity, one of those talk-show hosts or news anchorwomen types, the kind where you know the face but not the name. So I'm looking at the bottom where it says photographed by Vivian Yi and I feel so tense that I rest my knees against the window and say, *God help me,* again. Then I walk in.

The store is small and fancy with very expensive make-up samples, brushes and creams of all kinds on display. It feels more like it should be in Beverly Hills than Melrose. There is a very Ritzy-type woman with her silver hair in a bun at the counter buying products from Sophie. She gives a look when Shnooky follows me in.

"Shouldn't that dog be on a leash?" Oh, no, don't test me, not right away, I think, as Sophie says to her, "Don't worry about it, honey." She gives a quick wink to me. "That's my close friend, Dave, with his sweet dog..." And I chime in right away saying, "Shnooky..."

"Yeah, Shnooky," Sophie says. "How are you, my sweet?"

And Shnooky knows how to behave; she wags her tail politely like she's known Sophie for years.

"She's in the back," Sophie says, pointing to a half-drawn curtain that partitions the shop, then she beams at her customer and says, "Now where were we, honey? Anti-wrinkle cream?"

I walk around the edge of the curtain with Shnooky trotting behind me to see Vivian, sitting on an indigo and purple cushioned couch against the wall, sipping her coffee, browsing through a fashion magazine. Elle, Vogue, I don't know because I'm seeing how stunning she still looks, barely a line on her smooth, satin-skin face and her thick, straight, glossy black hair is long, past her shoulders now.

She's dressed in some wide-cuffed, brown and blue-striped pants with a white linen blouse and thin, blue suede jacket over. Her strong hands, which I remember she didn't like (but I did), are manicured with soft pink nail polish, as are the nails on her dainty feet, popping out of her dark blue platform sandals.

"Hi," I say and she smiles, reserved but polite.

"Hello."

And right away that voice, I forgot how cute it sounded with the slight trace of Korean accent she still had. I remember how she told me her mother whisked her over here from Seoul at thirteen when her parents got divorced. She was immediately thrown into eighth grade English classes, knowing only a few words of the language so she never learned it properly and would always get her articles mixed up.

She would say things like, "You're getting on my nerve," or, "You're a pain on my ass," or, "You're not paying attentioning," and she would say it very seriously but her voice, so cute...

And I wanna pick her up and hug her. But she isn't jumping up for joy to see me. So, it's awkward. Shnooky breaks the ice a bit by sauntering over and sniffing Vivian's coffee.

"You like coffee?" she says as she strokes Shnooky's head. No big deal. Cool. Casual. Shnooky takes to her right away.

"It's the milk and the sugar."

"I drink soy milk," Vivian says.

"Ah, so do I. She likes that too..."

Then some more silence, a page or two flipped in the magazine.

"You look the same," I say.

"I don't think so," she says. "I'm forty."

"Well, you look beautiful."

She looks up and smiles. It's a real smile. Not a big one but a real one. And her deep, soulful brown eyes are serious. Truthful.

"Thank you. You look pretty good, too."

"I like your hair long. Do you like mine bald?" I say trying to make her laugh.

"Excuse me?"

Oh, fuck, this is so hard. Why? Why? Why?

"I'm just joking around because I'm going bald."

"Oh," she says. "I can't see because you're standing up."

So I sit down on the couch next to her and tip my head.

"Oh, it's not that bad," she says, looking and touching around a little with her fingers. "I don't remember you being that vain."

"Well, I had my hair..." and I laugh but she doesn't.

Silence. Nervous. Awkward.

"You wouldn't happen to have a cigarette?" she says.

"No, I quit... but I could go out on the street and get you one if..."

"No, no, no, I'm trying to quit too," she says. "How did you do it? I remember you smoked a lot."

"I don't know, it just happened," I say. "I did chew the gum for a while..."

"I don't want to do that. I'm just going to quit one day."

"Good, I hope you do."

"Thank you."

And we're just rolling along. Chatting it up.

"So..." I say.

"So..." she says.

"So... how have you been? Still doing photography?"

"No."

"Oh, I just saw that photo in front and I thought…"

"I was just helping Sophie. She tells me you are still off drugs."

"Yeah, things are different, I'm different."

"So is she or I wouldn't be helping her out. So how is your son?"

"He's good. I just dropped him and his friends off at the skateboard shop up on Melrose…" And I tell her about Max being in a good school and how he's a good artist.

"I went to the Art Centre in Pasadena you know," she says. "That would be a good college for him to go to if he is serious about art."

"I didn't know that," I say.

"I think I told you that, Dave," she says. "I mean I had only graduated a few years before I met you."

"I don't remember that."

"I think we remember different things," she says.

"I remember talking to you before I got married."

"I remember that," she says.

"And I wanted to make amends if I did anything to upset you or hurt you in any way."

"I think you were only hurting yourself," she says.

"I know…"

"But you don't owe me any amends. You just talked and I listened and you left."

"And at that after-hours club when I was with Keri…"

"I don't really remember that one and you don't have to tell me," she says.

"Okay," I say. "I just want to feel comfortable around you and if there is anything…"

"Well, we can't feel that comfortable," she says. "We haven't seen each other more than a few times in fifteen years."

"Holy shit! Fifteen years, and you don't look a day older."

"Oh, stop it," she says, but now she laughs.

"So your son is good?" she asks again. "It must have been very hard to bring him up."

"Yeah, and I did it pretty much alone… and about that time I saw you at that café, it was only about six months after the accident and I'm sorry if I…"

"It's okay, it's okay," she says. "It was an awkward situation."

"Are you still with that guy, that handsome guy? What was he, French? English? Some European…"

"No, I'm not."

"Are you with anybody? I thought you'd be living in some villa on the French Riviera…"

"Oh, stop it. That is so not my style. You must have me confused with someone else."

"Well, you were in that club scene with all those international celebrities and famous people."

"So what? It was a job. I hated being around most of those people."

"So are you seeing anybody?"

"I'm dating, nothing serious. So tell me what happened again with Keri. Max was with her, right?"

I tell her the whole story about the accident and Max on the road next to his mom and what he said to me in the hospital about wanting to go to heaven with her and how he had to be in the body cast for months while I struggled to get us by... and Vivian starts quietly sobbing.

"I'm sorry, I'm sorry," I say. "I didn't mean to upset you."

"It's okay, it's okay," she says wiping away her tears. "It's just so heartbreaking..."

And as I reach out to touch her shoulder, and Shnooky licks her hand, Sophie walks back.

"So... you two getting along okay? Doing a little reminiscing?"

48

So we talked a little longer and I told her I was living in Studio City. I caught myself saying, "I own a house there," and felt stupid but she let it slide. Well, I don't know what she thought but she didn't say anything. She told me she had been living with somebody in Nichols Canyon for the past three years but she moved out a few months ago. He wanted to get married. She didn't.

I asked why and she said even though he was handsome, intelligent, successful and wealthy, he was very stubborn, was abusive to his two children from a previous marriage and still drank a bottle of wine a night and snorted cocaine occasionally. She said he made minimal efforts to change and she couldn't see herself spending the rest of her life with him.

I wasn't really paying attention to the reasons because I was busy envisioning this rich stud in a silk robe sauntering around a sprawling Nichols Canyon mansion, drinking Chateau-Lafite and snorting pink Peruvian flake, but I managed to say, "I'm sorry it didn't work out."

"I also don't do drugs anymore. Not that I had a problem with them like you, Dave, but I just don't want them in my life."

And how could I get defensive? She was right so I just said, "Me either," then she told me she was living in a friend's guest-house now, near the top of Laurel Canyon off Green Valley road, that she liked the solitude, peace and quiet and went for walks every morning.

"So we live kinda close to each other, I mean I'm just over the hill," I said. "And I run with Shnooky every morning." Then I told her I was trying to find a trail where Shnooky could run off leash like she did at Bronson Canyon. Vivian said she knew a trail by Fryman Canyon. And when I said I had already been to Fryman Canyon, she said, "You're not paying attentioning to me. I said a trail by Fryman Canyon." And I almost laughed and kissed her when she said 'attentioning' but I held it back. I mean, we had just met again.

"Can you show me?" I said.

"Oh, I guess so."

And we made plans to meet at the bottom of Fryman road in the morning.

"Nine o'clock?" I asked.

"No, ten would be better. I have some plans tonight and might be out late."

"One of those late night dates?" I said, then I caught myself and admitted it was none of my business and she confirmed that it wasn't but she gave me her number and told me to call her in the morning when I was leaving, "your house that you own," she added with a smile.

And when I picked up the kids at the skateboard shop and Max said they were spending the night at Simon's, I wanted to call Vivian right away and tell her to cancel her date. So I had to say, "God help me," out loud in the car because my head was just screaming with justification to call her.

"Dad, please, do that after you drop us off," Max said, and I did like a mantra all the way home. And I cleaned the house in case I got to show it to Vivian the next day after our walk, read a few ruthless Paul Bowles stories that so masterfully transport me right into his world of Morocco, then I prayed again not to call her. And I fell asleep.

It's almost nine in the morning now. Should I call her yet? No. Wait until nine. No, nine-thirty at least. It's only a ten-minute drive to Fryman. I don't usually take a shower before I run but maybe I should. Shave or no shave? T-shirt or long sleeve? My arms look too skinny in T-shirts. I mean I do push-ups but only twenty or thirty after I run. Maybe I should do ten sets of ten push-ups and then some reps with my dusty ten-pound dumb-bells. Yeah, do a bunch of curls, get my arms a little buffed. I can wear shorts because my legs are strong and muscular from years of running, but they're so hairy. Should I wear sweatpants instead? Someone told me once I looked like I had sweaters on my legs. Vivian's seen 'em before. It's no big deal. What am I worrying about? Be nice. Be kind. It's not like I'm some young Adonis. I'm okay. She said I looked good. Maybe I should run first and then go meet her. This is so silly. Maybe she's hung over and can't make it. Maybe she slept over at her date's house. Come on, don't go there. Try a little meditation. Get calm. Call Vivian and meet her.

And she's home when I call which is such a good sign and she says she's ready to meet me. So I throw on my green skateboard shorts with the little alien face-tag on the pocket that Max got me for Christmas, mainly because they make my ass look good, and a plain white t-shirt because white makes me look less skinny. The Shnook is already dressed.

"Aren't you? You're always dressed and ready," I say as I lace up my running shoes. And we head out the door.

I make the right off Laurel onto Fryman and look for Vivian. The parking lot for the Canyon looks full and the road is already lined up with cars. It's Sunday and it's crowded. All regular, law-abiding citizens are going for their hikes up Fryman Canyon with their poop bags and their nice doggies on leashes. I glance back at Shnooky who gazes out the window with sadness in her eyes.

"We're going to a secret trail, don't worry. Vivian is taking us to one."

I hope so, Daddy…

Then I see Vivian about twenty yards up the road. She has on an oversized white, floppy hat, light blue tank top and tight bellbottom jeans, flaring over a pair of white Nikes. She looks so cute leaning against an enormous beige coloured Citröen. I pull up next to her.

"Hi, your car looks like a big beige shark."

"That's what I call it," she says. "The Sharkmobile." And she opens the door of mine. "We'll go in your car. It's just up the street."

"Okay," I say as she gets in and says, "Hi, Shnooky, ready to go up a nice trail?" And I hear the happy tail thumping on the back seat.

"Take a right here," Vivian says at a stop sign and I make a mental note to remember the turn as we go up a steep private road with big beautiful houses on either side. *Bigger than mine. It's okay. Bigger than mine. It's okay. Bigger than mine. I said it's okay!*

"I never pictured you in one of these SUV's," Vivian says.

"It was a carpool mom thing."

"You look good in it."

"Normal?"

"I didn't say normal, I said good."

"Sorry, I mean, thanks. You look good too, I mean you look pretty."

"You can't even see my face with this hat."

"I can see," I say, as I look over at her and I see her dark nipples popping through her tank top. I remember how they popped out of all her shirts like thick pencil erasers.

"Does it make you uncomfortable that I'm not wearing a bra?" she says. Oh, my God!

"I'm not uncomfortable, I can just... see."

"I have such small breasts anyway," she says. "It's not that big a deal. Park here."

And I wanna say, "Okay just take the shirt off then," but I take a breath and I pull over to the curb.

Vivian tells me to keep Shnooky on the leash as we walk across the street to what looks like a long private dirt and gravel driveway heading up into the hills.

"Most people don't know about this," she says as she surveys the street like a spy. Then she unhooks Shnooky's leash herself. "Let's go." And just as we start walking up the trail a pair of huge German Shepherds barrel down a steep, wooded hill area to the right that is separated by a tall metal and mesh fence. Shnooky just trots along, happy to be free, maybe shaking her ass a little extra, as the Shepherds bang against the fence, barking and growling. Vivian and I watch as one of them viciously lunges at the other.

"That's the female," Vivian says. "What a tease you are Shnooky," and she laughs, and Shnooky wags her tail as she stops to munch on some tall blades of green grass. "That's quite a dog you have there, Dave," and Shnooky looks back at me.

I like her, Daddy, I like her.

Then I feel comfortable enough to ask, "So how was your date last night?"

"Not very interesting."

"Oh? What happened?"

"That's all you need to know," she says. "Do you want to tell me about all your dates?"

Oh, it's awkward again. I feel awkward. I shouldn't have asked that.

"I don't go on many. I'm with Max pretty much of the time and when I'm not I... can't find the... I don't know... I'm sorry..."

"No, I'm sorry," she says. "I'm just getting tired of most men. Can we just walk for a while?"

"Okay," I say, as we pass a few Eucalyptus trees to the side with their long leaves hanging low enough to touch.

May I, Eucalyptus?

Yes, of course you may.

I reach up, grab one and crunch it between my fingers so the sweet, clean menthol aroma flows out. I offer it to Vivian to smell, holding it under her nose. She accepts.

"Nice."

"Yeah."

"I didn't mean you, when I said most men."

"Okay."

That's all we have to say and we keep walking to where the trail seems to end into a wide clearing off to the right where there could have been a house planned to be built at one time but it's all grown over with tall weeds and grass. In front of us seems to be all wild bushes and past them a view of the San Fernando Valley and the mountains beyond, some tops still covered with snow.

"This is where some people stop too, because they don't know where to go," Vivian says as Shnooky walks over to a narrow path in-between the bushes. Vivian smiles. "She knows where to go."

And we follow her down the path that winds around then widens again, up a steep hill with thick, wood beam steps wedged into the dirt with fat little brown lizards hopping off them as Shnooky runs up. Then Vivian runs up and I run up right behind her, so close that it makes her scream out in mock fright and run faster. And the hill levels out about a hundred yards up where Vivian stops to catch her breath. I'm breathing easy.

"You're in good shape."

"I was running up Bronson Canyon almost everyday with Shnooky for six years."

"I go to the Runyon sometimes," she says. "That's a really steep one."

"Yeah, I've been there," I say, smiling. "I'll go with you sometime if you like."

"Why are you smiling?"

"Because you said, the Runyon, instead of just Runyon."

"I guess you forgot how I talk."

"No, I just... I like it."

"I can't help it you know. I don't do it on purpose."

"I know. I think it's cute."

"I'm not always so cute either, you know."

"Okay."

"I don't think I've ever seen you so straight and together either," she says, and then she gives me a quick kiss on the lips and continues on the trail that turns back into a narrow path with daisies and ten-foot tall mustard flowers on either side. And I follow her through with my arms stretched out like I'm floating through them. Then there is a line of poison sumac bushes, shiny red and green up ahead.

"Careful," Vivian says, as she looks back at me.

"I see 'em," I say, as I smile and bring my arms in. And I see Shnooky, yards ahead, contentedly trotting along, sniffing all the fresh new smells, stopping to dribble her scent and gobble more blades of grass. Then Vivian points to some wild sage and says, "You should pick some for your house."

"To do what?"

"You wrap a string around a bunch and dry it, then you light it and purify your home with the sage smoke. You've never done that?"

"No."

"Well, pick some and I'll show you how."

"I have to ask first."

"Excuse me?"

"Ask the sage if I can pick it."

And Vivian doesn't look at me like I'm insane, she just says, "Okay, ask."

So I do and the sage says, *Of course,* and I pick a bunch and put it in my pocket. Then we continue on for another half-mile or so, seeing red-tailed hawks above and bunnies hopping under bushes and fields of more daisies, light yellow and deep yellow in colour mixed with other wild flowers of purple and orange, until the trail dips down into a narrow stream, then up and through a wooded area that turns into a shaded eucalyptus forest, the trees tremendous and tall, with another wider, rushing stream that has two long, fallen eucalyptus across it as a bridge. Shnooky wades into the water, lapping up her fill as Vivian stops by the edge and does some yoga stretches. Not showing off, just doing them, and then she squats down with her hands clasped together in meditation.

"I love it here," she says. "When I was little in Korea, just before my parents got divorced, I used to go in the woods and spend hours there because it was where I found peace." And she closes her eyes and I feel myself on my knees, close to her, hands clasped together on my lap, eyes closed, hearing the water flowing, flowing through me, through my mind, through my soul. And we both stay there, I don't know; two minutes, five minutes, ten minutes. No questions of, what are you doing? Then we both seem to stand up at the same time.

"The trail continues up to Mulholland but I'd like to head back now."

"Okay."

"Maybe get something to eat if you want."

"We could go to the store and bring food back to my house."

"Okay. I'd like that," she says, and now I give her a little kiss on the lips, a little longer one, before we start back.

49

Vivian follows me to drop off her car at my house so we can go to the market together. I get panicky when we get to my street. I have to go in and take a piss. Should I invite her in now? What is she gonna think? It's just natural that she will want to come in and see it, right? I could hold off until we come back from the market but what will that do? She is gonna see it anyway. I'm sure she's seen better, much better. Lived in 'em, too. She was living in Nichol's Canyon, for Christ's sake, of course she's seen better! So what? If she doesn't like it... fuck her! Fucking snob! I'll tell her to get the fuck out and go back to her mansion life. Who gives a shit about her anyway? Stuck-up, better-than bitch! Yeah, that's what I'll do, that's it, that's the old Dave of self-destruction coming to the rescue. Why don't you just slam your car into a tree?

Okay. Relax. Just take it easy and invite her in. This is your house. Be proud of it. Be proud and humble. Be happy proud and humble... and grateful. Yes. Be grateful too.

"Oh, shut up and get out of the car!" I say as I park in my driveway. Shnooky thumps her tail with her ears down and eyes squinted in worry.

I didn't do anything, Daddy...

"I know, I know. I'm not talking to you, silly!" I say, as I open the back door and Vivian is there.

"Excuse me?"

"I was just talking to Shnooky."

And Shnooky eyes Vivian as she hops onto the driveway.

Daddy is a little crazy. You'll find out.

"Did she do something wrong?" Vivian says.

"No..." and I start laughing. I mean, have to.

"Is something funny?"

"Okay," I say. "I was just talking to myself because I was nervous about bringing you here. You wanna come in? I just have to use the bathroom before we go to the market."

"It looks cute."

"What does?

"Your house. Your house looks cute from the outside. I like the sage colour and the plants in front. I love lavender."

"Thanks. Inside is a little sparse," I say, as I open the door and she follows me in. I watch for her first reaction.

"It's airy. I feel a good energy," she says. I pull the sage out of my pocket.

"Should we burn this?"

"You have to let that dry," she says, laughing at me. "Why are you so nervous? I think it's charming in here. That's a nice style couch and the wood table is nice. Both tables are."

"Yeah, the couch and the dinning table are Keri's. The other is some antique... well, not really." Then she sees the boxes.

"How long have you been living here?"

"A couple of months. They need to be moved, I know."

"I didn't say that they did. I just asked..."

"Max was supposed to do it. Listen, I have to pee...I'll ah... feel free to walk around." And I go to the bathroom and pee and blame Max for not moving the boxes, no I blame myself. I even cleaned last night and I cleaned around them. So what? She likes it. I like her. I like Vivian. I know I do. Look in the mirror and say it. And I smile at my reflection and say, "I like her."

"What? Are you talking to me?" I hear Vivian say, so she must be in my bedroom. I come out to find her looking at the bed with Shnooky's hair thick on the blanket over the frayed, faded white sheets.

"I said I like you and I need new sheets," then I kiss her. It lasts a little longer than the first one on the trail or the second and both of our lips soften into it.

"I need a lot of new stuff," I say after the kiss, feeling my voice deeper and relaxed. "I just haven't gotten around to doing it. Ya know, two men and a dog, we just kinda let things slide a little. I'm gonna fix it up, though."

"Do you want help?"

"When?" I say, and as I wonder if I answered the question too fast, she says, "I guess we could do it today."

And we're in Bed, Bath and Beyond, a place I would usually run from just because of its name, but there's one a few blocks away on Ventura and I'm in it with Vivian, in the 'Bath' section, buying bath mats, towels, green for Max, blue for me, with face towels to match and a shower curtain. Then over to the 'Bed' section for pillows, pillowcases, comforters, comforter covers and thousand thread count cotton sheets. I don't know about thread counts. I never knew about 'em. Vivian says the thread count is important and soft sheets are always well worth the price.

Then I remember Keri was particular about sheets too, and at that moment when I'm thinking of her, I hear her voice say, *Dave, I like this girl*. And I look at Vivian picking out white ones for me and some red and light brown checked ones for Max.

"You think Max would like these?" she says.

"Yeah, I think so."

And I don't know where the 'Beyond' section is in this store, but I know I just got a message from it.

Then we stop at Whole Foods for a baguette, fresh sliced Soppresata, Swiss Gruyère, some country mix Greek olives, vine ripe tomatoes, basil, and a couple of homemade macaroons, half covered with bitter-sweet chocolate. We both have similar tastes in food, and pick everything together as if we've done it before many times. It is comfortable and strange, and I tell myself, don't get in the way; just let this be how it is.

And back at my house I make us sandwiches while Vivian unpacks all the bed and bath stuff. Then she offers to empty out one of the boxes in the living room and pulls out a few of my old plays and some unfinished movie scripts from the top.

"I didn't know you were a writer."

"Well, I am. I produced a few plays, good ones, and got close with a movie but I really haven't written anything from my heart yet. I will, though, I know I will." And as I say it, I believe it myself for the first time.

"I'd like to read some of these."

"Yeah, I still do commercials too, I mean I just did one."

"Do you like doing those? They seem so silly."

"Well, they are silly but the residuals help earn enough so Max and I get health insurance through the Screen Actors Guild. I guess I do it because I have to."

"Well, I'm getting back into the club business," she says. "I'm going to open one with some partners in Hollywood soon. It will have two dance floors, a great restaurant and entertainment also. It's going to be a big deal."

"Will you let me in?"

"Why not?"

Then I look to see if she remembers that time in front of her old club, downtown, with me nodding out in the back of the crowd. No. She doesn't. She would have let me in if she saw me, I know it now.

"I was just asking," I say and I bring out the sandwiches. Vivian likes to eat. She's no little bird that pecks away at the bread, she takes a big bite into the baguette and I like watching her enjoy it. I like a woman who likes to eat good food.

"I was thinking," she says in between bites, "now that I know you're a writer, your desk should be in the den where the TV is, instead of the way you have it up against your bedroom wall. I can't see how you can feel creative that way."

"I thought that when I first moved in, too. Maybe I'll do that. Maybe you'll help me?"

"Maybe." Then she nods towards the mantle and says, "I love that piece."

"What? The Ivory Buddha woman? My father left me that."

"It's not just a woman. It's Kwan Yin. She is the Buddhist goddess of compassion and mercy."

"Really?" I say and I think, no wonder my father got it.

After we eat, I show Vivian the back patio and the plants I put in the flowerbeds.

"Birds of Paradise aren't my favourites," she says.

"Well, they were Keri's favourite."

"Oh…" she says and she looks down at her feet. Then she puts her hand to her mouth and says, "I'm sorry."

"Please, don't be sorry. I shouldn't have answered like that either. Max just likes to look at them sometimes." And I put my hand to my mouth in a loose fist and bite on my knuckles while Vivian blinks fast and stares at the flowerbed.

"I mean, I don't hate them… I like the roses better but I don't hate them…" and I start laughing and she starts laughing and I hug her.

"We're both so sensitive, aren't we?" I say. "Come on, let me show you some of Max's sensitive art work."

I open the garage and show her the old desk Jay left us, cluttered with coloured pens, pencils, paints and a sloppy stack of drawing paper. The first drawing I pull out says, 'My Monster' in thick black strokes of watercolour paint on the top. It's a drawing of a head of some horrifying black and red, longhaired, dripping demon man, with frightening greenish-yellow eyes with tiny blue pupils. His bloody mouth is stretched wide open in a scream with his tongue flying out over gnarled, pointed teeth. It is very detailed and scares me just to hold it.

"I don't know what's in his head, if it's about his mom… I mean, he seems fine but stuff does come out in his art," I say. I feel awkward. Ignorant actually.

"He's an artist, and I don't use that term lightly," Vivian says. "He has a sense of his own expression. It's wonderful."

She picks up some more drawings, one of a blue, green, white and red coloured sphere with orange fire around it over a black speckled background, then a black pen sketch of a long haired kid with aviator sunglasses, coloured in a red and black psychedelic type of maze in the centre and stylized drawings of guitars, skateboards, soda cans, portraits of Iggy Pop, Sid Vicious, Hendrix, Basquait and then he has drawings of funny little, brightly coloured birds and one of a cartoon-style, sweet-looking dog with long eye-lashes.

"I'm betting Shnooky was the model for that," Vivian says.

"I don't know… I just let him draw what he wants."

"Well, you should," she says.

"I mean, I just let him feel safe with who he is. My father never did that for me."

"Well, that's very important," she says. "Especially for an artist."

Okay. Can you move in right away? I think, but I just say, "Thanks," and when we walk back to the house, Dena, the tenant, comes out of the guest-house, barefoot, dressed in shorts and a Bob Marley t-shirt, her dreads dangling down, with her doggy by her side. Shnooky runs over and bullies her a little.

I'm the landlord here. Remember that, honey. But then they get into playing and chasing each other up and down the driveway as Dena hands me a small Fed-Ex package.

"Hey, Dave, this came for you yesterday but the guy brought it back here, so I just signed. Hope you don't mind."

"No, that's cool, thanks."

"Love your hair," Vivian says to Dena as I take the package.

"Mine? What about yours?" Dena says. "It's beautiful. You're beautiful." And she smiles at me, nodding her head. "Lucky guy, Dave."

I open the package as we walk inside and find a little blue felt ring box with a note rubber-banded around it. I take it off and open it while Vivian gets busy laying out the towels and sheets for Max and me. The note reads: 'Just in case you find someone, Love Margaret'. Then I flip the box open, and inside is my mom's wedding ring. It's a simple ring, a gold band with a dainty antique setting of a quarter carat diamond or so, surrounded by a circle of smaller ones. I remember it on my mom's hand. It looked so beautiful. Now I have it for...

I flip it closed, fast. I stand there immobile, with the box cupped in my hand, trying to swallow.

"You get something in the mail?" Vivian asks, her head down, separating the green towels from the blue ones.

"Huh?"

Then Shnooky barks at the door, and as Max walks in, I slip the box in my pocket.

"Dad, whose car is that outside? It is so cool."

"That's mine. Hi, I'm Vivian."

Max looks at her, mildly interested. "What kind is it?"

"It's called a Citroën. It's a French car, made in 1969."

"Cool." Then he looks at me, not accusingly, but he feels something in the air.

"Dad, you look different."

"What are you talking about? How come you're back so early?"

"Homework, Dad, something you don't know about."

Vivian obviously sees he is not the shy type. Perhaps not the most polite either but he is who he is and she doesn't seem bothered by it.

"I saw some of your art work," she says. "I really like it."

"She liked, 'My Monster'," I say.

"She did?" Max says, his lips curling up into a smile.

"I hope one day you could do drawing for me," Vivian says, and Max shrugs and says, "Okay. What's all this stuff?"

"What does it look like? Pick yours up and put the towels in your bathroom and the sheets on the…"

"Dad, I have homework like I said, okay."

Then Vivian gets up with Max's things already in her arms.

"I'll help you," she says. "We can do it really quick."

And he shrugs again and says, "Okay," as he follows her into his room.

So I put up the shower curtain in my bathroom as Vivian helps Max and when I'm finished, I look in his room and she's showing him how to put his comforter in the casing. I just stand in the hall and watch them, with Shnooky at my side, my hand in my pocket around my mother's ring box, and I think that something might happen here. This could work out. And I have hope that it does.

Thanks to:

Franc Roddam

Billy Wirth

Sue Choi

Nick D

Schnooky

Jack Grapes

Nicole Arlyn

Cynthia Thayer

and to the memory of my mom and Sandi